About the Author

Krishnan Doyle lives in London with his partner and twin daughters. *Dirty Angel: The Angel Rises* is the second part of the series with input from both Krishnan's daughters in terms of creative and artwork. He is passionate about diversity and inclusion and would like future books to focus on strong science-based stories, with strong female role models. Krishnan is founder of an international recruitment business with offices in six countries, the non-executive of a public relations business and a patron of several charities within the homeless/workplace sector.

Dirty Angel: The Angel Rises

Krishnan Doyle

Dirty Angel: The Angel Rises

Olympia Publishers
London

www.olympiapublishers.com
OLYMPIA PAPERBACK EDITION

A CIP catalogue record for this title is
available from the British Library.

ISBN: 978-1-80439-501-1

This is a work of fiction.
Names, characters, places and incidents originate from the writer's
imagination. Any resemblance to actual persons, living or dead, is
purely coincidental.

First Published in 2023

Olympia Publishers
Tallis House
2 Tallis Street
London
EC4Y 0AB

Printed in Great Britain

Dedication

To my two little angels Ella and Scarlett. I look forward to seeing where you take this on your adventures. Dad xxx
And my ever-supportive husband.

Acknowledgments

Thank you to Gary for all your support. And thank you to all who helped to create this series and for all the positive comments and feedback on book one.

Chapter 1

The Times
10th July

How Going to Space Could Help You Live Longer

Zero gravity could hold the key to people living longer — and MethusalaCo intends to prove it with a series of missions to space, says tech giant Max Bing.

"Our scientists believe zero gravity can open the doors to a whole range of new possibilities for extending our lifespans. And where better to develop that theory than in space?" Bing, the CEO of Synoplex, the world's biggest technology company, asked.

Max Bing has been dubbed 'Peter Pan' owing to his youthful looks and his unwillingness to age, and these space missions are his latest step in his search for immortality.

The first mission will send human stem cells — developed from human blood or skin cells — into space, then explore new treatments in zero gravity that could be used to treat diseases back on earth. In space, the stem cells will not be under pressure from the effect of gravity, meaning they could multiply faster. The results will help scientists who focus on diseases of the heart and brain, as well those who study the effect zero gravity has on the deterioration of muscles.

MethusalaCo has been at the forefront of new developments into the process of aging since Synoplex launched the ambitious start-up four years ago. For the mercurial Max Bing, to use the words of Neil Armstrong, this truly could be the "one giant leap for mankind".

The day is just starting at the exclusive St. Edith's School for Girls and Miss Rossington is still bleary eyed. Breakfast will be served in five minutes. As she walks through the hallway that leads to the dining room, she notices some movement in the exercise studio. The teacher stops and stares through the small glass panel of the door at the young girl exercising vigorously. Miss Rossington has been teaching English at the school for fifteen years and has never come across a girl quite like her before. She is unusual. No, she is *very* unusual.

Eleven-year-old Jane is working out in the exercise studio, a room that had once been a drawing room in this old manor house. Miss Rossington has always found the metal, state-of-the-art exercise equipment and bright blue mats incongruous with the neoclassical eighteenth-century room and its high, stucco-decorated ceilings, gilded with gold paint, and huge windows framing garden views.

Jane works out like this every day. This is her training regime. With a combination of aggression and grace, she twists, turns, and jumps through her exercises, constantly twirling the aged hickory hockey stick she uses for balance. At least she is not using that rusty old spear any more, the teacher thinks. Every so often Jane stops, frozen into position with her posture rigid. Firm, balanced, focused, and determined. From what Miss Rossington can see, she is now using the hockey stick as a weapon — as if it still *was* that spear — fiercely thrusting it at invisible opponents to the front, back, and side of her. This way and that the girl flies, legs and arms flailing in seemingly random directions. And yet, her bare feet always land firmly and confidently on the polished solid-oak floorboards following each jump, and the landings never make a sound. It is as if she is a feather floating to the ground.

"If that was me," Miss Rossington mutters to herself, "I'd make more noise than a herd of elephants."

"That's if you landed on your feet, Miss Rossington."

She turns around to see Abigail Thomas standing beside her, already dressed for a quick game of hockey the girls are going to squeeze in after breakfast. Red top, white skirt, and white socks — the famous colors of St. Edith's, a boarding school that has had been educating young girls to the highest standards for a hundred and sixty-two years, in a building that is even older than that. Her lower legs bulge with the large shinpads she's inserted into her socks to protect her from errant, or deliberately aimed hockey sticks. It is a rough game, after all.

"What *is* that crazy girl Jane doing this morning, miss? She thinks she one of those Mutant Ninja Turtles."

"How do you know about them?" Miss Rossington asks, deflecting the conversation away from Jane. "They were around way before your time."

"My papa told me about them, miss. They sounded very, er, interesting. Were they, miss?"

"Were they what Abigail?"

"Interesting, miss?"

"They were of their time, Abigail. Now, go on. Get your breakfast, then outside to enjoy the nice weather and your game. But make sure you are back in and ready for Speech Day."

The rest of the girls come skipping down the arched hallway, looking to get breakfast out of the way quickly before heading into the morning sun for hockey. They don't even glance at the impressive collection of art that lines the walls of the corridor. The paintings that show scenes of the local area: farmers working the field, gentry enjoying picnics in the open fields, or happily riding their horses. The maps that show the local area at different times through history. Religious artefacts, including crosses, goblets, candles, and framed stained-glass panels pilfered from churches. And plenty of other random historical items from across the world. The spoils of colonial conquest.

The other girls pass by, some glancing through the glass panel of the door to the exercise studio and shaking their heads in bemusement. Most muttering a few derogatory words.

"She's mad!"

"What *is* she doing?"

"Waste of a good hockey stick, I'd say."

Then they are gone, one by one disappearing into the canteen.

The girls don't dislike Jane. They just find her odd. Unlike the other girls, she never seeks popularity — and that is odd enough in itself. Why would anyone not want to be popular? And although none of them admit it, they are scared of her and a little in awe.

Three years earlier…

Jane's first day at St. Edith's is a daze. She's just turned nine and is alone in the world. Her mummy and daddy are both dead and her grandmother has insisted she changes her name. She is no longer Jane Travers but Jane Banks. Her world has been turned upside down. The teachers are fully briefed prior to her arrival by the headmistress Miss Fernsby and instructed to read her file, just as they are with every other new girl. St. Edith's takes great pride in knowing what every girl needs, and this goes way beyond just their academic needs. At least that's what headmistress Miss Fernsby keeps telling everyone who will listen.

Jane's file is a lot thicker than the others the teachers receive for the new intake of pupils, and the headmistress has obviously taken great care with it. It is no surprise; Jane is the granddaughter of Lorraine Meaden, renowned alma mater of St. Edith's, Miss Fernsby's former classmate, and more significantly, the school's biggest benefactor. Inside Jane's file are her school reports, a number of newspaper articles, and an overview from Miss Fernsby to ensure everyone is of the same mind. Her mind, of course.

14

Letter from Miss Fernsby
Subject: New pupil Jane Banks

Dear Ladies,

I enclose an information pack on our new pupil, Jane Banks. As well as the usual school reports and relevant information on her background, hobbies, and so on, I have also included some rather disturbing newspaper reports. I am sure you will have heard of this case, although Jane's name was not published at the time. I urge you to treat this information with the utmost confidentially. I have also received permission to share with you a recent (false) health diagnosis Jane received, as it could materially affect her psychological progress at the school. Again, your confidentiality is paramount. Please read all the information carefully and prepare yourself to receive Jane to our family at St. Edith's. I will remind you that Jane is the granddaughter of Lorraine Meaden.

• Jane is a pupil of average ability, usually achieving grades of between C and C+. Her schooling has been at a mediocre private school in North London, so I have no doubt we can improve on these grades significantly.

• When Jane was just eight, her mother was killed during a burglary at the house and father has been declared missing, presumed dead.

• Jane may have been witnessed rituals of Satanic worship, although I am assured there is no evidence that Jane was included in these.

• A few months ago, Jane was diagnosed with Duchenne muscular dystrophy, a muscle wasting disease that affects only one in fifty million girls. Subsequent examinations have proved this diagnosis to be incorrect.

• Jane will be receiving counseling once a week for the trauma she has undoubtedly suffered. Under no circumstances is this to be revealed to any of the other girls.

Take these points into consideration, but please ensure you welcome Jane to St. Edith's in the same way you do with every other girl.

Yours faithfully,
        Miss Fernsby
        Headmistress, St. Edith's School for Girls

From the Daily Telegraph Archives
Young Girl Escapes Grasp of Devil Worshippers

Satanic witchcraft has been linked to two deaths after an eight-year-old girl — who was found asleep alone on a hiking trail in the Brecon Beacons — told police she had gone there with her father so he could give her a magic potion.

Her mother, age thirty-four, was shot in the garden of her home by armed burglars in Cherry Tree Lane, Woodside Park, North London on the 10th November, only a couple of days before the young girl was found. Although the couple were estranged, the father, age thirty-six, was at the house at the time and is believed to have escaped with his young daughter, who cannot be named because of her age. The girl had been found by hikers, covered in a blanket, on the popular Pen Y Fan walking trail, two hundred miles from her family home. Her father was nowhere to be found and a manhunt, with the help of helicopters and dogs, was launched.

Three days later, the man was declared missing, presumed dead, by police. The young girl told police that her father promised her the magic potion would make her better; doctors had recently diagnosed the girl with muscular dystrophy.

"This is a double tragedy for this family, and especially for the young girl who has lost her mother and father within days," Inspector Ken Hughes of Dyfed-Powys Police said.

"It is made all the more frightening because it appears that the father was connected with a group that practiced Satanic worship. We believe that, following the diagnosis of his daughter's illness, he turned to the group in desperation. The girl was found by hikers in a popular area for walking, but she has no memory of how she got there. She informed one of our female officers that her father was going to perform magic on her. We discovered items used by Satanic worshippers at a nearby site that backs up the girl's story. We immediately dispatched helicopters, sniffer dogs, and a search team to track down this dangerous man to ensure no harm could come to any other children. After an extensive search, the man has been officially declared missing, presumed dead. We ask for privacy for the family at this difficult time."

Inspector Hughes would not comment on the issue of witchcraft any further, but it has struck fear into locals.

"Frankly, it makes me scared to go out," one resident, who refused to give her name for fear of repercussions from the Satanists, said. "If a young girl can be taken from London for this, then what about us? We only live a couple of miles from where she was found."

The man worked as an associate for Cooper & McKenzie in the City of London, but he was recently dismissed and was understood to be after immense stress after a multi-million pounds deal he had brokered on behalf of steel magnate Anil Kapoor had collapsed.

"He was behaving erratically recently and could not be trusted. But we are all shocked to hear he was associated with such evil practices," Andrew Ransome, a junior partner at Cooper & McKenzie, said.

Soon after arriving at St. Edith's, Jane realizes she is one of the smallest girls in the school, but she has a determination to get stronger. She can feel something has changed inside her since her the medical procedure with her daddy that was performed by the Indian man. She remembers her daddy saying she needed a magic potion to make her better. He was shouting when the Indian man arrived and put a tube in her arm. Then a tube into her daddy's arm. A machine was whirring and green liquid came down the tube.

Her mind is a whirlwind and after a few days Jane is in trouble at her new school. Miss Gilbert, the music teacher, walks into the exercise studio to see what this new girl is doing jumping about on her own and holding two short sticks. To her horror, the teacher sees they are not sticks at all, but a short nineteenth-century spear and a miniature farming scythe she has taken from the wall of the corridor.

Jane is taken immediately to the headmistress's office. Miss Rossington herself, as Jane's house tutor, is called and she has to suppress a smile at Jane's spirit and cheekiness.

"What were you thinking, Jane Banks? You've been here only a few days and you steal a spear and scythe from the wall," the headmistress says.

"*Iklwa*, Miss Fernsby."

"Excuse me, Jane?"

"The spear is an *iklwa*."

"Yes, I know. It's a spear from Shaka Zulu."

"Shaka kaSenzangakhona, Miss Fernsby."

"That's enough from you, Jane. We have a duty of care for all our girls. Whatever it is called and whoever it came from, it has a sharp, metal end, and you could do yourself serious damage. The same as this scythe. Do you understand? I will have to inform your grandmother, of course. Heaven knows what she will think."

"Yes, Miss Fernsby."

Once Jane leaves the room, remarkably without even a single demerit, the head turns to the teachers, her face reddening

18

in frustration and embarrassment.

"Miss Gilbert, will you instruct Mr. Thomas to screw these to the wall so they cannot be removed. And Miss Rossington. Will you find one of the history teachers and tell them to come to my office immediately. What did she call that spear again?"

A week after the spear and scythe incident, Miss Rossington is in the headmistress's office with Jane again. She is embroiled in Jane's troubles personally this time.

Walking down the corridor near the science labs, Miss Rossington spots a small girl being poked and taunted by fourteen-year-old Charlotte Carter. She shouts at the girls to stop their nonsense, but before she can get there the younger girl crouches down, swings her right leg around and knocks the bigger girl off her feet in a style the teacher has only previously seen in Jackie Chan movies. In a seamless movement, the younger girl catches a flailing arm of her victim, flips her around and pins her to the floor, face down, with her arm twisted against her back.

Miss Rossington realizes who the younger girl is.

"Jane Banks, let that girl go this instant. Do you hear me?" she shouts with all the authority she can muster.

Shouting at girls is certainly not something she has to do at St. Edith's very often.

Jane lets go and stands up calmly, but not before twisting Charlotte Carter's arm in its socket, forcing the older girl to let out a squeal of pain. The high-pitched baying from the other girls falls silent as they stare on in disbelief. Charlotte is nearly a foot taller than Jane and probably three stone heavier. For a moment, Miss Rossington just stands there with them, staring. Trying to make sense of what she has seen.

Jane is calm, breathing normally. Charlotte is shaking, taking in huge gulps of air, with tears streaming down her face.

"To Miss Fernsby's office. Now! The pair of you!"

"Well, Jane Banks," Miss Fernsby says, annoyed that her

ritual of afternoon tea and biscuits has been disturbed. A plate of Harrods shortbread biscuits rests untouched on a china plate on her desk. Fernsby is a traditional woman, always dressed in a tweed two-piece, who just wishes the world could return to the way it was in 1970s.

"I can truly say that in all my years at St. Edith's I have never encountered this before. A new girl in my office twice within days of just starting at the school. First the spear... and I don't want to hear you correcting me! First the spear... and now this. Needless to say, there will be consequences this time."

"It's outrageous, Miss Fernsby," Charlotte Carter's house tutor pipes up. "Attacking another girl like that."

The head ignores her.

"As for you, Charlotte Carter. You are nearly a senior and should know better. And don't think that because I sit in this office that I don't know what goes on among you girls. You can both go back to your rooms and I shall speak to each one of you in private after dinner. Now go! And both of you think carefully about what you have done."

Oh, how she wishes she could deprive girls of their dinner, as had happened in her day. And for a lot less than this, that's for sure! Such silly, soft rules these days. How can she instruct these girls how to be ladies if she cannot discipline them properly?

Transcript of e-mail to Alexandra Burton, Private Secretary to Mrs. Lorraine Meaden

To: alexandraburton@westleyhall.co.uk
Cc/Bcc:
From: judithfernsby@stedithsschool.co.uk
Subject: To reschedule my call with Mrs. Meaden

Dear Ms. Burton,

As arranged, I have a scheduled call with Mrs. Meaden at seven p.m. on Thursday. However, a matter of some urgency regarding Jane has arisen. Please could I ask you to put in a request to Mrs. Meaden for our call to be rescheduled to this evening?

Please assure Mrs. Meaden that there is no need to concern herself, and that Jane is perfectly well. However, as this is a serious matter regarding Jane's behavior it is important that I speak with Mrs. Meaden tonight, if at all possible.

I understand that Mrs. Meaden is a busy lady and has a schedule, so I would like to thank you in advance for your assistance in this matter.

Yours sincerely,

Miss Fernsby
　　Headmistress, St. Edith's School for Girls
　　Alpin Road
　　Wilton
　　Nr. Salisbury
　　Wiltshire

Lorraine settles down in her favorite chair and rings her bell. A tall, middle-aged, bronzed Mediterranean butler appears and she nods toward the drinks cabinet behind her. The butler pours out a healthy dose of Grey Goose vodka into a crystal highball glass, topping it up not that liberally with tonic water. A quick squeeze of lime and it is ready.

Lorraine sighs. What does that weaselly woman want that is so important? They have specifically arranged that she will call on Thursdays to present an update on Jane's progress at the school. What is so urgent that the call has to be brought forward?

The two women were at school there together in the 1970s. Fernsby — Lorraine has always found it amusing that she carries a name of such a common plant — had latched onto her at school. The other girls nicknamed Fernsby "Lorraine's poodle" because

21

she always scuttled along behind her like a dog after scraps. But Lorraine had found her useful and it suited her to let Fernsby think they were friends. It had been no surprise to Lorraine that she had spent virtually her whole life at the school, hidden away from the real world. Nine years as a pupil, then returning as a teacher after a few years at university in Bath, before finally becoming headmistress two years ago.

The phone rings, and Lorraine takes another sip of her vodka, making sure to let the phone ring a few times before answering. While the headmistress goes through her usual ritual of fawning over their friendship and their days together at the school, Lorraine squeezes a touch more lime into her drink. She can't resist smiling as she hears the story of Jane's day. It serves that older girl right, Lorraine thinks. It seems those self-protection classes she sent Jane to have already proved useful.

Of course, there had to be some form of punishment she agrees with the headteacher. And no, no, it just wouldn't do for the other girls to see this go unpunished. There was clearly no question of a suspension, even though such an offense certainly warranted it. The women agree on a suitable punishment for Jane. It is, of course, Lorraine who tells the headmistress what the punishment will be. She also outlines the punishment for Charlotte Carter, which even the headmistress, with her old-fashioned views on discipline, thinks very harsh. How is she to explain everything to Mr. and Mrs. Carter? She will have to find a way; they certainly don't donate as much to the school as her old friend.

Before finishing the call, the headmistress adds one more thing.

"Oh, Lorraine, just to let you know: Jane will be needing a new hockey stick. A couple of days after we stopped her using that spear, she started using her hockey stick to exercise. Now the face has broken off."

Lorraine rings her bell to order another vodka tonic and

opens her folder on Jane. She makes a few notes concerning the telephone call and rereads some of the documents inside.

I have a lot to answer for, Lorraine thinks, taking an extra-large gulp of vodka tonic to dull the guilt.

"The pain my granddaughter has been through..." she mutters to herself.

Jane's punishment is to spend every Sunday for the next six weeks in the library, after she has attended the church service with the other girls, from noon till six. She will only be allowed to leave the library to use the bathroom and for lunch. At the end of the six weeks she has to present as essay on something of relevance to St. Edith's or Wilton. She will be allowed out of the school only once, accompanied by a teacher, if she needs to conduct research for the essay. Charlotte Carter is suspended for two weeks and banned from playing hockey for the rest of the year.

Jane accepts her punishment without complaint. She even seems to relish it. On the first Sunday, she is waiting outside the library when Miss Rossington arrives.

"Jane, what are you doing here? You are allowed to have tea and biscuits after the church service before your, er, before you come to the library."

"That's OK, Miss Rossington," Jane replies as the teacher pushes the door to the library open.

Miss Rossington spreads out her papers and points to a desk nearby.

"Please sit there, Jane. This will be your home for the next six Sundays."

Jane sets down her white Moleskin notepad and strokes it with affection before heading off to the local history section. The teacher notes a Mont Blanc pencil and a new, bright white eraser next to Moleskin. It is all very stark.

Crack!

Miss Rossington sits bolt upright in shock.

"What was that? I heard a crack."

Crack!

Jane shows her the source of the noise.

"Sorry, Miss Rossington, it was my knuckles. I'm just preparing to start."

Jane had seen her daddy do the same thing before he started an important job (or when he was nervous) and now she has adopted the habit herself.

"Well, stop it. You'll get arthritis when you get older."

For the next three weeks, Jane works in silence (apart from the occasional crack of knuckles), reading, making notes, and occasionally getting up to take a different book from the shelves. She has to be prompted to take her breaks and is reluctant to leave when the bell sounds for dinner.

"Just a few more minutes please, Miss Rossington?" she always asks.

Some punishment, the teacher thinks to herself. This girl is actually enjoying herself locked up in the library each Sunday while the other girls are outside, playing. For Jane, the quiet of the library is a chance to make sense of the numbers that have been running though her head ever since she woke up on that hill in Wales.

"...Swiss National Bank, account Number 339809089, sort code 907081. Harrods, London, safe deposit box 31. Access code 0497..."

The words and numbers had been jumbled at first, but now they seem to be falling into place. But what are they?

Toward the end of the fourth week, Jane looks up from her notepad.

"Miss Rossington," she says. "Miss Fernsby told me I could go out on one short, local field trip if I needed it for research."

"That's right, Jane. Where do you need to go?"

"Wilton House, Miss Rossington."

"I gained strength from my army exercises on Salisbury Plain. There is a big house nearby. I took your mummy there many times. She always said it reminded her of the house where she grew up."

"OK, Jane. It is open to the public, so it shouldn't be a problem. I will have to get it approved by Miss Fernsby first. What information do you need from there?"

"I'm not sure, Miss Rossington. I have all the information I need, but it's just too, er, historical."

"Too historical? You think your essay will be too dry and boring?"

"Too dry, that's it!" Jane exclaims, like she has discovered the secret to eternal life.

It is the first time the teacher has seen her show any emotion.

"It needs some *real* life."

"Writers would say it needs some color to bring it to life. Well, Wilton Hall has certainly seen lots of color in its life over the years," Miss Rossington says.

The trip to Wilton House is largely uneventful. Jane just sits on the grass most of the time, staring into space. Well, it is more like she is staring into herself. For a moment, Miss Rossington wonders if Jane has somehow connected with her subject, Edith Oliver, a woman who reportedly had many paranormal experiences herself, and who some called a psychic. The teacher laughs off such a silly idea.

Halfway through the field trip, Jane asks if she can go for a walk alone, so she can "imagine what it was like for Oliver", who spent so much of her time alone in the gardens. The teacher is reluctant, but she is so delighted that Jane is showing an interest in something other than her workouts, that she agrees. She still wouldn't describe Jane as *animated* — she continues to show no emotion — but she certainly is interested.

Jane wanders off, and once she is sure she is out of sight of the teacher, she rolls up the bottom of her skirt and removes a Marlboro Red she hid in its hem with a couple of Diamond Light Strike Anywhere matches. She runs a match down the bark of the tree and the flame pops out with a fizz. She tries to picture her mummy and daddy walking around the gardens together. So, her mummy grew up in a place like this? Jane knows nothing about her mummy's childhood because she never spoke about it. Almost like she was hiding something. She coughs as she draws on the cigarette, then glances around to make sure no one is looking. Her daddy's voice races through her head.

"I really enjoy these fags. They are strong, and you will get used to them quickly. But they are bad for you Jane. Take care my darling. And keep your mind focused on the job in hand."

Her daddy's words jolt Jane into action. She has a job to do and no time to waste with cigarettes now. She nonchalantly flicks down the Marlboro Red, as she'd seen her daddy do on countless occasions, and grinds it into the base of the tree. Then, after a quick look to make sure Miss Rossington is not looking in her direction, she heads past the gift shop and now-defunct Wilton Abbey on the edge of the estate and toward to small town of Wilton. Jane enjoys feeling the power in her legs as she runs and pushes herself a little bit harder. Faster, she thinks to herself. Feel the power in your legs. You can go faster.

"I loved running around here during our exercises. They had been giving me special food rations and I was feeling stronger and more alert than ever at that time."

It's only a couple of minutes to the town but Jane quickly builds up a sweat in the warm summer sun. A couple of people glance at her as she passes the Pembroke Arms and the police station and heads into Russell Street, but most are too busy with their own chores to notice a small girl.

"Hot out there, is it?" the man behind the small counter at Keys4U says in that stating-the-obvious way some people use as he looks at the beads of sweat running down Jane's face.

She hands him two keys and smiles sweetly. He pulls copies of the standard keys off the pre-cut rack and a couple of minutes later Jane is back at Wilton House, using the same sweet smile to answer her teacher's questions about the hot afternoon sun. She will have the original keys she took from the school earlier back in their place this afternoon before anyone even notices they are missing.

On the sixth and final week of Jane's punishment, she turns up at the library with her laptop.

"Have you not started writing your essay yet, Jane?" Miss Rossington asks.

"No, Miss Rossington. But I have done all the research."

"OK, I'll leave you to get on with it. Sit in the usual place please."

Jane works through the day, typing steadily, and only stopping to refer to her notes every so often. She checks everything twice, sometimes three times, to make sure she has got her facts correct. This essay may have been a punishment, but she wants no errors. There is no room for mistakes in anything she does if she is going to achieve what she wants.

At four o'clock Jane looks up.

"I've finished it, Miss Rossington," she says, showing not even a glimmer of satisfaction.

"Well done, Jane. Load it onto this memory stick and I'll get it printed for you."

Crack! Crack!

"Jane! You really must stop doing that with your knuckles."

Miss Rossington reads through the essay and smiles. This girl is good. She'd come to St. Edith's as an average pupil from an average school, but now, even after a few weeks, she is head and shoulders above anyone in her English class. In fact, having seen this essay, the teacher concludes that her research and writing skills are probably better than any other girl in the school. If she hadn't been sitting with her and watching her for the past six weeks, she'd swear this was written by someone much older. The teacher takes some pleasure in her teaching skills, then admonishes herself for her pride.

"Jane, please clear up your things, and wait here for me. I need to take this to Miss Fernsby."

The headmistress seems engrossed in the essay. She puts it down on her desk next to her afternoon tea and Harrods shortbread biscuits, which she nibbles on daintily every so often. Far from being annoyed that her little tea and biscuit ritual has been disturbed, she seems puzzled. She glances down at the essay one more time.

"Miss Rossington, I have to ask if you have corrected this already? As you know, I always like to see what the girls can do themselves without your help."

"No, no," the English teacher replies. "This is what Jane put together. I was with her the whole time and she never asked for help once."

"Well, I have to say, Jane seems have done very well. *We* have certainly brought on her on a huge amount in the few weeks since she joined us."

"Yes, *we* have, Miss Fernsby."

"Well, this will have to go in the school magazine, of course. Will you see to that? But I will also contact Mr. Alberton, the editor at *Wiltshire Alive* magazine. I'm sure he would be very interested in publishing this. It would be excellent publicity for the school."

"That's quite an achievement for a nine-year-old girl if he does."

"Quite an achievement for St. Edith's, Miss Rossington. It shows what *we* achieve here with our girls."

Wiltshire Alive
A special magazine for a special county

Edith Oliver — a Lady Ahead of Her Time
By Jane Banks, aged 9, of St. Edith's School for Girls, Wilton
(Published with kind permission of Miss Fernsby, Headmistress of St. Edith's School for Girls)

Edith Oliver was a lady who challenged traditional boundaries for women in the late-nineteenth century and early twentieth century. Oliver pushed back perceptions of women's roles in society to become a role model for young ladies in Wilton and across the country.

Oliver was awarded an MBE for her work on the Wiltshire Women's Land Army, became the first woman to serve on the Wilton Town Council in 1934 and the county's first mayoress in 1938.

But writing and art remained her great love and she frequently organized gatherings where she brought together renowned names such as Cecil Beaton, Osbert Sitwell, Sir John Betjeman, and Siegfried Sassoon...

Chapter 2

Once all the other girls have headed to the breakfast hall before their game of hockey, Miss Rossington steps back and thinks about their comments about Jane.

"She's mad!"

"What is she doing?"

"Waste of a good hockey stick, I'd say."

At that moment, the door creaks outwards and Jane walks into the hallway. Her long blonde hair is covered in a black head wrap, with a knot tied at the back to catch the sweat. Despite the wrap, the salty liquid has seeped through and soaked the spine of her burgundy Dri-FIT top, which clings to her toned body as if it has been sprayed on. She has grown stronger in her three years at the school and is now of average height for a girl about to turn twelve, but she is incredibly well-toned compared to the others.

"Hello, Miss Rossington," Jane says.

"I just saw the other girls. They are already kitted out for hockey," she replies, even though Jane had not asked her a question. "Now I'm admiring the school's artefacts, but you know all about them, don't you, Jane?"

Miss Rossington eyes a short stabbing-spear and small replica scythe on the wall, the only artefacts that have been bolted to the wall so they cannot be removed following Jane's actions a few years earlier. There is generally no need for such security measures in St. Edith's.

"Yes, Miss Rossington. May I go for a shower now?"

"Yes, Jane."

Jane is always polite, thinks Miss Rossington, but never says more than she needs to. And she certainly *never* opens up and talks about the terrible things that happened to her and her family.

"Why don't you join the other girls in their game outside later?"

Miss Rossington knows she is wasting her time. Jane is good at hockey but will only play when she has to. Jane nods and strides down the halfway to the shower rooms. Miss Rossington eyes the old-style hickory hockey stick in her right hand. One end, the end where the face had been broken off, has been taped up carefully, to avoid her hands getting splinters. No doubt by the caretaker Mr. Thomas. He likes Jane. She is the only girl who treats him with respect; treats him like a man, rather than an invisible caretaker.

Mr. Thomas is one of the few people Jane actually speaks to. She always seems to be looking at bits of machinery with him, even though she's been told numerous times to keep away. Enquiring, questioning, learning; that is Jane.

From Angela West's WhatsApp account.
18ᵗʰ July

Angela West: typing…
Simone Grant: online

Angela: Hey Simone, I've found an article on that thing we were chatting about on Thursday. You know, the stuff of chemtrails?

Simone: Wow! Can you send me the link?

Angela: Will do. www.thetruescience.com

Simone: Cheers, I'll read it in my break. I'm due a latte soon anyway!

Angela: You're always due a latte babe!!

Simone: Only skinny tho!

Angela: Haha! Did you ever do anything about getting in touch with Jane?

Simone: I was drunk when I said I'd do that! It's been over three years since I've seen her so I think it's best left alone. I don't think I'll ever see her again to be honest.

Angela: That's a shame. You always got on well with her.

Simone: Yeah, when George was around.

Angela: Sorry to remind you babe.

Simone: That's OK. I'm over it now.

Angela: You sure?

Simone: Yeah. Anyway, I'll check out that article later. You still on for a drink later?

Angela: You bet! First margarita on me!

Jane takes off her gym kit, her chest still heaving with the intensity of the physical training she has just put herself through. She has trained every day since coming to the school just over three years ago. She showers alone in the St. Edith's modern changing room, running her left hand down her right arm as she flexes it, taking pleasure in feeling her muscles tighten.

"Not bad for an eleven-year-old," she thinks. "And they told me I had a muscle wasting disease! A few more years and I'll be even fitter and stronger."

"You are strong, Jane. Stronger than you think. There is nothing you can't do. Don't let anyone tell you otherwise."

Jane is obsessed with getting fitter and stronger. Her teachers tell her grandmother that it's down to whatever it was that made her weak when she was younger. The problem the doctors thought was muscular dystrophy. They tell her that she's compensating for all those years when she had to struggle, working her body hard to ensure she will never return to the fragile thing she was before. And they can't blame her.

Jane sits in endless hospital appointments and inwardly laughs at the surgeons' pub psychology. She knows the real reason she's training her powerful body. For revenge.

She dries herself and pulls her school uniform on over her muscular legs and well-defined arms, then glances around before opening her locker. It's full of unused medication. The doctors have instructed her to continue taking it just in case, and although a voice in her head keeps telling her there is no need, she's kept them all the same. It's the same voice that tells her to train early every morning. The same voice that tells her to keep Simone Grant close. And Lorraine, her grandmother, closer. The same voice that told her to acquire the small pistol she takes from behind the stash of pills, before strapping it to her thigh.

"Make sure it is secure. Check everything three times. That's what they taught me in the army."

She looks in the mirror to make sure that the gun can't be seen beneath the pleats of her red skirt as Lorraine walks in.

"Darling. I thought I'd come early so we could have some time together before Speech Day. Are you nearly ready?"

"Coming, Grandmother."

Lorraine looks unamused.

"Lorraine. You know I prefer Lorraine."

Jane smirks. She calls Lorraine "Grandmother" just to annoy her. She finds herself taking a peek down her impressive cleavage. She has no idea why, but it both amuses and disturbs her at the same time.

"I'm proud of you. It's the biggest award of the day, you know," Lorraine says, tapping at the headline in the local newspaper she is holding.

Salisbury Recorder
18th July
Tech Tycoon Max Bing to Present Award to Outstanding Student

Jane shrugs coolly and takes her grandmother's hand, though her heart begins to speed up again at the prospect of finally coming face to face with *him*...

Max Bing looks out the window of his top-of-the-range silver Tesla Model S as they enter the quaint country town of Salisbury. An old lady with a green shopping bag scuttles along the pavement with a newspaper.

"This is Salisbury, sir," his chauffeur confirms. "The school is about fifteen minutes from here."

Bing looks down at the folder on Jane Banks. He had spent his life dedicated to the study of aging. To the study of stopping aging and extending life. And now he is to meet one of his greatest experiments. This little girl might have hopes and dreams of her own, but Bing has other plans for her future.

Medical and wellbeing report

Jane Banks

Age: 11

Physical: The subject's physical fitness is well above average for a girl of her age.

Resting heart rate: 60bpm, the lower end for a female of her age.

Strength: Maximum of 5 using the Medical Research Council Manual Muscle Testing scale. The subject displays muscle activation against the examiner's full resistance and a full range of motion. The tests reveal that the subject has the strength of an average eighteen-year-old female.

Visual acuity: Exceptional 20/10 vision. This means the subject can see at 20 feet what other people can only see at ten feet. Less than one per cent of the population have 20/10 vision.

Hearing acuity: Perfect hearing. There is no evidence of hyperacusis (sound sensitivity).

Medication: Corticosteroids. The subject continues to take corticosteroids — used to delay the progression of Duchenne muscular dystrophy — under instruction from her doctors. The actual mechanism of corticosteroids on the wasting disease is not yet fully understood and we recommend the subject be removed from this medication as soon as possible.

Psychological: According to reports from her psychologist, the subject continues to suffer memory loss relating to her mother's death and the incident at Anno Methusala HQ. The last thing the subject remembers is her father taking her somewhere to make her better before being woken up by strangers on a hill. The psychologist believes this is a full memory loss brought on by the lysosomal transfusion procedure, although there remains a possibility that this is dissociative amnesia (repressed memory loss) brought on by the trauma of the events.

Academic: High. She excels in mechanics and English, and her understanding of all sciences can be equated to a high-performing under-graduate.

Intelligence quotient: 131 (Extremely High for Children). The Wechsler Intelligence Scale for Children measures Verbal Comprehension, Visual Spatial, Fluid Reasoning, Working Memory, and Processing Speed. Despite the problems noted above with memory loss, this places the subject in the top two-and-half per cent of children of her age.

Emotional intelligence: Low. The subject displays the same low EI traits as her father. She is a loner and believes she is always right. She gets irritated by small talk and is intensely focused on what she wants to achieve. "Driven by a hidden force" is how the psychologist describes it. The subject has no social media accounts.

Things are going very well, except for this worrying link to her father's traits, Bing thinks. *This girl could be the breakthrough that takes our research to a new level.* Who would have thought that a lysosomal transfusion — previously only tested on mice — would work so perfectly on a young girl. But she was given a huge dose, a dose never considered safe by the scientists before. We now need to get her into the laboratory to experiment on her fully and see just what that huge dose did to her. She will be the perfect specimen for us. It all came about thanks to the actions of Anil Kapoor.

MethusalaCo has been Bing's baby during the last three and a half years, following the announcement that his tech giant Synoplex would launch the life science company that, as *Time Magazine* put it: "hopes to cure death".

The media dubbed it an audacious start-up, but Bing knew it was anything but that. At its launch, it already had many years of research behind it. And unlike other companies of its ilk, it had already tested its technology on people. Illegally, of course, but that was the only way they could know what worked. There was just the little matter of making people 'disappear' when they needed new specimens. But who really misses a handful of useless people? They should think themselves lucky that their bodies are helping develop some of the greatest research ever conducted by mankind.

New York Times
18th July
Space, the Final Affordable Frontier, Thanks to a Skyhook and the Egyptians

For years, we have been told that flying to space was about to become possible for all of us. But now, British tech entrepreneur Max Bing says it will become a reality using a skyhook and a surprising partner in Egypt's national space program. Big thinkers like Richard Branson and Elon Musk have talked up commercial space flights in the past — but it has always come at a cost that is out of the reach of ordinary people. Visits to space have remained a dream belonging to the super rich. But following Synoplex's audacious takeover of the US rocket company Blast for six billion dollars yesterday, Bing is promising that trips to space will soon cost no more than a return ticket to London on a jumbo jet.

It was Bing's choice of partner in the venture that raised eyebrows. Although formed in 1950, Egypt's National Authority for Remote Sensing and Space Sciences (NARSS) is not the first name investors would have expected to hear when this new venture was announced.

"Blast has the skyhook technology that we were looking for. NARSS has been a ground breaker in remote sensing in space and has long had ambitions for a building a ladder into space. Our partners' expertise coupled with our technology and access to capital can make trips to space affordable for everyone," Bing told wide-eyed journalists at a press conference in the ballroom of Manhattan's Four Seasons Hotel.

"Once we are up and running, people won't be checking online to find flights to London to see where the King lives. They will be looking for flights to see the stars. And I don't mean Hollywood."

Bing, a man known for his revolutionary ideas, added that, "Science and technology always has the answers. We may have bought a rocket company, but we will be using non-rocket space launches."

A skyhook, or a momentum exchange tether to give it its correct name, is a tether that can be used for space launches without the high costs of rockets. A cable would be connected to an orbiting station and would go down into the atmosphere of earth. The spacecraft would be attached to the tether and effectively pulled into space using centrifugal force by the system's rotation.

Blast started as a company in 1992 that offered little more than compact, fun rockets that interested only a small group of amateur launch enthusiasts. But following the arrival of mercurial engineer Reginald Bloom ten years ago, things changed. Known as the 'bird man' for his eccentric habit of feeding the pigeons around St. Paul's Cathedral in his lunch break, Bloom set about revolutionizing the company's ambitions. Their share price soared along with his new designs, which grew more ambitious by the year, and the company's move into building orbiting stations. This culminated in a test flight two years ago that successfully sent three monkeys into space and safely back in a rocket that even some NASA scientists have marveled at. But the real breakthrough came when Bloom started working on the skyhook.

Max Bing has for many years been pushing boundaries. Now it seems he is determined to push back the ultimate frontier.

The Tesla crunches its was up the driveway to the school. A discreet sign set back in the perfectly trimmed bushes announces its presence.

St. Edith's School for Girls
Since 1860
Founded by Rev. Charles Witheringham

Max Bing doesn't normally bother himself with events such as this. He never has the time. He receives hundreds of requests, most of them much more high profile than something as trivial as a School Speech Day. His assistant just bats them away politely.

But this one is different. Jane Banks is important. She is *very* important. To Synoplex. To MethusalaCo. And most importantly to Anno Methusala and the members of the society who have

38

invested billions in his research into aging.

He can read all the reports into Jane, checking the facts and analyzing the figures till he is dizzy with excitement. But nothing replaces seeing your experiment in person. He won't be able to examine her like he does his other experiments, of course. But he can see her up close. See how those muscles had recovered and got stronger.

Lorraine Meaden has made it all happen, telling the excited headmistress that she met him at a function and casually asked him whether he would honor the school with his presence. The headmistress had naturally been delighted.

Top-of-the-range cars fill the car park and spill onto the temporary parking area that has been cordoned off on part of the hockey field. Most are old-style petrol guzzlers, simply expensive calling cards to display the owners' wealth. Few are eco-friendly.

"Such a shame," Bing thinks.

A space has been reserved for Bing, and the headmistress is waiting excitedly by it with Lorraine. She clasps the make-shift red rope attached to the gaudy gold-colored barrier that makes up the school's VIP parking place for her guest of honor. The chauffeur slides the Tesla into the space as if he is pulling up to the entrance to a downtown nightclub.

"Mr. Bing!" the headmistress exclaims moments after the chauffeur opens his door. "We are honored to have you here at St. Edith's School for Girls. What a stroke of luck that my good friend Mrs. Meaden was able to meet you recently. We appreciate you are a busy…"

Bing cuts her off.

"Miss Fernsby. I am happy to be here and support this very important event," he lies.

39

The headmistress blushes at the mere mention of her name.

"Mrs. Meaden. It's nice to see you again," Bing says, extending his hand in greeting.

Bing strolls to the high-arched stone entrance with Lorraine while the headmistress skips along behind them, desperately trying to run through the evening's proceedings. He stops on the top step and turns around.

"Miss Fernsby, shall we do the honors for the photographers?"

Lorraine slips away, ensuring she will not be in the official photographs.

The photographer from the local paper and an agency photographer, covering the event for the national dailies, click away. A few of the parents, who have hung around the car park despite being asked to move inside to the hall, sheepishly capture the moment on their phones.

"That's fine," Bing assures them. "If the gentlemen from the press have finished, you are welcome to come up for a photograph. Synoplex is a company for everyone. And I'm sure you all have Synoplex phones!"

One by one the parents scuttle up the steps to get their photograph taken with the man who leads the world's largest tech company. The headmistress looks crestfallen as the parents check the images on their phone screens to make sure they are good enough to impress their friends. Her moment has been stolen from her.

The hall is packed. Even parents that never normally bother with Speech Day have made the effort. All because Max Bing is there to present the certificates. The girls receiving awards are seated in the front row, with the other girls in the rows behind them. The parents, all dressed up as if it was a day at the races, sit in the back rows. The teachers are on the stage.

After an introduction and welcome from the headmistress,

Bing speaks about his multi-national company. He keeps it general at first: Synoplex phones, laptops, how their technology leads the world. But he soon switches to his baby: MethusalaCo. There are some very rich people in this hall. All potential sources of money for his research.

"This is the company that is changing the way the world thinks about aging," he says.

Lorraine smiles. She knows what is coming. She has heard it all before.

First comes Ray Kurzweil — Bing's hero — the man who created the concept of Singularity, a theoretical tipping point when the very fabric of humankind's existence changes after technology reaches a hypothetical tipping point.

Then come the questions.

"Would you like to live longer? Would you like to live healthier? Would you like to have a total sense of wellbeing even well into your nineties?"

Who could say no?

"MethusalaCo can achieve all of these things."

Lorraine readies herself for the punchline.

"Some of the most forward-thinking people in the world — people like David Rogerson, the world's youngest billionaire, renowned investor Carl Sachs, and GeeTel chief executive Stephen Trent — have contributed to our work. This is the biggest challenge facing mankind. Now it is time for you to get involved."

And there it is. Lorraine groans inwardly. Max Bing never misses an opportunity when it is presented to him. The headmistress is too overwhelmed by Bing's arrival to realize that her Speech Day is being hijacked by a consummate fundraiser, and she simply applauds enthusiastically along with the parents.

It is time for the awards. The teacher in charge of each award steps forward and hands the relevant framed certificate to Max Bing. The headmistress then reads out the name of the girl receiving the award to more applause and the girl makes her way to the stage for a handshake and a photograph.

Jane counts the time it takes for each girl to walk from her seat, up the stairs, and across the stage to Max Bing.

"One, two, three…" she counts. "One, two, three…"

Just as she had thought. There is only one opportunity to get the gun from under her skirt and shoot Bing — the man who murdered her mummy and daddy. It has to be just after she climbs the last step. He always turns sideways to the audience to face the girl coming up the steps. She'll have to be quick and smooth as she reaches down to pull out the gun. Miss Fernsby will be alongside him when she gets her award. The girls who have already received their awards stay on the stage with the teachers. There will be too many other people up there for her to make a mistake. It is Bing she wants.

"This is your chance, Jane. Be brave. You are ready."

Hockey, athletics, mathematics, ancient history, she ticks them off in her head. Her award for Outstanding Achievement will be the last one presented.

Then her moment arrives.

"Finally, we come to our most prestigious award," the headmistress gushes. "It goes to a girl who is just eleven years old — the youngest girl to ever receive this award at St. Edith's. I am pleased to announce that the award for Outstanding Achievement this year, goes to… Jane Banks."

Jane readies herself, pausing briefly before standing up. Lorraine will be soaking up the applause, no doubt, she thinks. But she dismisses thoughts of her grandmother. She *has* to concentrate. She makes her way slowly to the stage and lowers her right hand onto her skirt, carefully taking each step one by one. Does this make her look unnatural? Who walks like this?

She has practiced this in her head dozens of times. But now, when the moment is here, she is starting to question herself.

This is it. Jane's mind races with images of her daddy. The times he took her swimming and urged her on in her matches at chess club. The gentle way he promised her he would make her better when she was sick. Now he was gone. His voice reverberates in her head and strengthens her resolve for what she is about to do.

"It's now or never."

As she takes the last step onto the stage, she bends forward and slides her hand up her skirt. But she fumbles briefly before getting a grip on the gun. The movement is quick, but it isn't smooth. She points the gun at Max Bing and fires without hesitation. But her fumble has given Bing a split second to react and he starts moving backwards. He reels back as the shot hits him.

Jane stares at her target. She's got him. Her eyes are fixed on Bing and she can't see the teachers jumping from their chairs and diving for cover at the back of the stage. She can't even hear the screams behind her. The focus is Max Bing.

She *has* got him, but only in his shoulder. Why did I fumble? I needed to be smoother withdrawing the gun from its holster.

Bing grabs the girl who is standing closest to him — Judith Pearson, who'd won the Latin award — and hides behind her. Even from ten yards, Jane can see the fear in Judith's piercing blue eyes. It is the first time she's taken her focus from Max Bing. She can't shoot again. It is too risky.

Without hesitation, Jane runs back down the stairs of the stage to the floor of the hall. The room is in panic. She darts, gun in hand along the side of the stage, past the area that is used for costume changes during plays, into the kitchen and pulls out the key she needs. Over the years, she has gotten keys for all exits of

43

the school so she can come and go as she pleases, and despite her growing anger at not getting Bing, she is grateful for this foresight at least. She has planned her escape route in advance. This is the nearest exit and the easiest to reach.

Jane doesn't even pause to look back as she runs. She crosses a small grassy area, heads up a narrow pathway and through a wooded area to a clearing. This is where Mr. Thomas keeps all his equipment. In the unlocked shed she finds what she is looking for: the quad bike he uses to get from one part of the school grounds to the another. The key is in a gardening glove on the seat.

The quad bike starts with ease. Although Jane has never ridden this bike, Mr. Thomas has shown her exactly how it works, and she has used a similar bike at her grandmother's estate often enough. About four hundred yards further on through the woodland is the perimeter wall. There is a small gate. Mr. Thomas once told Jane that it was probably the entrance the servants had used many years ago. The gate is rarely opened these days, but it opens easily enough with a sharp pull. Once the quad bike has been eased through the gateway, Jane pulls the gate shut. She can't get the images of the failed shooting out her head. The approach. The shot. Bing hiding behind Judith Pearson. Why did she fail?

She speeds off. Jane heads through some more woodland before reaching a small road. After a few meters, she turns right into the entrance to a field. The gate is ajar. What is it with people in the countryside and not locking things?

Making sure to keep to the edge of the field, mostly so she has cover from the trees, but also so the farmer, whose house is on the other side, can't hear the quad bike, she crosses to more woodland. The area is wild and the pathways erratic and overgrown. But Jane knows the way. She walked it many times while planning her escape. Finally, after a couple of miles, she stops and turns off the quad bike. There is no point wasting time hiding it; they will find it anyway. Once the police realize it is missing, there'll look for it, and once they find it, they will know her escape route. It doesn't matter anyway, as she will be circling back on herself. She knows exactly where she is going. And they won't find her there.

Jane reaches down into the open roots of a large tree and drags out a bag. She pulls out a pair of Japanese Unbranded jeans, a cheap, gray hooded sweatshirt, a gray baseball cap and some Allbird sneakers. There are no logos on anything. Nothing to help identify her. She strips off her school uniform, stuffs it in the bag and changes into her casual clothes.

She stares at the gun. She nearly got him. Why did she fumble? She was trying to be too quick. What an evil, cowardly man to hide behind Judith Pearson like that. It proved everything she knew about him and why she wanted him dead. He'd do anything to get what he wanted and sacrifice anyone to survive.

She looks down at her Smith & Wesson Bodyguard 380 and strokes it with her fingers and thumb, enjoying the rough texture of its fish-scale grip. The semi-automatic fits well into her small hands and is ideal for concealing. If only she'd been quicker and smoother removing the gun when she needed it most...

Before she walks away from the quad bike, she slides her hand into the side pocket of her bag and pulls out the pack of Marlboro Reds she'd put in there. How she would like one of those right now. But she has to keep moving. She puts them back, smiling as she feels the shaft of the *iklwa* she'd taken from the wall. She runs again, steadily, breathing comfortably. First, Jane heads north, putting more distance between her and the school, then she jags eastwards.

She approaches the edge of the fruit farm cautiously, being sure to stay hidden, deep in the bushes. It is here that she will wait for the darkness. The pickers work late on these summer nights packing well into the night, so she has a few hours. She settles down for her wait and tries to calm her racing mind. She watches as workers stack boxes of fresh fruit so they are ready to be loaded onto the trucks later that night. The trucks will be heading to the supermarket distribution center in south London with the fresh country produce. And Jane will be on one of them.

The presenter straightens his tie before the producer brings down his hand to signal that he is live on air.

NEWS FROM THE SOUTH
Breaking News

"Welcome to News from the South. We are reporting outside St. Edith's School for Girls near Salisbury, where the dramatic news coming in is that there are unconfirmed reports of a shooting incident at an event attended by the tech giant Max Bing."

"How much do we know about the shooting at this stage, James? Does the shooting involve Max Bing himself?" the anchor back in the London studio asks.

"This has not been confirmed yet," the local presenter replies, barely concealing his excitement at being front and center of such a big story.

He knows the big boys are already racing down to the school from London to cover the event, but he will be the face everyone sees on their TV screens until they arrive. *This sure beats reporting on prize marrows and agricultural fairs.*

"The police have released very little information at this stage but judging from the amount of activity around the school, this certainly appears to be a very serious incident."

"Do we know how many shots were fired, James? The *Daily Mail* website is reporting that this could be a terrorist attack. The work of immigrants left unchecked by the Home Office." the anchor prompts.

"We should emphasize that those reports remain unconfirmed by the police at this stage. Any scenario is possible. But we do have this photo of Max Bing on stage with a young girl."

"James," the anchor says, missing the photo prompt in her desperate effort to wrest control of the broadcast from the regional stringer. "Usually, with incidents such as this a lot of information emerges from the people on the ground, but all of the Synoplex social media sites are down and no information at all is coming out. Do you think that is a coincidence?"

"It's certainly strange that Synoplex is down at a time like this! If this is linked then it would give us some indication of exactly when the incident occurred. Synoplex sites may be down. But here at News from the South, we are still able to bring you information on the ground. I am here with local resident, Mary Kaye, who was due to be at the school to help clean up after the event..."

St. Edith's Mumsnet

Charlotte Aston: For mums and dads who couldn't get back for Speech Day. There has been a shooting at the school!

Meera Dev: OMG! We couldn't get back from LA. What happened?

Jennifer Wilson: We are stuck in Dubai. What the hell!

Charlotte Aston: Some girl had a gun. She shot Max Bing I think!

Alice Thompson: We are all outside now. It's crazy here!!

...ERROR: Connection to Server Interrupted or Message Stuck in Loading...

47

Lorraine Meaden sits bolt upright, aghast as the sound of the gunfire echoes around the hall. She knows the sound only too well. But had she really just seen what she had seen? As Jane had stepped onto the stage she had bent over briefly. What was she doing? This was no time to be pulling up her socks. Then there was a loud bang and Max Bing had recoiled backwards, before grabbing a small girl near him on the stage. Jane paused briefly but then ran down the stairs quickly. For a moment everyone else in the hall had frozen. Then someone shouted: "She's shot him! She's shot him!"

Lorraine sits frozen, unable to move as chairs scatter around her. Some parents run to grab their daughters; others just run. The woman next to her is cowering behind the chair in front of her and screaming. Lorraine's eyes remain fixed on the doorway where Jane exited the hall.

Wiltshire Police
18th July

Scanning feed...
999 call received... Shooting reported at St. Edith's School for Girls, Alpin Road, Wilton... One possible victim... 80+ public still on scene... Armed response requested... Do not enter building until armed response on scene...
Scanning feed...

Minutes later the armed response unit arrives. Many of the parents, children, and school staff are standing outside and the local police are trying to calm them down. Others are revving up their car engines in a mixture of fear and frustration despite the loud shouts from the constables who were first to arrive at the school.

"What's the situation? Is the shooter still inside? Are there any civilians still inside or on other parts of the grounds?" the section sergeant of the armed response unit asks.

"We believe the shooter left the building immediately after

firing, sir. According to witnesses, it was a young girl in school uniform."

"A young bloody girl! Are you sure?"

"Yes, sir. We have been told that by everyone we have spoken to. We have also been assured that the shooter exited from the back of the building within seconds and has not been seen since the shooting."

"*I'll* be the one assuring you what the situation is, constable!" the sergeant exclaims loudly.

"And the victim?"

"He was brought out by his staff, treated in the car by one of his own men, and driven away. They had already left by the time we arrived. We understand he was hit in the shoulder but was walking and conscious apparently."

The sergeant waves his hand and his team fan out, ready to approach the building.

"Right, constable, we are going to sweep the building. Keep these people back. Don't let anyone leave. And stop those bloody people revving their engines! It's driving me mad!"

Crouching, but moving swiftly, the armed response unit storms the building from all sides on their sergeant's signal.

"Where the hell are we going?" Max Bing screams to the medic who is part of his security team.

"Your facility in Southampton, Mr. Bing."

"Are you mad? I don't have time for that. You've seen the back of my shoulder? There's a hole in it. The bullet has passed through. You've patched me up and I'm not losing blood. Turn this eco-warrior car around and take me to Wales. I need to be at A.M. HQ."

Bing picks up his phone and dials his assistant.

"Have the Synoplex social media sites been shut down?" Max Bing asks, without bothering with the greeting formalities.

"Yes, Mr. Bing. We received the call within thirty seconds of you being shot. Are you all right, Mr. Bing?"

"Yes, yes, I'm fine. And you shut everything down immediately?"

"Yes, Mr. Bing. We have told the media that it's due to a loading problem, but our press team are receiving questions about the timing, of course."

"Call all the editors and sort that out. And leave all social media sites down until the team has had time to sort everything out with word and phrase blocking."

"Mr. Bing, some MPs are already saying it's a disgrace that these essential services can be disrupted by one company. They are raising the usual questions about monopolies."

"*Essential? Essential?* This is social media. It's just for people talking rubbish and sending each other photos of their dogs and babies. How is that an essential service?"

The owner of the tech giant doesn't wait for an answer because he doesn't want one.

"Ignore them. A couple more things..." he tells his assistant. "Get hold of Lorraine Meaden. Tell her to be at A.M. HQ tomorrow evening. And find the parents of the girl that I grabbed on stage. We need to keep them quiet. Money as usual. And that bloody image of me on stage behind the girl. How the hell did that get out? Get our spin doctors onto it. Tell them to use the angle of me saving her and making sure she was safe."

Bing calls David Rogerson next.

"David, I assume you have heard the news? ...Yes, yes, I'm fine... I agree, something with that transfusion may have affected her. It was a huge dose, after all. Too much of her stubborn father in her blood now. We need to find her and run some tests. ...No, no, she's not dangerous, just a little girl... yes, yes, we've certainly dealt with tougher characters in our time... oh good, you've contacted our people in the police force already. And they'll hand her over as soon as they find her? I've summoned Lorraine Meaden to A.M. HQ for a meeting with us tomorrow... excellent, if you can be there tonight we'll have a late supper and talk about what we are going to do. We need Granny Meaden on our side for now so we can find Jane. Then, as the mafia say… *basta!*"

As Bing talks, the medic rolls up his sleeve and inserts a cannula into a vein in his arm. Bing winces and stares at the man as it enters. The medic holds up the bag and the green liquid slowly starts flowing into his body.

"This will speed up your recovery, Mr. Bing," the medic tells him.

"Yes, yes, I know. Who do you think owns this company?" Bing snaps as he settles back into his seat.

The police have left the scene. The girls have already left with their parents and the other staff have been told to go home. Only the teachers who live at the school remain and they can finally go to their rooms.

Miss Rossington always hates the school at the end of term. It feels like a body without a heart once the girls have gone. Tonight, it feels as if the body has died. She walks through the corridors and looks at the mess. The girls' lockers have been opened and checked by the police. There was nothing in Jane's locker except for some unopened foil packets of pills. It was as if she was saying goodbye to her muscular dystrophy for good.

Miss Rossington was questioned about Jane, just like all the teachers. Has she shown signs of violence before? Has she made any threats before? Do they know where she could have got the gun?

What could she say? This was St. Edith's, not some inner-city comprehensive full of troubled children. This sort of thing just never happened at St. Edith's. Just because Jane exercised every day, it didn't mean she would shoot someone. The police were particularly interested to hear that Jane had trained with the African spear, though. But when they went to the hallway to find it, the spear had gone. Had Jane taken it? Had she meant to stab Max Bing with it?

Miss Rossington returns to her office to clear up. All the

51

offices have been searched too. It looks as if it has been burgled. She carefully picks up her books and puts them back on the shelf. Then she picks up an old book she does not recognize.

As Far as Jane's Grandmother's
    Edith Oliver
    Published 1928

Miss Rossington sits down behind her desk and opens the book. It must be from Jane. Tucked in the inside cover is a piece of paper. She takes it out and reads it. It is short and concise and in Jane's handwriting.

From one strong woman to another.
    Thanks for everything.
    J
    PS. I've taken the iklwa as a souvenir. Nobody else knew what it was called anyway!

Just a few miles away, Jane makes her way through the bushes and around the perimeter of the fruit farm. The trucks, piled high with produce for London, are parked just a few meters from the bushes. This is the moment she has been waiting for. The pickers and loaders have finished. There are just a couple of people around — still ticking off lists on clipboards — but they are all over by the main farm buildings about a hundred yards away.

Jane creeps out of the bushes and makes her way to the nearest truck. She carefully releases two of the restraint straps on the curtainsider truck so there is enough room for her to crawl under the canvas side. Jane tucks her head under and wiggles her lithe body through the small gap before reaching back through to tighten the straps as best she can. From the inside, she can't get them as tight as they were, so they flap slightly, but hopefully not enough that the driver will notice.

She slides into a gap behind the boxes, smelling the fresh

produce as she inches her way carefully out of sight in case anyone looks into the truck. She hasn't eaten for hours and longs to bite into an apple, but she will have to wait until they are on the move and the roar of the engines can hide the sounds of her crunching her late supper.

A few minutes later, she hears the sound of footsteps and men's voices. She holds her breath, making sure not to make a sound.

"There are a couple of loose straps here, John."

Jane gulps quietly. Would they discover her?

"That's them loaders. They don't know how to tie 'em prop'ly. Lazy beggars they are. Only do eighteen-hour days, you know!"

The truck driver laughs at his own joke, which was really just admiration for how hard the mostly foreign army of pickers and loaders worked.

"Tighten 'em up. And makes sure you check the rest of 'em. Then let's hit the road. Hopefully we can be in and out of London before that place wakes up," he tells his co-driver.

"Wakes up?" his co-driver asks. "I thought it was the city that never sleeps?"

"Haha. That's New York, you silly boy."

"Not for me it isn't!"

"Did, did, did-did-der
Did, did, did-did-der
Start singing our song, We're driving away
... London, London..."

I'm going to drive to a place
And find, it's busy as hell, full of people
... London, London..."

The two men laugh as their voices trail off into the night air. Jane smiles. They won't be checking the truck tonight.

They are soon on their way. The journey is bumpy as they drive along farm tracks for a couple of minutes and Jane has to cling onto the crates to stop bouncing about. It is a wonder these apples make it all the way to London, Jane thinks. But as soon as they hit the tarmac they are speeding along smoothly. The reality of her failure to shoot Bing is really sinking in. Her whole body feels heavy. It had been her big chance and she failed. Every so often, Jane checks her watch so she can work out where they are. It will be less than three hours if things run smoothly. Up the A360 before turning onto the A303, first passing Stonehenge, then near her grandmother's estate in Surrey, before looping south around the M25 toward Kent, and finally heading into London along the A2 and the supermarket's distribution center in Charlton, south of the river.

During the trip, Jane recites the numbers that have been running through her head. They come clearly and smoothly now.

"...Swiss National Bank. Account Number 339809089, sort code 907081. Lloyds Gracechurch Street, London. Safe deposit box 31. Access code 0497..."

She knows when they hit the M25 as the lights from the other vehicles start to flash by more frequently. The canvas sides of the truck flicker as the sun rises and its early morning light pierces through the trees and onto the sides of the truck. About thirty minutes out from the distribution center, Jane makes her way to the side of the truck. The canvas sides would be tied tight now and there would be no gap she could wiggle through.

The gap is tight, but the give in the canvas between the ties allows her to slide her forearm out. Feeling along the canvas on the outside, she fumbles for a clasp, her face squashed against the side of the truck on the inside. Eventually she locates the clip, flicks it open and feeds the tie through it so it is loose. She pushes the flapping canvas to see how much room she has created. It isn't enough. She'll be jumping out when they stop at a junction or at traffic lights, so she will only have seconds to avoid getting caught up in the wheels. She loosens another strap and checks her watch. Only a few minutes. She can tell from the speed they are driving that they are now off the A2. Anytime now. She turns around and balances herself on her knees so she can slide out backwards.

Before long, she hears the driver work down the gears and the growling hiss of the brakes being applied. They are about to stop.

Jane slides out effortlessly through the gap in the canvas side of the truck, yanking her bag out once she is down. There are only a couple of people around. She is at the Charlton retail park. Apart from a couple of cars, the only vehicles around are delivery drivers. It is still too early for people to be going to be out shopping.

Jane crosses over to the huge, empty car park. In a few of hours it will be full of people looking for bargains. Asda, McDonald's, Specsavers, Sports Direct, and Makro.

It is too early for the trains, so Jane heads down to the river. A couple of river barges chug along; the early birds getting their work done in the early morning light. As she approaches Greenwich, an early Thames Clipper, emblazoned with "Uber Boat" slides its way westwards, ferrying workers and tourists who want to get the most from their day into central London. That's perfect, Jane thinks. Fewer cameras. Jane buys a ticket and waits with a handful of other people for the boat to work its way safely to dock at Greenwich Pier.

To try to clear the images of her failure from her mind, Jane opens a copy of the *Metro* she's picked up from the dispenser bin at the pier. Nobody bothers a person who is reading. As they pass the towering financial buildings of Canary Wharf, she flicks through to see if there is any news about yesterday. It is impossible for her to stop her mind from racing. She finds what she is looking for, tucked away on page eight. Bing's team had been hard at work downplaying the story; there is just a small stock photograph and the basic information about the incident.

Metro
19th July
Bing Injured in Shooting at School

Tech boss Max Bing was caught up in a shooting incident yesterday while attending an event at a private girls' school near Salisbury. Police reported that a firearm was discharged at the annual Speech Day being held at the exclusive St. Edith's School for Girls in Wilshire.

Police are still investigating whether the gun was fired in accident, although some people who were at the scene are suggesting that it may have been deliberate.

Paul Ashton, Chief Constable of Wiltshire Police said: "It is understandable in the chaos of the event that some people may be reaching for the worst possible answer, but our investigations lead us to believe this was simply a bizarre accident. What does worry us, of course, is why a school of such esteem had a firearm on its premises. Questions will rightly be asked of the school."

Bing is reported to be in good health and has been treated by his personal doctor. He is reported to have pulled one of the girls on stage to safety despite being shot.

Analysts say that while shares in Synoplex may fall initially when the markets open, they are expected to recover later in the day.

Those people can even adjust the truth, Jane thinks. She knows their influence reaches far into the police force and the media,

56

but surely the people at the event know what they saw? He couldn't have paid off all of them.

Jane squints into the rising sun at the back of the City Clipper as it speeds its way along the Thames, passing the glut of sights that attract millions of visitors to the city each year — the Tower of London, London Bridge, and the South Bank — before pulling into the pier at Embankment. The boat staff are too busy making the boat secure for people getting on and off to take any notice of a small person in a hoodie. London is the perfect place to hide, Jane reminds herself.

She quickly becomes just another anonymous figure in the city as she heads up the Strand. She will soon be back at her secret hideout — a flat she'd only discovered a month earlier on a school trip.

Chapter 3

One month earlier…

Jane can hear the squeals of the other girls from the end of the hallway.

"Year Seven has a field trip to London!" one girl shouts.

"Hurray!"

A few of the girls jump around as if they have won the lottery.

Jane waits until most of the girls have moved away from the noticeboard and reads the announcement.

Announcement
Year Seven Field Trip

Year Seven's field trip this term will be to London on the 20th June. All your parents or guardians have been contacted.

<u>Itinerary for the day</u>

6.30 a.m.: Coach leaves the school. You will have a packed breakfast on the coach.

8 a.m.: Stop for a break and coffee.

10 a.m.: Arrive in Trafalgar Square.

10.30 a.m.: Visit to the National Gallery.

12.30 p.m.: A fifteen-minute walk across the Golden Jubilee Bridge for lunch at the Riverside Terrace Café at the Southbank Centre (lunch is booked for 1 p.m.).

2.30 p.m.: A fifteen-minute walk across Garden Bridge to Covent Garden and the London Transport Museum.

4 p.m.: Free time for shopping (accompanied by a teacher).
6 p.m.: Meet in Covent Garden for a short walk back to the coach for the journey back to St. Edith's.

<u>Please remember to bring</u>
Day bag
School jacket
Formal school hat (no sports caps)
Sunglasses
Notebook and pen
Phone
Bottles of water will be provided
Note: School uniforms must be worn. Remember, you are representing St. Edith's!
All Year Sevens must stay behind following dinner on Friday for a briefing on the trip. Any questions can be asked then.

Great, Jane thinks. Any reason to get out of this place.

The days before the trip pass quickly. Most of the girls can't concentrate in classes. The very idea that they will be allowed to walk around Covent Garden and go shopping is all they can think about.

"I'll be going to Chanel and Dior," one girl boasts.

"No, no," her friend says. "It has to be Atelier Cologne!"

The only thing they agree on is they will all spend a lot of time in Hotel Chocolat.

Most of the girls spend their time closeted in this ancient girls' school and their holidays in the country with family. For them, this trip to London — most have only been to the capital with their parents — is another step forward in their blossoming womanhood.

For Jane, of course, London was home for the first few years of her life. She went to school there, played with her friends there, and went shopping with her parents there. The crowded streets and the grand tourist attractions were simply the backdrop to her life. She is happy to be going home.

The girls are all waiting outside long before the coach arrives. Nobody is missing the chance to go shopping in London.

"If only you were all so eager to get to your classes, girls," Miss Rossington smiles. "Here comes the coach now. No rushing now, there's plenty of room for everyone."

Once the girls have all boarded the coach, Miss Rossington and the other staff supervising the girls on the field trip load up the boxes full of the packed breakfasts. Once they are on the road, they hand them out: a croissant, apple, muesli bar, and bottle of orange juice.

"There's a loo at the back if you need it, girls."

Occasionally, one of the teachers points out something of interest along the way. But none of the girls is listening. Who cares about Stonehenge and Swanley Forest when they are going to London?

Jane is engrossed in a book — *A Wild Sheep Chase* by Haruki Murakami — and the girl next to her hardly utters a word to her for the whole trip, except for when she offers Jane her muesli bar. The girl is much more comfortable turning and talking to the girls across the aisle. Jane is just too weird and scary.

The volume of the young, excited voices grows louder as the coach reaches the outskirts of the capital.

"Papa will only ever use Terminal 5," one girl says as they pass the signs for Heathrow Airport. "We went to St. Bart's last summer. It's a much more like a private terminal than the others, you know. And the lounges are top notch."

Jane rolls her eyes.

The coach rounds Trafalgar Square and the girls jump up, poised for their day.

"Now, we must be ready to get off quickly, girls. We only have a couple of minutes. Once you are off, you *must* wait together until everybody else is off. And *don't* forget your bags!"

60

"Thank you, driver. Thank you," the girls recite as they tumble down the steps.

"Calm down, girls, calm down," the teachers say as they each count heads to make sure nobody is missing.

"This is, of course, Nelson's Column. I know you have been studying the Napoleonic Wars with Miss Trent this year. You will see paintings of him once we are in the National Gallery. It's just a short walk across the square."

The girls wander through the gallery in groups, following the pre-assigned routes they have been given. It isn't long before the groups fracture and the girls are moving from artwork to artwork in twos and threes. Every so often, a teacher will appear from behind them and ask them what they think of a particular painting.

Jane is on her own as usual. She has other things on her mind. Access code 04970787#, Mews off Conduit Street 4A. It's only a short walk away. There is no opportunity to sneak away on the museum visits. It will have to be during their free time for shopping. She can get away from Harriet, Ashley, and Emma easily enough. They'll never say a thing. But how does she shake off the teacher?

Jane moves into the Porter Gallery. She stops at one particularly striking portrait of a young woman.

Cordelia Charrier
by Jean Paul Domergue.
Oil on board, 1952

The eyes of the woman in the portrait are striking blue, her nose small and cute, her lips red and seductive. Cordelia Charrier, Jane thinks. She looks familiar. Has she seen her before? But this was painted in 1952. It can't be someone she has met.

"Watch this woman, Jane. She is not what she seems. Do not trust her."

61

The rest of the day passes without incident. Lots of paintings, a short walk over the Golden Jubilee Bridge to the Southbank Centre, lunch in the Riverside Terrace Café, then another short walk back across the Thames to Covent Garden and the London Transport Museum. Just as the itinerary has dictated. But now the time looking at old buses and trams is coming to an end. It is time for a change in the itinerary, Jane thinks. It is time for access code 04970787#, Mews off Conduit Street 4A. Jane cracks her knuckles in nervous anticipation.

The girls gather in Covent Garden once their tour of the London Transport Museum has finished.

"Get into your groups of four, please, girls. You should all know which group you are in," Miss Rossington says. "As you know, we have received permission from Miss Fernsby to give you some free time. But you *must* stay with your assigned teacher in your groups of four. If you lose any of your group, you must ring one of us immediately. Do you have our numbers in your phones?

The girls nod.

"OK, enjoy yourselves and don't go too far. You are to stay in this area. And girls. You don't have to spend all of your time shopping! There are plenty of other things to do and see."

Jane's group wanders awkwardly into The Tea Shop — the nearest shop they see. The other three girls had not been pleased when their names were read out in the same group as Jane at the meeting about the field trip. All three of them groaned while the rest of Year Seven collectively sighed in relief.

"Oh no!" Harriet said. "How are we supposed to enjoy our day with that weird girl?"

"*Scary* girl!" Ashley added. "If we go in the wrong shop, she'll probably give us one of her kung fu kicks."

The other girls looked around and shrugged in sympathy.

"Why are we in a shop selling tea?" Jane asks the girls.

The other girls step back. Maybe she would be giving them that kung fu kick after all. Jane has been stretching her body all day. She hated missing her workout, but the six a.m. start meant she had no option as the exercise room was closed.

"Look," Jane says to the other three girls, checking that the teacher with their group is out of earshot. "I know you don't want me in your group, and you know I prefer being on my own."

The other girls don't know whether to nod or not so they just stand staring at Jane.

"That's a yes then?" Jane asks.

This time they nod.

"Right. I'm going to split. Cover for me as best you can."

"We can't. You heard what Miss Rossington told us," Harriet says.

"What are we supposed to say?"

"Say I'm in the loo or something. Make up something."

The three girls look at each other, then back at Jane.

"OK," they reply in unison.

"Remember," Jane says as the rest of her group walk over to shelf with teas from Ceylon. "We are all in trouble if anyone finds out it is planned. So, this is just our little secret."

Harriet, Ashley, and Emma feel thrilled to be sharing a secret with Jane. Maybe she wasn't too bad after all. In truth, the other girls admire Jane. She is strong and clever. She doesn't care what other people think of her. She does what just she wants. Secretly, they all want to know more about her. Maybe they could be friends with her after all.

Jane wastes no time. After checking her supervising teacher is not looking, she quickly exits The Tea Shop and makes her way toward Seven Dials, then through the winding streets of Soho. The array of shops — Pixi, Subdued, Stuart Weizman — would be a magnet to the other girls, but Jane is focused as she half-marches, half-jogs toward her destination. Only a street artist's work catches her eye, and she stops to admire his chalk drawings on the paving slabs. There are eight of them, in vivid colors. She is astonished at how good they are. *Almost real.*

"Hello, young lady. Do you like my drawings?" the artist asks.

"They are *very* lifelike," Jane replies.

"Yes, I start early in the morning to make sure they are perfect. I believe if you look into the scene you want to visit then you will be transported there when the time is right. Where do you want to go?"

Jane smiles and looks down at a scene of a large country house.

"I can see you like this one. I draw it every day, so you can come and look at it any time you want to. Go on, take a look at it. Look long and hard now."

Jane giggles nervously as she stares at the drawing of the large country house before dropping a few coins into the man's hat.

"Thank you. You are sure to visit that house now," he says smiling.

Early finishers, or late lunchers who never returned to the office, are spilling onto the streets outside the pubs, drinking frothy beer. Jane's daddy, George, liked beer. She'd seen him drunk a few times. He was funny. She'd heard her mummy, Winnie, shouting at him when he got home drunk. She wonders if he'd ever been outside any of these pubs. If he were still alive today, she'd be able to run over to him and hug him. She feels her anger for Max Bing grow inside her. She stops and pulls a Marlborough Red from the hem of her skirt, lights it, then slips on a plain blue jacket to hide the St. Edith's logo on her shirt, but nobody takes any notice of her anyway.

Jane crosses over Regent Street and into Conduit Street, walking slowly and steadily as she looks for the entrance to the Mews. She pops down a small alleyway framed by a trestle arch seemingly held up by a tangle of thin branches and leaves. The cobbled pathway leads to five converted carriage houses, all adorned with touches of the countryside: plants, wooden gates serving no purpose, and black pendant hanging lamps.

The door to 4A is plain black, in contrast to the others in the Mews, with their mock Georgian oak doors and ornate black door knockers. There is no keyhole in the door and no handle — just a keypad in the wall behind a glass cover. Jane tries to open it. Nothing. It won't flip open. It won't slide. No amount or tapping or banging will budge the case. There is a small blueish-black button below the case. It flickers as Jane presses it. It is a sensor. Jane lights up another Marlborough Red and thinks. It's just a deep blueish-black darkness.

"Hello," she says. "It's Jane. Zero-four-nine-seven-zero-seven-eight-seven-hash. Nought-four-nine-seven-zero-seven-eight-seven-hash!"

Jane bangs the glass in frustration. It is solid. She would need a sledgehammer to break it. She cracks her knuckles. She recites all the numbers that have been running through her head again and again, searching for something.

"Access code 04970787#, Mews off Conduit Street 4A, look into it."

Look into it! Jane crouches down and stares into the sensor. It flashes brightly this time and the glass panel slides open as the scanner registers the pattern of Jane's retina. How does it know *her* eyes? The glass panel slides back, revealing a keypad. Jane quickly types in the numbers and the door clicks open.

Inside, immediately in front of her, there is steep, black metal curved staircase, with a corridor to the right. On the exposed brick wall there are several framed newspaper cuttings. Jane scans them quickly, keeping her ears peeled for the noise of anyone else in the building. The door slides quietly shut behind her as Jane looks at the cuttings. She turns around and sees an identical keypad to the one outside. She hopes it works in the same way when she wants to get out.

65

The Daily Telegraph
MethusalaCo Announces Move into Producing Human Organs

There is a good chance you have a Synoplex phone, computer, and TV. Soon you might have a new organ from one of Synoplex's medical companies. MethusalaCo, which was launched to pursue solutions for aging and its associated diseases, has now announced that it is developing human organs.

Max Bing, CEO of Synoplex and the business brain behind the new development said, "Millions of people die from heart, lung, and kidney disease every year. We are looking at developing organs so these people can continue living a healthy life. We will no longer need to wait for suitable donor and transplants. Instead, we will make brand new organs from the stem cells injected into embryos — all taken from the very person who needs it."

The ability to grow replacement organs for people from their own cells in a lab could transform thousands of lives, doctors say.

"Organ donors are in short supply and people in need of replacement organs can wait years for a suitable organ. Sadly, for some people a suitable organ never arrives," Doctor Julie Awbuck of the Porton Medical Institute in Cambridge said.

Developments in this exciting field have been gathering pace in recent years and positive results from experiments of developing stem cells for the organs of larger animals such as pigs has been reported. For Bing and his company MethusalaCo, the time is now right for humans to benefit from this stem cell research.

Was this Max Bing's place? What was it for? Why did she have those numbers in her head? At least she'd cracked the meaning of one code.

She hasn't heard a sound in the house, but still steps

cautiously into the small lounge, which houses a modern, open-plan kitchen. Everything is spotless. Beautiful Rajasthani silk paintings cover the walls, depicting scenes from the eighteenth- and nineteenth-century, showing women with young children, elephants carrying rich men in howdahs, war scenes, and Hindu religious ceremonies. Jane stares at them for a while. The hand paintings are immaculate. Her grandmother has some of these in her home — but nothing as detailed and fine as these.

The open-plan kitchen has a bright white counter and cabinets, and the only things on show are shiny Japanese steel knives. Jane takes the largest one in her hand, weighs it up, then twirls it around, before finishing with a high kick and a thrust at an invisible enemy. It feels good to be back in action.

She opens the cupboards and sees that they are stacked full of dried food and cans. The fridge is also stacked full. Fresh items, including cheese, milk, meat, and vegetables. Someone obviously lives here, but it seems too perfect. Maybe it is a London bolthole for a business person with a house in the country?

Time is ticking, so Jane puts the knife away and heads upstairs. She is sure no one is in the house. She's heard nothing. The opening at the top of the stairs opens up into a large room with TV screen, and a comfortable looking white couch flanked by elaborately carved, hand-painted chairs. The fittings are stainless steel. It is also spotless. There are two bedrooms to the right — one larger than the other, although both are very spacious. The beds are made, and as with the other rooms, there is a nothing out of place.

Jane checks the cupboards. Suits, jackets, shirts, ties, some traditional formal Indian outfits, and a few casual items such as jeans and T-shirts. It is a man's place, that is for sure. But why the Indian influence?

Next to the bed there are photos in silver frames. Jane sits on the bed and picks them up, one by one. She stops, shocked. It's her grandmother. She is standing with her grandfather on a yacht with a teenage Indian boy and an older man, maybe the younger boy's father. Lorraine is much younger in the photo, but it is definitely her. Jane recognizes her grandmother and grandfather from other photos she has seen. She used to joke to her mummy that she looked exactly like her grandmother at that age — almost like they were sisters.

There is another photo of her grandmother. She is older. It looks more recent. She is with a tall, handsome Indian man. They are in a restaurant, with the sea sparkling behind them, and they have their heads together, as if they are in love. Was this one of the men in the other picture? Jane stares at the photo. The man's dark, hazelnut eyes glint back at her from the photo. She recognizes him as the man who performed the operation on her with her daddy. It was the man who had repeated the numbers to her, over and over again. Her head starts to spin.

Jane frantically searches for clues. Her memories have been hazy since the operation and she is still, even years later, piecing the pieces together. She knows it was Max Bing who had been responsible for her killing her mummy and daddy. But where did this man fit in?

She rifles through the drawers at the bottom of the cupboard. Cufflinks, tie pins, collar stiffeners, another photograph of the man with her grandmother. This one leaves her in no doubt that they were lovers, even though he is much younger than her. She picks up a small metallic name badge.

Anil Kapoor
Chairman
KapoorLakshmi Steel

This has to be him. She remembers her daddy talking about him before he was killed by Bing. It was about a big deal they were doing together. It was a deal that meant he would make enough money to get her anything she wanted. Her daddy knew him as well. Were they friends? She pulls out the drawer and puts it on the bed, looking for more clues.

As Jane tries to fit the drawers back in place, she spots a shiny steel plate at the back and realizes suddenly that the drawer does not go all the way back to the wall. There is a false back behind the drawers, hiding something. There is a sensor, just like the one by the front door. She leans in and stares into it. It opens. No need for numbers this time.

Inside are two guns, blank passports for India, the UK, South Africa, and various Caribbean islands, other assorted ID documents, books, and more photos. She handles one of the guns. It is small and light, and it fits perfectly in her hand, as if it has been selected for her personally. There is a pile of magazines for the gun in the hidden compartment.

Jane pulls out a baby blue box and opens it. The lid is embossed with gold lettering.

EST 1887
SMYTHSON
OF BOND STREET

Inside are a pile of identical black books, each embossed with a gold letter on the front.

"A, B, C, D, E, F, G, H, I, J..." Jane says, out loud to herself. "J! There's one for every letter of the alphabet and here's mine."

Then she sees a folder marked 'Confidential' sitting at the bottom of the hidden compartment. Jane opens it and scans the titles of some of the documents. She has no time to read through all of them now.

Report on Failed Clones
Six crucial causes of clone failure

Disposal of Eliminated Clones

New procedures for the clean-up of failed clone experiments

Project J
Success of first lysosomal transfusion

A.M. Mortality Charges
Updated fee for mortality through the cloning program

Targeting HNWI
Recruitment for high-net-worth individuals to A.M. program

This is clearly Bing's doing. He's not only a murderer but he's also crazy. He was 'eliminating' clones and 'disposing' of them. What did it mean? What was her daddy involved with? What did Kapoor have to do with it? This must be connected to the place they had visited for her operation. The operation that made her well. That made her strong again. She remembers the grotesque specimens she had seen: the bodies sewn together and the woman with all her skin removed and no eyelids.

Project J? A quick glance at the first paragraph soon reveals that J is Jane. She is just another 'project' to Bing and his rich friends — like those specimens she had seen at his big country house. Well, I'm not ending up like them, she thinks. This man Bing has to be stopped. Not only because he killed my parents — but because he's a danger to everyone.

Jane desperately wants to read more, but she knows she has to get back to Covent Garden and meet up with the group she was supposed to have stayed with. She pulls out her digital camera and photographs some of the documents. Time is ticking, so she will have to come back later to check the rest of the documents. She *has* to know more.

Jane briefly wonders if she should keep the J book from Smythson but decides to leave everything exactly how it is so the person who uses the house doesn't notice anything. She puts back all the items into the hidden compartment, hearing it lock with a whirr as she pushes the door shut. Then she tidies up the items in the drawers, places the photographs carefully back in place and smooths down the bed. She has to come back. And soon.

Jane hurries out of the house and the door locks automatically behind her. She walks briskly through the streets, weaving her way back to Covent Garden. The pavements outside the pubs are packed now and workers are spilling onto the streets from all directions as they celebrate the end of another day. Some of the men have removed their ties, as if they were shackles, and unbuttoned their shirts in a small show of rebellion. Most of the women have taken off the shoes they wear in the office and replaced them with comfortable white trainers for their walk back to the Tube and the journey home. The streets are noisy and alive but still not one person takes any notice of Jane.

The other three girls are waiting for Jane when she arrives at their meeting place. So is the teacher. And she is not happy.

"Where have you been, Jane? I will have to report this to Miss Fernsby. You were strictly told not to go off on your own," Miss Albert says.

"I went to buy something for my grandmother — you know, *Miss Fernsby's friend* — and when I turned around, I couldn't see anyone. It was an honest mistake," Jane lies.

The teacher pauses and considers her dilemma. After all, she would be in as much trouble as Jane.

"Well, that is nice of you to think of your grandmother. And I suppose you weren't gone that long. Anyway, you're here now. Maybe we should just keep this between ourselves?"

Jane nods as Miss Albert speaks to the other girls. Jane smiles and heads off to meet the main group. The other three girls scuttle behind Jane, still nervous they will get into trouble as well. Where *has* she been?

"Jane, Jane, you haven't bought anything. Everyone else will

71

have loads of shopping bags. It'll look strange. You told Miss Albert you bought something for your grandmother. Where is it?" Harriet asks.

Jane stops.

"You're right," she says. "Give me one of yours. You can have it back later."

Jane grabs one of Harriet's bags and marches off again.

"Jane Banks! I can't believe you bought something! That's a real surprise," Miss Rossington says as Jane's group walk toward her. Miss Albert smiles nervously.

Jane feeds her the story she has concocted, leaving out the bit about her disappearance.

"That it is sweet of you to get something for your grandmother. I didn't take you for a Chanel girl, though."

Jane looks down at the bag she is holding, then shoots a look at Harriet as if it was her fault for letting her Chanel bag be snatched from her.

"Oh, yes. I love Chanel. I mean, my grandmother loves Chanel. I was hoping to go to visit her next weekend so I could give it to her. I was going to ask you if you could put in a request with Miss Fernsby for a weekend pass for me."

Jane knows Miss Fernsby will do anything to keep Lorraine happy. And the teachers know it as well.

"I will certainly ask. Anyway, what did you get for your grandmother?"

Jane freezes. Quickly, Harriet comes to her rescue.

"It's Chanel No. 5, Miss Rossington. The classic eau de parfum… It's perfect for grandmothers. We were all *sooo* jealous when she told us she was going to buy it."

"Well, Jane, you surprise me more every day. And there was me thinking you'd come back with a tent or something."

As the girls walk back toward Trafalgar Square and the pick-up point for the coach, Jane hands Harriet her Chanel bag and whispers a grateful "thank you." Harriet smiles, not knowing if the thank you was for letting Jane wander off on her own, 'lending' her the Chanel bag, or saving her by answering Miss Rossington's question. Either way, a "thank you" from Jane is like gold dust, so she smiles broadly. Maybe Jane wasn't so bad after all?

On the way home, Jane scans through the documents she had photographed in the secret house, starting with the one about her.

Project J

The subject, Jane Travers (now Banks), was diagnosed with Duchenne muscular dystrophy, caused by a mutation of the dystrophin gene, when she was eight years old. Without intervention, it is unlikely that she would have survived beyond her twenties. The negative effects from the muscular dystrophy on the subject were reversed with a lysosomal transfusion. The donor, the subject's father, George Travers, was a fit and healthy thirty-six-year-old male at the time, with a military background. He had previously responded exceptionally well to the experiments A.M. conducted with the MOD (Hercules trial testing) to improve his strength, stamina, and mental awareness. He was the perfect donor both physically and psychologically, although he displayed worrying levels of single mindedness and resolve that may affect the subject as she gets older. The development of this will have to be monitored closely. Project J's mother was the aborted Clone C23 of Recipient 17.

Report on Failed Clones

To date, one thousand, four hundred and twenty-five clones have failed to meet the standards needed to be used. More than half of these had to be disposed of before the age of ten. We have identified six significant causes for the failure of clones.

1. A high level of stress in the recipient at the time of the

73

DNA extraction. In these instances, the clone's neural pathways within their brains can suffer malfunctions, a problem that particularly affects the visual cortex.

2. A level of interaction between the recipient and the clone that falls below the recommended levels by more than fifteen per cent before the clone reaches the age of six. In these instances, the clone will develop self-direction, autonomy, and initiative — effectively developing their own personality. In such cases, it is impossible for us to consider continuing the process.

Disposal of Clones

The original method of incineration of clones will be discontinued and will be replaced by a new chemical decomposition process. The new process, using sodium hydroxide, has been found to leave fewer traces of the clones' existence. It works more effectively if the clone is immersed in the caustic soda while still functioning. Once a clone has been broken down by this process, the remnants will be cleaned up and added to a mixture of hydrohalic acids. What is left will be disposed of at sea by one of our research vessels.

Targeting HNWI

The recruitment program of high-net-worth individuals to the A.M. program in order to raise capital for research and development, and to increase profits, will be extended into Paraguay, Argentina, Taiwan, South Africa, Saudi Arabia, and Yemen. Individuals identified include presidents, generals, heads of secret services, diamond and gold dealers, financiers, social media innovators, and owners of TV stations. The criteria for selection not only include very high levels of assets but also the ability to control and influence the people in their country. As usual, no moral judgments will be made on how their money is made or what methods they use to control or influence their populations.

Jane sits back stunned. But before she has a chance to absorb all of the information, Miss Rossington's voice comes over the microphone with an announcement.

"Girls, I have just received a very exciting call from Miss Fernsby. She has had a meeting with the rest of school tonight but she wanted me to tell you all that she has managed to secure a very special VIP guest for this year's Speech Day, which I'm sure you all know is only a few weeks away."

"Probably some boring person like last year," one of the girls mutters at the back of the coach, but certainly not loud enough that any of the teachers could hear her. A few of the other girls groan at the idea of having to sit through another dull speech just before they break for the summer holidays.

"Our special guest this year…" Miss Rossington continues, with a pause for dramatic effect, "…is none other than Max Bing himself. He is almost certainly one the most influential men in the world of technology and this is a huge honor for St. Edith's."

The girls gasp. Almost all of them have Synoplex phones and computers. Max Bing's company makes everything. They produce some of the coolest tech products young people can get their hands on.

"I don't need to tell you girls that we will all be working extra hard to ensure that this year's Speech Day goes with a bang!" Miss Rossington concludes.

It certainly will if I get my way, Jane thinks. This was her chance. All her worries about how she was going to get close to the man who was responsible for ruining her life were solved. *He* was coming to her.

Her mind races. She *has* to get the weekend pass to visit Lorraine so she can get back to the secret flat in London. She needs that gun. She needs to make a plan with Simone.

"Hello, darling, how are you?" Lorraine says, as Jane climbs into her car. "This is such a lovely surprise. Miss Fernsby rang me to say you had requested a weekend pass to visit me. Did you fancy a nice relaxing weekend in our country house?"

"Actually, I was thinking we could go up to London," Jane says, as the car speeds down the driveway of St. Edith's.

"Oh, but you were only there a few days ago."

"I know, but I had such a good time, I thought it would be nice to go back. There is *soooo* much to see," Jane adds, as if she is in awe of the city, like most young children following their first visit.

"OK darling, if that's what you want. Maybe we could meet my friend Elizabeth for lunch at Quaglino's?"

"That would be nice," Jane says, knowing full well she'll be wriggling out of lunch so she can go back to the secret house. Lorraine and Elizabeth will be perfectly happy without her while they are eating in the old-style brasserie and downing champagne. Jane would be bored stiff as they talk about what they own and which Caribbean island they'll be visiting next in order to top up the tans on their leathery skin. It was conversation like this that drove her daddy mad. She'd heard her parents arguing about it many times.

"She's just trying to belittle me," her daddy would say. "Your mother is just trying to remind me that I'm not good enough for her daughter."

Her mummy would just laugh and tell him to ignore her.

The rest of the journey back to Lorraine's country house in Surrey passes in a blur of questions about schoolwork, her health, her sessions with the psychologist, and whether she has made any friends. As they arrive, Lorraine changes tack.

"I hear you have a present for me, Jane. Miss Fernsby told me you picked it up on the school trip. They were very impressed that you thought of me. Most of the girls just bought things for themselves."

Jane pauses for moment, then stutters her reply. Miss

76

Fernsby had obviously told her about the Chanel she'd 'borrowed' from Harriet.

"Oh, er, yes. I just need to wrap it up. Can I give it to you later?"

"Of course you can."

The next morning the executive taxi picks up Lorraine and Jane at ten-thirty.

"Just so I can enjoy a couple of glasses of bubbly with Elizabeth," Lorraine tells her granddaughter on more than one occasion.

Lorraine does most of the talking on the drive to London, fussing about Jane's clothes and how she is doing at St. Edith's. But Jane is curious about the photographs she saw in the Mews house, so when there is a lull in the Lorraine's monologue, she takes her opportunity.

"You must have been lonely after Grandpa died. Did you ever find anyone else? You *were* still very young and attractive," Jane whispers in flattery, cocking her head and opening her eyes wide in feigned innocence.

Lorraine is taken aback and stutters slightly before replying.

"I really loved your grandpa," Lorraine replies earnestly. "We had a wonderful life together. Nobody could replace him, you know that. Why do you ask?"

"Oh, I just wondered," Jane replies as if it were a throwaway question. "I just know how you love your holidays. And they are so much more fun when you are with someone else," Jane adds, remembering the photograph of her grandmother and Kapoor at a restaurant overlooking the sea.

Lorraine looks at Jane curiously, but by now Jane has looked away as if she doesn't really care about the subject.

"She's just young and curious, like all young people. There's no way she could know anything. *Surely?*" Lorraine thinks as they speed on in silence.

"She's growing up so fast and she's just like Winnie,"

Elizabeth says when they arrive at her apartment.

"Yes, but unfortunately she's also very much like her father in many ways," Lorraine whispers.

"Shall we have tea first before then head off for lunch?" Elizabeth asks.

The old friends are soon into full flow, chatting as they sip tea and nibble on biscuits. But when Elizabeth turns to ask Jane a question, she puts her plan into place.

"I'm not feeling too well," she says, putting her hand on her stomach. "Would you mind if I went to lie down?"

"Oh no, Jane, what's wrong? What about lunch?" Lorraine asks.

"I just need to rest a bit. Would you mind if I missed lunch? I'm so sorry."

"Oh Jane, I was so looking forward to having lunch with my granddaughter. But we understand. Elizabeth, would you mind?"

Lorraine fusses over Jane as Elizabeth shows her to a comfortable spare bedroom. The walls are covered in old photographs and Jane notices that a younger Lorraine features in many of them.

Once they have settled Jane under a blanket, Lorraine and Elizabeth head off for lunch.

"You've got my number so just call if you want anything. I'll come straight back if you need me," Lorraine adds to assuage her guilt.

Once outside the house, Jane cracks her knuckles before lighting up a Marlborough Red and dragging on it hard. I'm like my daddy and I'm proud of it, she smiles. She pulls a baseball cap from her bag, slips it on and heads toward Conduit Street.

Once inside the Mews house, Jane goes through the process of listening for noises to make sure the house is empty. When she is sure nobody else is in the house, she checks the kitchen. It is spotless as before, and the fridge is still fully stocked. She smells the milk. It is unopened but fresh. Someone is definitely living here.

Once upstairs she takes snaps of the photographs of Anil Kapoor and Lorraine. Everything in the bedroom is in exactly the same place. The clothes look untouched. There is a laundry basket in the cupboard but it is empty, as before. Whoever lives here is the neatest person ever. Or they hardly ever use the place. Jane pulls out the documents and photographs and finds the ones she had not captured before. She picks up the gun and weighs it in her hand. It feels good. There is a black holster. Jane quickly works out it is for the thigh. With her jeans on, this would not work today, so she wraps it with the gun in her lightweight jacket and slides them into her bag. She has what she wants but still takes one more look around. She likes this place. And if things go as planned, she'll be spending a lot more time here.

Back on the streets of London, the atmosphere is a lot different to the last time she had been here. The office workers and their end-of-day tensions are gone — replaced by the bustle of weekend tourists and shoppers.

Jane has a niggling feeling that she has forgotten something. She stops. Then she remembers the perfume. But she is certainly in the right place for luxury goods. She pops into the first department store she sees — House of Fraser in Oxford Street — and asks the overly made-up assistant for a classic Chanel perfume that her grandmother would like.

"Could you gift wrap it, please?" Jane asks, once the Chanel No. 5 eau de parfum has been presented to her with a flourish.

Chapter 4

Max Bing climbs out of his Tesla as the chauffeur pulls the car up to the entrance of the A.M. headquarters in the Brecon Beacons. It's been four hours since Bing was shot by Jane and he winces at the pain from the gunshot wound as he wriggles through the door awkwardly. He raises his good arm to comfort the pain with his hand.

"Sir, sir, please keep your arm as steady as possible. Your body will be in shock," the doctor waiting for him says.

"Mr. Bing, are you OK? We were so worried," his assistant fusses.

"I'm fine, I'm fine. Walk with me while the doctor sorts this wound out. I need a full update on the Synoplex lockdown and how we are tidying up this mess with the parents and teachers who witnessed the shooting."

"There were eighty-five parents at the Speech Day and twelve teachers, including the headmistress. All of those have been sorted. The girls are, of course, a bit more difficult, but the parents have been instructed to talk to their daughters. That headmistress has been very accommodating with the teachers. We had to offer to build the school some new hockey facilities. There are a few leaks on the smaller social media sites that Synoplex doesn't control, but those are already being shot down as crazy conspiracy theories. We have the mainstream media on message, so all the while these leaks remain as fringe stories, we should be fine."

"OK, good work. Open up all Synoplex sites again, assuming all the relevant blocks are in place for anything negative," Bing instructs him.

He then turns to the doctor who is guiding him to the treatment room.

"How close are you to being ready to test our development into battlefield injuries? I want this to heal quickly."

"We could certainly use PRP — platelet-rich plasma — injections to help with the inflammation and cell proliferation of the tendons. That's a tried and tested technique many athletes already use," the doctor replies.

"Come on, we are here to develop revolutionary medical techniques, not use existing ones. I'm talking about the new technique that will radically change healing. You always refer to it as treatment of live tissue trauma."

"We combine AMD3100 and tacrolimus. It can reduce the scar tissue. Research centers have only tested it on mice so far. We have, of course, tried it on our human specimens in the lab. But we are not fully ready yet."

"Go ahead, Henry. I have been watching your speeches so you know I am familiar with your work. I am familiar with the work of all my scientists," Bing tells him, a faint smile creeping across his face just to make sure the doctor understands who is in charge.

"I'll be first that isn't one of those grotesque specimens you keep poking about with your needles and knives."

"Sir, it's not ready. You can't be the first," the doctor pleads.

"Of course not. Get me a clone."

The doctor returns with a clone, who smiles and greets Bing like a father.

Bing pulls out a handgun, and without hesitation, shoots the clone in the shoulder, then smiles with perverse pleasure as he recoils in pain.

"There you go. Test it on that injury and if you are happy, come back to me if it works."

The doctor steps back in horror at Bing's attitude to watching others suffer. Even after years of working with him, he

81

is still not immune to the blasé way Bing sees the clones and other people just as tools to serve his needs.

Bing heads to the laboratory. He likes nothing more than to visit the specimens. And perform a few of his own little 'experiments' when none of the doctors are around. He approaches one of the specimens strapped to a bed and filled with tubes and pipes. She can't move but she is conscious and her eyes are imploring for mercy. Bing turns up one of the dials and watches as her body starts to heat up. Gently at first, then her naked skin starts to redden and her eyes bulge in pain. Bing turns up the dial more and watches, taking pleasure in the specimen's pain as she wriggles uncontrollably before passing out. Bing knows there is nothing medical to be gained from boiling her blood but it amuses him nonetheless.

He moves to the corner of the room and logs into his computer. He has some work to do on the dark web. After typing in his encrypted password, he clicks through to his favorite marketplace and scrolls the menu down to the medical section. He has some items he wants to sell…

DarkWEbNET
MammonBay
Menu>>>>
Child pornography
Drugs
Snuff movies
Guns
Heavy duty weapons
Medical>>>>
For sale>>>>
Human heart (20yo)
Human lung (18yo)
Human kidney (28yo)
Assorted human body parts (various ages)

* Organs will only be removed from the body when ordered and delivered by dark courier in a frozen pack. Quality guaranteed.

A few hours later, it is Bing who is waiting at the main door to the headquarters as a car pulls up.

"How are you, Max? That is one crazy girl we have got on our hands. Let me see that wound," David Rogerson says, smiling as he strides toward Bing.

Bing laughs as he greets his friend and proceeds to update him on the afternoon's events at the school.

"Everything is in hand, then, and I must say you are looking well. We certainly can't afford to lose A.M.'s main man as we explore so many new projects," Rogerson says, when Bing has finished.

"David, David, you know only too well that this project would not exist without you. We will have dinner soon, but first, let's visit the young boy."

The two men catch the lift up three stories, then walk down a corridor, passing door after door all marked in a similar fashion.

RECIPIENT 12
    CLONES A, B, C, D, E, G, H, I, J, K

RECIPIENT 13
    CLONES A, B, C, D, E, F, G, H

RECIPIENT 14
    CLONES A, B, C, D, E

At the end of the corridor is a door without a sign. As the two men enter, a nurse jumps up and smooths down her tunic.

"You can leave us with the boy," Bing tells the nurse.

Adam is only three years old. He looks up with his big brown eyes but says nothing before turning back to his toys.

"He looks well," Rogerson says.

"Who would have thought that George Travers would contribute so much to our research eh, Max? Running off with one of our clones and fu…"

Rogerson looks down at the boy before correcting himself.

"So nice of him to have sex with Dee. The dirty dog. It was lucky that the doctors picked up the early stages of her pregnancy before we disposed of her body."

"Absolutely. It meant we had to keep Dee alive until it was old enough to cut out. She was pretty weak because we transferred so many of her enzymes to Cordelia, but it was important we kept her going a bit longer so we could make use of this little lad. A baby born of Travers and a clone. A nice half-clone for our research. And the son of the explosives expert who responded so well to our experimental drug research program with the MOD too. The boy is a useful specimen for us."

"And what about his temperament? Is it something we can work with?" Rogerson asks.

"So far, so good," Bing replies. "He seems very compliant. Unlike his sister! Her father was the perfect physical specimen. That's why we paired him with Lorraine's clone Winnie, of course. Little did we know that the daughter they produced would be so bloody single-minded like her father. We need clones who are followers and do what we tell them. It's very frustrating. We thought we had it just right this time," Bing continues.

"It seems that Jane is more like her father than Adam is, then. Even more of a reason that we need to get to her. Some proper, in-depth experiments on Jane could help us so much," Rogerson replies.

"Yes, she's important. We need to find her. The doctors have been carefully increasing Adam's levels of the catalyst that Kapoor used on Jane. They report he's getting stronger and sharper already, even at this young age. This boy could turn into a monster soldier for us at this rate."

"Just be careful with the doses, Max. Don't overdo it! Now, let's call the nurse back in to get this boy to bed. I know you kept him up past his bedtime just so I could see him," he adds, patting the boy on his head and smiling.

DarkWEbNET
Battlefield Secrets Can Unlock Your Inner Strength and Power

Forget weapons of mass destruction. Reports from our sources say that the latest deadly weapon will be a new battalion of crack soldiers pumped to peak condition by a specially developed cocktail of performance-enhancing drugs — anabolic steroids, ergogenic aids, adaptogens, nootropics, and stimulants. And we have the formula! The MOD, working with an unnamed partner company, have been testing the drugs on soldiers for a few years in a bid to boost soldiers' strength, stamina, and mental awareness.

It is believed that although there was only limited success initially, scientists have now perfected the mix and doses of the drugs — all thanks to the success they had with just one man! We have only been able to identify this subject as GT Explosives, who is now believed to be dead — but GT responded so well to the drugs that he improved in all areas by over sixty per cent within just a year of taking them. Scientists were able to use the data from an intense study of GT to perfect the formula that will now be used by the military to make their crack troops fitter, faster, and sharper than previously thought possible. Buy the formula here!

Anabolic steroids derive from testosterone, and after being modified they act by pushing more nitrogen to the muscles. This stops the muscles breaking down as it would in normal conditions and ultimately preserves its mass. A secret mixture of well-known steroids — nandrolone, stanozolol, and oxandrolone — are in this special formula, so you can be sure of quick results and bigger muscles.

Ergogenic aids include methylphenidate and amphetamine that maintain strength levels over extended periods of exertion and are widely used by athletes looking to delay fatigue. It's not difficult to see why the military can see the advantages of their use. And now you can enjoy those benefits too!

Adaptogens are used in herbal medicine to promote general health and reduce stress, while stimulants and nootropics (sometimes called smart drugs or brain boosters) sharpen up the brain and increase memory capacity, attention span, and concentration, while at the same time masking boredom, sleepiness, and fatigue. What's not to like?

All the usual side effects that doctors warn us about are associated with these drugs but after seeing how they helped GT Explosives turn into a super soldier, our buyers are already telling us: "we want this too!"

• Click here to purchase. All orders are fulfilled through dark courier and delivered in plain packaging.

"I want to talk to you about the exclusivity of the society. Too many members mean a greater chance of the word getting out — we need to get the timing right. Apart from anything else, where will we store so many clones?" Rogerson says.

Max Bing turns to his partner.

"We are getting better at producing and developing them. We no longer need so many attempts before perfecting a clone that is ready for a recipient to use and the numbers are coming down all the time. We have capacity here. And apart from anything else, if we are to put the A.M. program up for sale, we need the expansion."

"Max, I understand you want to maximize the profit from the sale of A.M.," Rogerson replies. "But we agreed at the outset on the number of people we would consider for clone transfers. We are already above that number. And that's just the people we know about. What about the older ones who were involved before us we don't know about? What the fuck will they make of all this? Not to mention the quality of the people we are taking is dropping. Just look at that awful chap from Cooper & McKenzie."

"Bruce McKenzie? He's a senior partner at one of the largest investment firms in the City. He paid *waaay* over the odds to join. He'll be dead long before we get a clone ready for him in any case."

Rogerson shakes his head. He really didn't like Bruce McKenzie. It was as if the original exclusive club they had dreamt of years ago was being diluted in quality with the likes of him joining. With the likes of him benefitting from their work on mortality.

"We have to stick with this McKenzie obviously. He knows too much and we've taken his money already. But from now on, I want the character of the person to outweigh their bank balance when it comes to new admissions. Yes, I want to sell this for a huge amount of money. But if we are going to give people the ability to live forever then we must choose people who are going to contribute positively to the world. We have risked too much to just give a bunch of rich idiots eternal life."

"Next you'll be saying we should develop clones for someone who is penniless because they paint nice pictures. David, you are getting soft. Let's go to dinner. We need to discuss Lorraine Meaden. She will be here tomorrow."

Lorraine knows there is trouble ahead and tries to mentally prepare herself before heading off to meet Bing and Rogerson. She knows they are dangerous. Jane is *certainly* in danger now.

Is there anything she can do to save her granddaughter? She reads through her file again — more in desperation than hope that she will see something from the report on Jane's transfusion three years ago.

Highly confidential

Security Level 3 A.M.

Incident: A.M. Headquarters

George Travers accessed A.M. Headquarters for the purpose of performing a lysosomal transfusion with his daughter, Jane. He initially refused the offer from Mr. Bing to conduct the procedure under our care but broke into the building a day later. He was assisted by Simone Grant, his assistant at Cooper & McKenzie (we continue to track her communications), and his friend and neighbor Alex Littlefield (now eliminated with his wife and two children), who contacted the police about the matter.

Anil Kapoor conducted the procedure. Following the procedure, our doctors entered the laboratory. Jane was still not conscious.

The next day, Anil Kapoor was killed in a car crash. The body of George Travers, who was put in the car with him, was not recovered at the crash site. Despite a search, he remains missing. He is highly unlikely to have survived and has been declared "missing, presumed dead" by police.

Initial tests on Jane showed the high levels of CK (creatine kinase) recorded by the Portland Hospital only days before had returned to normal. This indicates that the breakdown of muscles caused by the Duchenne muscular dystrophy had been halted and even reversed.

Once stabilized, Jane was taken to a popular hiking route at 10.32 a.m. and covered in a blanket, where she was found by a group of hikers thirteen minutes later.

At the hospital, the initial diagnosis has been declared false and the doctor who made the diagnosis will be struck off for malpractice. Jane will be monitored by our doctor at St. Edith's School for Girls, where she will be placed.

Inspector Ken Hughes of Dyfed-Powys Police has raised the issue of Satanic worship with the media for the purposes of discrediting anything George Travers may have revealed to other people.

Animal Safety Web News
19th July
Breeders Fined for Genetically Altering Personality of Dogs

A syndicate of illegal dog breeders has been fined two hundred and eighty thousand pounds for animal welfare offenses, leading to calls from animal lovers for a clampdown on breeders.

The syndicate, known as DocileDogs, specialized in breeding dogs specifically for their personality traits. Breeders commonly breed dogs for their appearance — which opponents of the practice say leads to genetic diseases and abnormalities — but breeding them for specific personality characteristics that appeal to owners is less known.

The syndicate is said to have made nearly three hundred thousand pounds from their cruel breeding program. They promised owners that the dogs would be "more docile, obedient and loving". They are said to have told one buyer that "this is the closest thing you will get to a baby. It will be totally reliant on you and do exactly what you tell it to do".

Judge Tom Shave said, "There is no doubt that companion dogs help many people, especially with loneliness, but the idea that you should breed dogs simply as playthings for owners is abhorrent."

Three men, William Alberts, thirty-two, David Alberts, twenty-nine, and Anthony Simpson, forty-six, all from

Colchester, operated the breeding business from a small farm.

Animal rights lawyer Jasper Suki agreed that the idea of breeding dogs purely for their personality was an unusual one.

"People often buy a particular breed of dog because they associate them with certain personalities — Labradors are friendly, Alsatians are protective and so on. But this is nonsense. It's as stupid as saying all fat people are jolly. Each dog has its own personality, just as humans do. In this case, though, they weren't telling people to buy a breed for its personality, they were specifically *producing* personalities. So they were breeding a docile dam with a docile sire or pairing dogs that were loving and needed attention. This was a heartless way to manipulate a pup's personality through genetics."

Animal welfare groups such as PETA (People for the Ethical Treatment of Animals) has campaigned for many years against the practice of breeding. The group's website states: "Breeding dogs is cruel and irresponsible, especially given the extensiveness of companion dog overpopulation. Dog breeders treat living individuals as commodities to be genetically manipulated for profit."

The manipulation of genetics through breeding has been criticized for reducing genetic diversity among dogs, which lowers the ability of certain dog populations to survive. Groups of people or animals benefit from the widest gene pool possible when it comes to their continued survival.

Suki added, "Some dog owners need to think long and hard. How would they feel if their genetics had been altered so they were more compliant and loving just to satisfy the needs of their parents?"

• Does this story make you think twice about owning a dog? Join the discussion on our website at three p.m. on Tuesday.

Lorraine is shown into the lounge at the A.M. headquarters. Max Bing and David Rogerson are sitting on the couch with a large pot of coffee on the table in front of them.

"Sorry, I got held up with the police questioning," she tells them.

"Well, it's not every day that your eleven-year-old granddaughter shoots someone, is it?" Bing queries, not expecting an answer.

"But don't worry, we have everything in hand with the police."

"Where is she?" Rogerson asks Lorraine abruptly.

"I don't know. I'm worried sick about her."

"You are worried about *her*?" Bing asks. "I have a bloody hole in my shoulder thanks to your granddaughter. We have to find her. Now, where is she?"

"I really don't know. Do you think I wouldn't go and get her if I knew?" Lorraine responds.

"We need to go to every place you think she could have gone. It's an eleven-year-old girl, for goodness' sake. She can't survive for long on her own. We need a list of all the friends she has. People she may have kept in touch with from her past. Relatives. Everything. What about that Simone character her father used to work with?"

"No, no," Lorraine replies. "Most definitely not. And you already have a list of everyone she has been in contact with since you got your claws into her a few years ago."

"It's a very short list. She obviously doesn't get on with people very well," Bing says sarcastically, handing Lorraine a pad and pen.

"Here, write them all down again. Plus, any places she likes to visit. But first we seriously need to discuss your position."

"What do you mean?" Lorraine asks, rising out of the couch and staring at the two men. "I am one of the founder members of A.M."

"You are becoming a liability, Lorraine. We allowed this nonsense with your clone Winnie to pass. You know we should have destroyed her, not let her live. But now this. We have to ask where your loyalties lie," Bing says.

"I didn't know anything about what Jane was planning. Do you seriously think I would have let her do that if I had known? I have every right to take my place in our society. Are you saying I am disloyal because I wouldn't let you incinerate Winnie? You got rid of the twenty-two clones before her because you couldn't get the cloning right," Lorraine responds.

"You say that, but we must warn you, that you are getting very close to the edge, Lorraine. The only thing you can do now is help us find Jane. It will be bad for you and it will be bad for her if we do not find her *very* soon."

"I'll find her. Just give me a chance," Lorraine nods meekly, realizing she has lost the battle.

From Janes online
The Trusted Source for Defense Intelligence
19th July
Bing shooting inspires breakthrough for treating battlefield injuries

Most people would be convalescing after being shot. But for tech billionaire Max Bing, a bullet through the shoulder was seen as an opportunity to put his team to work.

Bing, who was accidentally shot by a ceremonial Victorian pistol during a ceremony on Thursday, today announced that his life sciences company MethusalaCo has set up a team to work on new treatments for battlefield injuries.

"War is a sad fact of the world we live in. But what we can do at MethusalaCo is ensure that the men and women who suffer injuries during battle get the best possible treatments our innovative technologies can develop."

MethusalaCo's scientists will be exploring the use of two types of treatments for the battlefield initially.

• Light-activated technology to supersede the traditional ways to close wounds such as glue, staples, or sutures. The technology to bond these war wounds is called Photochemical Tissue Bonding and it has the added benefit of not causing the irritation or inflammation conventional methods often create.

• Use of tourniquet and cooling technology to reduce the number of limb amputations on the battlefield. Tourniquets have to be used to reduce hemorrhaging and save lives, but their extended use and subsequent pressure often means that the limb has to be amputated. A new pneumatic alternating tourniquet which uses adjustable bladders can spread the pressure and help preserve more of the tissue. This, in conjunction with a cooling sock, fed by bottled gas, can reduce the requirements of the limb metabolically, giving doctors a better chance to save the limb once it can warmed-up again in better conditions away from the field of war.

Chapter 5

Jane still can't get the images of the shooting out of her head. *She should have got Bing!* Now she needs a new plan. The safety of the Mews house will give her time to think. She looks up at her new home. Her new secret home. Jane looks into the sensor to activate it and types in the code. Zero-four-nine-seven-zero-seven-eight-seven-hash. She can't go back the school after the shooting and she can't go to Lorraine's. This is all she has for now. Once inside, she listens carefully as before. Nothing. There is nobody here. What will she say if someone arrives? Does Lorraine know about this place? Has she been here? There's no evidence of a woman living here — no women's clothes in the wardrobe and no women's beauty products in the bathroom. The whole place is very masculine.

Once back in the Mews house and safe, tiredness floods over Jane. She hasn't slept for two days. It's the longest she has gone without sleep. Her mummy and daddy once let her stay up till just after midnight so she could watch as people out on the London streets let off fireworks on New Year's Eve, but this is the first time she's gone through a whole night without sleep. Her body feels heavy, and although it's a warm summer's day, she feels cold and shivery. In the main bedroom, she crawls under the duvet, its cover crisp and clean, and falls into a deep sleep.

She awakes refreshed a few hours later, her mind clear, and heads upstairs. Nothing has changed. It doesn't look as if anyone has been here since she first visited a few weeks ago. She runs her finger along the top of the coffee table. There's not a speck of dust. There is something very strange about this house. It's immaculate. There are clothes in the cupboard, photos by the side of the bed, and the fridge is always full — yet it doesn't look as if anyone ever comes here.

She retrieves her small bag which she dropped at the doorway and puts it in the spare bedroom. At least she assumes it is the spare bedroom. There are no private items in this room and no clothes in the cupboard. The bed is a double, but slightly smaller than the one in the main bedroom. There are framed Kashmiri silk paintings hanging on the walls just like the rest of the flat.

Jane wanders through the flat aimlessly; she isn't used to having nothing to do. She examines one of a warrior goddess fighting a huge buffalo then takes a book on Hindu deities from the bookshelf and flicks through it until she finds what is looking for. There is a similar image in the book although this one shows the goddess and buffalo just before the fight. The buffalo is evil-eyed and stares at the woman as it prepares for battle. The warrior is Durga, the goddess of preservation, power, energy, motherhood, strength, and unity. In the painting, Durga is swirling her sword as she ferociously fights the giant beast — the shape-shifting demon Mahishasura, who can only be defeated by a woman. She reads on. The goddess is worshipped for fighting evil forces that threaten peace and prosperity and liberating downtrodden people from their oppressors. Just like me, Jane thinks, smiling. She starts reading out loud from the book.

"Ashtottarshat Namavali of Goddess Durga — the undefeatable goddess."

Jane puts the book away and examines more of the paintings, but none grab her imagination like that of the warrior, so she returns to the files that she'd found in the hidden compartment on her first visit.

Anno Methusala Experiment 2346
<u>Confidential</u>
Brain Transplants and the Transfer of Consciousness

Although Clone F of Recipient 19 was physically healthy, she was exhibiting worrying signs of self-awareness. When the corrective procedures failed to reverse the problem, Clone F was formally rejected as a candidate for Recipient 19. As per the procedure of physically healthy clones, a complete examination was carried out prior to its disposal to assess use for other experiments. The examination revealed that the cranial cavity was of sufficient size to accommodate an adult brain and Experiment 2346 was signed off by the medical committee on 14th March to carry out a full transplant to further explore the transfer of consciousness.

It is pertinent to chart the progress of head transplants to date at this point.

• 1908: a full head of one dog's head was grafted onto another dog and the two-headed dog survived for three hours.

• 1954: several full head grafts, again using dogs, were successful and the animals were able to move, see, and drink with their two heads. Survival rates were usually within three days, although the longest was twenty-nine days. Immune system rejection was the cause of death in all cases.

• 1970: conducted by neurosurgeon Robert J White, the full head of a monkey was transplanted onto another monkey that had had its head removed. Initially the brain's cranial nerves were fed successfully by the circulatory system but within nine days the immune system was again the reason for the death of the animal, despite the use of immunosuppressive drugs.

• 1990s: the proposed full head transplants of humans by Robert J White in mortuaries did not go ahead as planned.

Experiment 2346 will go ahead on 11th November, subject to the successful immune system check with the donor. Clone F remains in good physical health and will be kept operational until such time as the experiment takes place. A full report will be released in the first quarter of the new year.

Jane shakes her head. Is there nothing these people won't do? She needs to clear her head. Some of the files make her feel physically sick when she reads them. Suddenly, Jane feels alone. A hollow feeling. She realizes it's her birthday; her twelfth birthday. It's the first birthday she has spent alone and she looks around as if someone will pop out suddenly with a big smile on their face and a cake with a row of candles burning brightly.

"Happy birthday to you. Happy birthday, my darling Jane."

Memories of her early birthdays with her mummy and daddy flood her mind. Even in St. Edith's, they made a point of acknowledging the girls' birthdays. This is different. There is nobody here. She is alone. In a bid to fight her sadness, she pumps her chest and smiles. She has herself and her new-found strength and confidence. Being alone on her birthday will not drag her down.

Jane changes into her training kit and heads downstairs to the kitchen. She knows a good workout will raise her spirits. There is a good open space in front of the breakfast counter and a firm floor. She removes the broom from the cupboard, and using her bare foot, kicks off the brush head. The handle would work just fine.

After stretching — she feels stiff — she effortlessly works her way through her routine. Twirling, twisting, kicking, and thrusting the broom handle into imaginary opponents, Jane soon works up a sweat. She wipes her neck with the back of her shirt and pretends she is Durga fighting the evil Mahishasura.

"Take that, you ugly demon-buffalo! Take that!" she shouts.

97

"I am the undefeatable goddess!"

Panting heavily at the end of the workout, Jane sits crossed-legged on the floor, enjoying the coolness of the tiling against her limbs. With her eyes closed, she runs through positive images in her head, first picturing Durga taking on the buffalo, then herself defeating the evil Max Bing. Then she meditates, letting her mind clear itself of all thoughts. Her breathing soon returns to normal. She grabs some kitchen roll and mops up the sweat drops on the floor, then gulps back mouthfuls of cold water straight from the tap.

The next morning, after another vigorous workout, she reads through more of the files. Clones, rich people living forever, experiments on people while they are still conscious, body parts being swapped between people. Slowly she is piecing together what Bing and A.M. are *really* doing. The promises in the newspaper articles about a brighter future for everyone are all rubbish; all they care about is money and their rich friends. *The rest of us are just here to be used.* Jane feels anger rising inside herself. She can't wait. She's going to get Bing now. She'll find that house and kill him. Right now. She doesn't what care what happens to herself.

"Never attack in anger. Make sure the time is right or you will hand the advantage to your enemy."

Her daddy's voice calms her. She flops back onto her bed. Her brain is frazzled. She's finding it all too much to take in. She decides to cook some food to clear her mind.

There are a few cookery books in the house and one has caught her eye. It's from Mother India, a restaurant in Glasgow. She's never cooked an Indian dish before — only basic dishes she was taught at St. Edith's — but she likes it. Her daddy used to love teasing her mummy by announcing, "Come on, let's take Jane for a curry" — then dragging them down to the Mogul on the corner.

Jane plumps for a simple-looking dish called King Prawns with Dill and Ginger. Following the recipe closely, she fries up the onions in butter and oil, then adds the chilies and garlic, followed by the spices. The cumin seeds, dill, fennel, and turmeric are all in a rack on the wall. Once it is all mixed together, she adds the prawns with the tomatoes and ginger. It smells fresh and she wolfs it down with a piece of ready-made Indian flatbread. The food makes her focused again. *"Do not attack in anger."*

She may have failed to get Bing at the school, but she can get him next time. She flicks on the television to look for news about the shooting. An image of her, dressed in her school uniform, flashes up on the screen.

GLOBAL NEWS
…Breaking News…
20th July
Twelve-Year-Old-Schoolgirl Missing

Jane Banks from Surrey missing for two days… Last seen at St. Edith's School for Girls in Wiltshire… Grandmother's heartfelt appeal for safe return on her twelfth birthday … Police appeal for information…
…Breaking News…

There is no connection to the shooting. Just the usual television stuff about a missing child. Jane wonders how many children go missing and never make it the television screens. Never warrant the attention, according to the media chiefs. Jane checks herself in the large, ornate mirror hanging on the wall. Even without her frumpy private school uniform, she is clearly recognizable. The photograph had only been taken a few weeks previously for the St. Edith's Yearbook.

It is time to change. She cracks her knuckles and lights up a Marlborough Red under the extractor in her bathroom. She sets out the items from her washbag: gloves, scissors, and the deep, black at-home hair color kit. Then, after staring intently into the mirror for a few seconds, Jane starts cutting her hair. She has to do whatever she can to change her appearance. She struggles to cut the back, but eventually can feel her hair is barely lower than her hairline and it feels straight enough. The top looks a mess but there is no doubt it is shorter. She'll be wearing a cap most of the time anyway. Pulling on the gloves, Jane suddenly feels nervous. She's never done anything like this before. She applies the color carefully, then lights up another cigarette. She has to wait for the color to take effect. She laughs. Staring, she pouts and poses, sarcastically mimicking the models she has seen on television, laughing at her reflection in the mirror. Her hair is a bit of a mess, but Jane doesn't care. It will do the job. She certainly looks different.

"Very good. That's it. Keep your eyes on the plan. Take it step by step."

From Simone.Grant83's Instagram Account.
22nd July

Simone.Grant83 Great win for Chelsea on the weekend. 4-0! That one was for my old boss and colleague, George Travers. @chelseafc
#sadlymissed #fanforever #chelsea #CFC

Andrew Ransome strides up to Simone's desk, flushed with anger. Since everyone in the office discovered he is actually the nephew of the boss, he has become even more rude and direct with the rest of the staff. He knows Uncle Bruce has his back whatever he does. The constant Instagram posts from Simone are riling him. He had hated George Travers and he doesn't like being reminded of how much Simone liked and admired him.

"Andrew, have you been running? You look hot," Simone says sarcastically.

"Simone, I need to have a word. Can we go into my office please?"

"It's OK, we can do it here," Simone replies, determined that the rest of the office will hear his pettiness.

"I'd prefer to do it in my office, but if that is what you want. These Instagram posts about George Travers simply have to stop. He was connected with some very bad people. You must have read the news and yet, years later, you continue to bring up old photographs of him as if he was a hero. We do not want our clients to be reminded that he was associated in any way with Cooper & McKenzie."

"It was my personal account. It has nothing to do with Cooper & McKenzie. At least it's not like that one of you drunk with your buddies at the weekend."

"That was a business meeting with clients, as you know only too well. You booked the table, remember? I want these posts to stop. People know that you work for us. And you are posting them in work time as well."

"Well, they shouldn't be looking at my personal account. Just like you shouldn't, Andrew. It's a personal account and I will post personal messages on it if I wish."

Simone is determined not to back down. She had really liked George. She'd certainly had a crush on him, even though he was older than her. He was good looking without a doubt, but it was more than that. It was his rugged, couldn't-care-less attitude that attracted her the most. He wasn't scared of anything or anyone. It was a characteristic she knew Jane had inherited from him.

"I will be speaking to Bruce about this. Don't be surprised if you receive a formal letter of warning," Ransome adds in one last defiant show of seniority before storming off.

Simone looks around. The rest of the office staff have heard everything. She doesn't really know what they think. They rarely speak about George any more. Do these idiots really believe that stuff about George being a Satanist? She knew George. He loved his daughter. He would never do anything to harm her. She knows it is all nonsense.

From Angela West's WhatsApp account.
22ⁿᵈ July

Angela West: typing…
Simone Grant: online
Angela: Hey Simone, another photo of George. Seriously?
Simone: You bet. I didn't realize what a great boss he was until I had to work for this Ransome idiot.
Angela: Only coz you fancied him! I bet your new boss is pissed off?
Simone: That's why I do it! And shut up! I didn't fancy George.
Angela: Any news on George's daughter? You always got on well with her. I'd love to know what's happening with her!!
Simone: No. Nothing. That's all in the past.
Angela: It's for the best, my lovely. You still on for tonight?
Simone: You bet!

Simone sighs. Angela may be her best friend, but there is no way she can tell her the truth. The truth that she's secretly been in touch with Jane ever since George was buried. She pulls out a small black phone from her handbag and makes her way to the ladies' toilets where she locks herself in the cubicle at the end. She holds the button and waits as the screen flashes into life.

NOKIA 105
    …Two new messages…

J. 10.23: Putting next plan into place.

J. 10.29: Need more info on what they know and what they have released to public. Will contact shortly for meeting.

Simone turns off the phone. She is taking no chances. The longer it is on, the more time Bing's security team has to trace its activity. The small phone has been her link to Jane since they had met in Oak Hill Park the night of her parents' funeral.

Simone had been taken aback by how much Jane had changed when she met her that night. The sweet, quiet eight-year-old girl of just a few days before had gone, to be replaced by an angry yet focused girl, fixed on revenge. Even in the darkness that night, Simone had seen the same fiery determination in Jane's eyes that her old boss George used to display when he was focused on something. *It was almost obsessive.*

Jane had told her how men had broken into her house and shot her mummy. How George had driven miles, then crawled through a muddy pipe to a large country house with Jane clinging to his back. The tortured specimens she had seen. How her daddy and another man had taken her into a room to make her strong again. How she had been told that her daddy was dead as well. Now she wanted to kill the people responsible. And she needed Simone's help.

In the years that followed, she had checked the phone Jane had given her every couple of days. Often there was nothing, but occasionally Jane had asked for Simone to search for information or to contact someone. She never wasted time with small talk or told Simone about her life. She was completely focused on the plan to get Bing. Then, suddenly the opportunity at the school had arisen. Simone had warned Jane that she was not ready and she should wait. But she was determined to go ahead. Now, after Jane's failure to kill him, they were back to square one. Except

Bing now knows they were gunning for him.

From an A.M. security investigation document.
22nd July

NOKIA 105
    1. Activity to Base Station 51.513°N 0.088°W 17 July 13.58
— 1 minute 15 seconds
    2. Activity to Base Station 51.513°N 0.088°W 17 July 14.44
— 2 minute 52 seconds
    3. Activity to Base Station 51.513°N 0.088°W 18 July 15.11
— 2 minutes 38 seconds
    4. Activity to Base Station 51.513°N 0.088°W 18 July 11.25
— 49 seconds
    5. Activity to Base Station 51.513°N 0.088°W 22 July 14.05
— 32 seconds

Identified as possible burner phone used by S. Grant. Action —
follow and investigate all future uses.

The Times
23rd July
Bing to Build a City in Space for 4,000 People

People will be living in space in a matter of years — that's
according to Synoplex CEO Max Bing, who announced
yesterday that his company would be building a city in space
called Stella Terra — meaning Star Land or Star Earth.

    "The stuff of science fiction movies is about to become a
reality. Together with our partners, we are investing hundreds of
billions of dollars into this project and in just a few years the first
residents will move into their homes among the stars," Bing
promised.

104

Unlike existing space habitats, like the International Space Station, Stella Terra will not just be home to astronauts. While there will be two hundred astronauts, scientists, and engineers living there, the rest of the four thousand-strong community will be drawn from all walks of life.

"What we have seen over the last few years is that more and more people can work remotely. Thanks to advances in technology, people are not only working from home but also from other countries. So why not space? It doesn't matter if you work in banking, insurance, teaching, or hospitality, Stella Terra can be a home for you," Bing added.

The tech tycoon showed he is particularly keen to attract families by emphasizing that Stella Terra will offer a crime-free environment, views of space from all family quarters, an opportunity for quality family time, free day-care facilities, schools, and numerous leisure facilities geared toward families. There are even Virtual Holiday Pods where families can be transported to a destination of their choice through virtual technology.

To get this audacious project off the ground, Synoplex are partnering with airline and spacecraft manufacturers MaxWing, defense technology Re-One, as well numerous space agencies including UKSA, NASA, CNES, ESA, JAXA, EgSA, ISRO, and SpaceMauritius. Live Buzz, the interior design company that specialize in layouts for small spaces like submarines and micro houses, will be consulting on the planning of the living quarters.

Everyone joining the community at Stella Terra will be expected to commit to two years in the new city but there will be regular connections to Earth for supplies and emergencies.

The city will comprise of a series of pods — the first of which is the control center manned by astronauts — and other pods can be added in space over time. Bing sees no limit to the size of the space city.

"Finally, technology has enabled us to allow people to live

in space. Our revolutionary pod system means the initial population of four thousand is just the start. We can add pods and expand the city when the time is right," he said.

• Anyone interested in applying for a life in space should apply via synoplexinspace.co.sp

On day five in the house, after following her usual morning routine, Jane gets to work with the files as usual. She methodically lays out the reports into groups: experiments, clones, the people involved, and money involved. What does it all mean? But before she has a chance to think any further, she hears a noise. Someone is in the house downstairs. She quickly gathers up the files, puts them back in the folder and runs into her bedroom to hide them in her bag. She stands at the doorway to the bedroom, as if guarding it. She can hear the person coming up the stairs.

"Hello," the young woman says. "It's lovely to see someone eating the food at last."

Jane is still standing in the doorway.

"Hello," she replies.

The woman is carrying a box of cleaning materials.

"I'm Eva," she says, pausing for Jane to reciprocate with her own name.

"I'm er, hello. It's nice to meet you."

Eva doesn't push Jane for her name but instead starts taking out the cleaning materials from her box and arranging them on the table.

"Do you know," Eva says, as if it was perfectly normal to see young girl alone in the house on a Wednesday morning, "I haven't seen anyone here for more than three years. I've been filling up the fridge all that time and throwing all the food away. That's why it's nice to see someone eating it at last."

"Yes, it's very nice, thank you," Jane says, stunned that the woman isn't asking who she is or what she is doing here.

"Between you and me, this has to be the easiest job ever. I get three hundred pounds a week to clean five rooms — although I haven't been able to get in the other room since I last saw Mr. Kapoor — and it's spotless anyway. Still, I'm not complaining. The money's is always is my account on time."

"I'm sorry. I hope I haven't made a mess," Jane says.

"Not at all. Are you going to be here next week? Is there any favorite food you want me to buy you? I normally just get the basics."

"No, everything is fine, thank you," Jane says, as Eva walks toward her.

"I see you've changed your hair color. I was always doing things like that at your age. Maybe I could help you tidy it up a bit? It's always difficult to do it on your own. You need to do your eyebrows too. They are still blonde."

"It's fine," Jane says, but Eva isn't listening and ushers her back into her bedroom and toward the bathroom.

Eva works away with the scissors, applies another layer of color to Jane's hair, then tips back her chin and gets to work on her eyebrows. It feels good to have someone taking care of her, even if it is a stranger.

"There," she says, when she has finished. "Leave it for twenty minutes, then rinse it out. It should look a bit more even now. Right, I must get on and earn my money!"

"Were you a hairdresser?" Jane asks.

"No! But you learn how to do these things over the years. Us girls must stick together!"

"Do you mind me asking how you get into the house? Do you have a key or something?" Jane asks, still wondering how the access panel at the door recognized her eyes.

"Goodness no! A place like this doesn't use keys. Mr. Kapoor scanned my retinas with his watch and uploaded it to his computer system."

107

Jane thinks back to her time in the medical room with Kapoor leaning over her. He ran the face of his watch over her face, its blue light flickering.

"That's how he got it. He scanned my eyes!" she mutters.

Once Jane has rinsed the excess color out of her hair, she heads back into the main room. Eva is polishing the frames of the Kashmiri silk paintings.

"These are lovely, aren't they?" she says, sensing Jane is behind her. "Worth a lot of money apparently. Mr. Kapoor told me they were originals from the eighteenth century."

"Yes, I like them," Jane says, before plucking up the courage to ask what she really wants to know.

"Eva, who else comes here? To the house, I mean."

The cleaner stops what she was doing and turns to look at Jane.

"Not many people really. As I said, I've not seen anyone for more than three years. Mr. Kapoor was here a lot at one time, but I haven't seen him for ages. There was a glamorous lady who used to visit sometimes."

Eva points to a photograph of Kapoor and Lorraine.

"She was here a lot at one stage. I accompanied them to a few events and realized they were very close. I think, um, she was Mr. Kapoor's girlfriend or something."

It confirms everything Jane has been thinking. The flat was Anil Kapoor's. The photograph in the hidden compartment in the main bedroom clearly shows he and Lorraine were more than *just* friends.

Eva finishes up her cleaning and goes to say goodbye, but Jane is intrigued by something Eva said. *"I accompanied them to a few events and saw they were very close."*

"Eva. I hope you don't mind me asking, but why would Mr. Kapoor get his cleaner to go with him and my... er, that lady to events?"

Eva just stares at Jane and smiles.

Jane can see something in her eyes. Since her operation, she has been able to weigh up people quickly and accurately. She can tell immediately whether she can trust them.

"You're not just a cleaner, are you?"

Eva pauses, taken aback at Jane's directness. It's not something you usually encounter with a girl so young.

"Are you not happy with my cleaning? Look at how spotless the place is."

"So?" Jane prompts, not letting Eva avoid her question so easily.

"OK. No, I'm not just a cleaner. I provided private security for Mr. Kapoor. That's why I accompanied him and the lady in the photographs to certain events. He did tell me that someone else might be coming here and that I was to help them, but I wanted to get to know you better before telling you. I have to go now, but I'll be back in a few days."

Once Eva has gone, Jane slumps on the couch. She has a lot to think through. Would Eva tell anyone she was here? It seems unlikely. Especially after what she told her about providing private security. If anything, she was someone she could trust. Another piece of the jigsaw Kapoor had provided her.

Jane thinks through what they had talked about. Then it strikes her. Eva mentioned a fifth room. But there are only four rooms: the kitchen, the lounge, and the two bedrooms. There isn't a fifth room. What did she mean?

It has to be hidden. It wouldn't be a surprise. Everything else about this house is secret, so why not a secret room?

Jane jumps up and looks around. The house isn't *that* big. How could she have missed an entrance to another room? There are certainly no doors. Nothing obvious. Maybe the room is under the house. She searches the kitchen but finds nothing that looks like it could lead to another room. Back upstairs, Jane scours the shelves, pulling back a few books on the bookshelf, as if one of them will spring open a door magically, then laughs at

109

the absurdity of it. Suddenly, just as Jane is running her hands along the back wall, she sees a sensor. Its blueish-black color means it isn't immediately obvious, but it is clearly a sensor, just like the one at the entrance to the house.

Jane braces herself, hoping this is what she has been searching for, then looks into it. It flashes and part of the wall slides to one side, revealing a door. There is a keypad. Jane runs through the codes in her head.

"Inside door, four-four-six-seven-two-two-three-seven-hash."

Jane breathes deeply at her success and steps inside a room of about six meters square. Screens fill one wall and there is a black, leather-topped desk facing them, with a large, modern shelving unit against the other wall. There is a mirror next to a glass door in the corner. A secret room leading to another secret room. Jane laughs. This whole house is a mystery.

Jane settles down into the leather desk chair, straightens her back in mock importance, and swivels around a few times before looking through the drawers. As well as the usual stationary and folders, there is a smart-looking watch and a big box of memory sticks. She shuts the drawers with a flourish then wanders over the mirror to re-check her hair.

"Not bad at all," she says, smoothing down her hair, then pushing it behind her ears

"Not bad at all, Jane. Welcome to Mr. Kapoor's tech room," a steady, firm staccato voice says.

Jane takes a step back. The voice is coming from her image.

"What? A talking mirror!" she exclaims.

"I'm a computer actually. You can call me Y_RAM."

"Cool. Can you play me some music?"

"I can if you wish. But please don't insult me by comparing me to a household virtual assistant!"

"How do you know who I am?" Jane asks with concern.

"Facial and voice recognition of course. You have nothing to fear from me. I am here to help you."

110

"OK. What are all the screens on the wall then?"

A long screen flashes into action to display share prices and market indices from around the world.

...FTSE 100 7,461.34 (-0.46%)... DOW 34,725.47 (+0.32%)... SYNP 13,400.01 (+0.02%)

"What about the other screens?" Jane asks.

"They will display whatever you want to see. I can access documents and images that are stored on other computers around the world," Y_RAM explains. "Unfortunately, some of them are heavily encrypted so it may take me some time to access them. Until you have decided what you want me to find, I'll show you how to access images from CCTV cameras. You might find them useful."

The other screens light up. The large middle screen shows a map covered in green dots and it is surrounded by eight other screens showing real-time images of the London streets. People are zipping around in all directions, going about their business as if they are ants sent out with a specific purpose for their nest. It strikes Jane that no one is standing still.

"Images from new cameras are available all the time. There are thousands erected in streets and buildings every day. You are currently looking at central London, but you can view anywhere in the world that has a camera. Simply ask me or use the control pad on the desk."

"Go to North London. Where I used to live," Jane instructs, quickly getting the hang of having a super computer at her command.

The screen shifts northwards and hundreds of dots form on the map.

"There are loads of them! Are they all CCTV cameras?"

"Yes. You have to realize how many of these cameras there are watching people every day. The UK government operates about fifty-two thousand of them, but there are about two million of these cameras in total around the country. You can see pretty much anywhere you like, especially in the cities and town. There are fewer in the rural areas."

"What am I looking for?" Jane asks.

"That's up to you. I just make the images available," the computer replies. "Obviously, if you can see these cameras then others can too, so there may be times when you out and about that you might want to turn them off. The average person gets seen by seventy CCTV cameras every day, so just be aware of that yourself."

"Do you have a big brain?" Jane asks smiling.

"I don't have a brain like you do, although I'm working on it. But I know lots of things. If you need me when you are not here then you can use the watch."

"This one!" Jane exclaims after rifling through the top drawer for the watch she saw earlier.

She looks into the blueish-black screen and the watch activates at the retina match.

"Is it one of those watches that can shoot people?" Jane asks, her eyes widening in youthful curiosity.

"Ah, like 007 you mean? No, It's nothing like that. But it means you can contact me at any time. You are the only one who can use it and it will deactivate thirty seconds after it is last used for security reasons. Now, remember I said you might need to turn off the CCTV cameras. You can do that by using the silver pen with the black top."

"How?"

"It works just like any other pen if you need to use it for writing, but if your press the button and twist the top, you will shut down all cameras within a half-mile radius. It will also shut down all internet connections and anything else that relies on technology to operate. Everything! So don't use it for fun!" Y_RAM adds.

"The small, black cylinder will open all locks — doors,

gates, safes, everything. Just hold it next to a lock. It takes a bit longer with electronic locks, but be patient. Now, you wanted something to shoot with, like in the movies, you said."

Jane smiles. She likes this computer.

"The blue memory sticks with the eight tiny pins in the end. You fire these by depressing the button on the side and sliding it. They have a range of ten meters. Whatever you hit will be immobilized immediately and won't be able to move for an hour. It won't harm them; just stop them moving for a while."

Jane pulls out one of the memory sticks and points it at the wall. The pins fire rapidly, splaying out as they travel and lodging themselves firmly into the wall.

"Wow!"

She sits back in the chair. Suddenly, swiveling around in it seems childish. She now has some tools that will help her get Bing. But how will she get to him? The whole country is looking for her and Bing's cronies almost certainly are. This is the only place she is safe but she can't get him sitting here. She needs a plan. She needs to flush him out. To make him so angry that he makes a mistake and gives her an opportunity.

Jane instructs Y_RAM to zoom in on the map and she spends some time looking at the CCTV images. Everyone is seemingly unaware, or simply don't care that they are being watched. Wherever she looks — London, Manchester, Edinburgh — she can see people shopping, chatting, laughing, arguing. Cameras inside buildings show people sitting at reception desks and traveling in lifts. There's nothing remarkable about it. She zooms into Salisbury and Wilton, where she went to school. Neither are covered by cameras as much as the cities but there are still images of ordinary people doing ordinary things. As she watches a woman with a green shopping bag, she suddenly feels dirty looking at people without them knowing they are being watched. Are there other people watching these images as well? What sort of job is that? Spying on people doing nothing.

By flicking between cameras, she practices her spy skills by following one man's movements from his office, down the lift and out of the building, walking to a shop to buy a sandwich, then stopping at the Red Lion on the corner to meet friends for a drink. If she can follow him, she can follow anyone.

Jane is still curious about Anil Kapoor. Who was he? What sort of person was he? What was he doing working with Bing? Why is he helping her from the grave?

"Y_RAM, call up all the information you have on Anil Kapoor."

Y_RAM search results… Anil Kapoor
    …Surface web post and mentions: 129,455…
    …Deep web posts: 16…
    …Dark web posts: 184…

Dark Web
The Hidden Secrets of Anil Kapoor

The death of Anil Kapoor in a road accident on the icy roads of Wales at the age of fifty-four completed a tragic life-cycle for the steel magnate. There is no doubting that fast cars and crashes played a central part in his life.

It was perhaps inevitable that a young man born in London to a rich family would enjoy the finer things in life. When studying chemical engineering at Queens' College, Cambridge, Kapoor was driving a sleek, jet-black Ferrari Testarossa. It was the one fastest road cars in the country at the time and his frequent crashes quickly earned him the nickname 'Crash Kappy'. It was a nickname that he relished, and some of his former university friends have since said it simply made him drive faster and wilder.

But it was back in India with his family that his mad driving would start to haunt him. While speeding through a village between Mumbai and Pune, he hit a young boy. The boy died instantly. Kapoor was never charged amid rumblings of a yet another cover-up from a rich family soon surfaced. All that is known for sure is that Kapoor was at a meeting in Mumbai earlier that day and neighbors of the family who lost their son reported that soon after his death, the family started building a new, much larger house. Two of their other sons still work for KapoorLakshmi steel company today.

Reports of another accident — this time resulting in the death of a young girl — ended with Kapoor's driver being imprisoned. Rumors swirled that he had taken the fall for his boss in return for a big pay out for his family. People who knew Kapoor pointed out that although his father insisted he had a driver, he would never let him drive.

Kapoor cleaned up his act when he took over the family business in 1998 but before long it was a business that consumed him. He worked tirelessly, spending long hours when at the office and spending much of his time away on business trips. Many people believe he was hiding from his past at this time.

It was while away on one of his business trips that his son, Amith, was killed after a short and unexplained illness. It was an incident that changed Kapoor forever. From that moment forward he dedicated his life — and wealth — to social responsibility programs and research into extending life. When he died, Kapoor left his fortune to the Bing Foundation, a foundation that is well-known for its work in finding ways to help people live longer. It's not hard to connect his financial legacy with the guilt he must have felt for the two young lives he took.

The attraction of the glass door in the corner is proving too much, so Jane deactivates the screens then heads to check it out. As usual, there is a blueish-black sensor she has to activate. The door slides back to reveal a lift door. It opens instantly. The lift senses her weight inside and starts to move without instruction. Jane calculates that she has gone down two floors. She's below the level of the kitchen. She's underground. The door opens and Jane can immediately feel it is cooler.

She steps out into a garage. It's bigger than the ones people have next to their suburban houses and there are no boxes or tools against the walls, just a huge black cupboard. It's more like a miniature underground car park. There are four vehicles. One is a black and white sports car. It looks like a racing car. Hardly discreet. There's a big off-road vehicle — a classic Land Rover. But it's the other two vehicles that catch Jane's eye: a tiny car that's more like a buggy, and a baby-blue scooter. Jane sits on the scooter and mock weaves through the traffic, leaning from left to right while making a smooth, purring engine noise. Then she gets into the smart EQ fortwo. It's snug and she can see out clearly. Through the window, she views a ramp and metal shutter gate that must lead to street level. Jane wants to head out and drive. But she doesn't know how. How can she learn? Maybe Simone can teach her? Or Eva?

Back upstairs, Jane's mind is racing. She flicks on the television to look for more news of her disappearance but soon spots a movie called *Fifth Estate*. It stars Benedict Cumberbatch, her mummy's favorite actor. The film charts the early days of Wikileaks, a website that releases secret information about big companies and governments so people can read what they are *really* up to. Although the film is mostly about the US government's actions in a war, Jane is fascinated with revelations of a big bank that helps rich people hide their money in offshore accounts. The blond-haired Cumberbatch calls them "rich arseholes".

If only I could do the same with Bing and MethusalaCo, she thinks. That will show people what *they* are really up to. Tell them the truth about how evil he is and how people are being experimented on so "rich arseholes" could live longer. She has some documents. She has been piecing them together so they make sense. Why not release the documents for people to read? The newspapers will call them the LiveForeverLeaks, she smiles.

"Y-RAM. Call up all the documents you can find on MethusalaCo and Anno Methusala. And show me the images from all the cameras around Max Bing's estate in Wales."

Chapter 6

The Daily Telegraph
24th July
How You Could Become a Reef in the Sea After Your Death

MethusalaCo, the life sciences company owned by tech behemoth Synoplex's CEO Max Bing, today launched a new division that offers people an alternative to burial or cremation when they die — becoming a reef in the sea.

Although MethusalaCo seeks solutions for aging and its associated diseases, Bing says dealing with death is a natural progression.

"MethusalaCo continues to lead in the field of extending the lifespan of people everywhere. But despite our innovations, death is still inevitable, and we recognize that many people want their burial to be eco-friendly. With our new division, your remains can now form part of the seabed, creating new habitats for sea life that will thrive long after you have gone."

The new division, called SeaLives, will offer a service of cremation, with the remains turned into marine friendly capsules that are placed onto the floor of the ocean, offering new habitats for a range of life, as well as encouraging reefs to develop.

SeaLives will initially be funded by two million dollars of capital and is expected to be profitable within one year. Shares in Synoplex finished at 13,402.34 up 0.23%.

From Angela West's WhatsApp account.

24th July

Angela: typing...

Simone: online

Angela: Hey Simone, you seen the latest about your favorite company?

Simone: Yeah, I was just reading it. They are taking over the world!!

Angela: I don't know. Becoming part of the seabed when you die sounds kind of cool, don't you think?

Simone: Yeah, I suppose so. I just don't trust them.

Angela: Come on, you're paranoid.

Simone: Yeah, maybe. Anyway, gotta run. Need to check something.

NOKIA 105

...One new message...

J. 14.20: Can you meet me at the Belgravia Park tonight? 9pm?

S. 15.47: Yes. See you there.

Simone hasn't been able to concentrate all day. Her mind is still racing with unanswered questions. What does Jane want? Where has she been hiding? How does she plan to get to Bing now? The sun has only just set and the night air is still warm. She's feeling quite sporty in her figure-hugging jeans, trainers, and a thin summer blouse as she approaches the private park. Simone has only ever been in a private park on their open days. It was the only way to get in if you didn't live in a house in a square next to a park. Is Jane staying in one of the houses in the square? She has refused to tell Simone where she is hiding.

The gate is open. Simone pauses before entering the rectangular park but after a few steps, she stops and squints into the half-light. Where is Jane?

"Simone, over here. It's me," a voice whispers from the

119

bushes.

She heads toward the voice and a strong arm yanks her through the foliage, quickly cupping a strong hand over her mouth.

"You were followed. Over there. Look!"

Two dark figures enter the park and are looking ahead intently. One of them looks into a device. They are only about thirty yards away.

"Over this fence, quick," Jane tells Simone.

Jane grabs Simone, putting one hand under her armpit and the other under her bum. With a sharp push, Simone is over. Her blouse rips on the spike, revealing her pert black breasts. She instinctively pulls the split together in embarrassment before turning to help Jane.

"Here, let me help," she says, reaching over the fence with her arm.

But Jane needs no help, and swiveling on her left hand, she swings over the fence in one smooth movement.

"Show off!" Simone says, impressed at Jane's flexibility and strength.

"Quick! Run! They are close just behind us. They must have traced our phones," Jane says.

They both toss their phones into the bushes as they exit the square and head toward Victoria Station.

"Bloody Bing. How did they crack those phones?" Simone queries.

"It must have been the day of the shooting. We used them a lot that day. Quick. Keep running. The Tube is over there," Jane says.

"They'll be over that fence by now," Jane shouts, urging Simone on. As they get closer to the station, it starts to get busier.

"Down here," Jane says when she spots a narrow service alleyway, before leaping down five steps in a single jump.

The alleyway leads to the back doors of the restaurants and

shops. Jane pushes Simone ahead of her, kicking some bins over in her wake as she runs. There is a lanky chef in his whites, sitting on a large, overturned white bucket enjoying a cigarette during his break. The door to his kitchen is propped open. Simone darts through it first at Jane's insistence.

"Hey! You can't go in there," the chef shouts.

"Sorry," Jane says, smiling sweetly before grabbing his cigarette and pulling the door shut. As the chef bangs on the door from the outside, Jane pops the cigarette in her mouth, takes a quick drag, then drops it into a hand basin.

"Through here, quick. They can't open the door from the outside. It's an emergency exit. They'll have to run round the block."

Jane and Simone weave their way through the restaurant kitchen, dodging chefs who are busy stirring pots over hot stoves and the kitchen porters running around with plates. They are moving fast, so despite their sudden appearance from the back there is barely murmur from the kitchen staff. A few astonished diners look up at the sight of a young girl and attractive woman with a ripped blouse pushing past them but only the maître d' shouts out a warning. It's immaterial because they exit the restaurant before he even has time to finish his tirade.

They skip down the steps to the station and both leap the barrier.

"Great leap!" Jane jokes. "Only one minute. Good. They won't know which line we get on, but we'll change at Embankment just in case."

They choose the quiet end carriage. Apart from a couple snuggling up to each other at the far end, there is no one else around.

"How's life in hiding?" Simone asks, grabbing her torn blouse to cover her breasts.

Jane leans over and gives Simone a hug. Simone is taken

121

aback by Jane's warmth. It's somehow soaking up love. For a brief moment, Simone senses a loneliness in the embrace before Jane pulls away suddenly and starts running though the details of what has been happening since the shooting.

Jane hugs Simone again as they change onto the Northern Line at Embankment. Once inside the end carriage again, Jane explains her plans to leak Bing's secret documents.

"I'll set up a website. It'll take a few days. Something they can't block or take down. And I'll release them to the media as well. You just need to get the documents to me. How are we are going to contact each other without the phones?"

"Go to Brookhaven in Roblox at nine in the evening every night. Go to the corner of Brookhaven Street and Maple Drive by the swimming pool. When I'm ready, I'll be there, waiting for you. Only talk to GeorgeExplo. Right, I'm going to jump off the train here," Jane says as the train pulls into Euston.

"OK. I'll meet you at, er, Brookhaven in a week. I'll stay on the train for a couple more stops."

"Nice boobs by the way," Jane laughs, before jumping off the train and disappearing through the tiled archway.

Simone pulls her ripped blouse together again and blushes as she repeats the details in her head.

"Go to Brookhaven in Roblox. The corner of Brookhaven Street and Maple Drive by the swimming pool. Only talk to GeorgeExplo."

She'd promised George she'd look after Jane before she died. *I bet he didn't mean I should help her kill Max Bing though!* Simone stays on the train until a couple of young, drunk girls get on at East Finchley. An hour later, Simone is knocking on Angela's door.

"What's up, girl? What are you doing here at this time?" Angela asks, answering her door in her dressing gown. "What the hell has happened to you? Your top is proper ripped."

Simone tells Angela that she has been mugged.

122

"What! Quick, get in here. Let's get you cleaned up," her friend says

Red wine is soon glugging its way out of the bottle into the glasses.

"Get that down you. It will make you feel better," Angela says with a cheeky wink.

"You're right, that's just what I needed," Simone tells her friend as she feels the red wine on the back of her throat and the alcohol relax her body. "By the way. Do you know what Brookhaven in Roblox is?"

Angela laughs.

"I didn't take you for a gamer, Simone! Yes, I do actually. It's a virtual world. Part of the metaverse you might have heard of. You can buy land, open shops, drive cars, all sorts."

"What? With real money?"

"With Robux, but people get those by using real money, yes."

"Ro-bucks? That's crazy. Another world within the real world?"

"Yeah. It's actually a lot of fun. Some people just explore the place and chat to other people. But there are stories of people who actually make a living in the metaverse. I'll get my laptop and show you how it works. It's pretty addictive though. We could be on it for hours. But it doesn't matter; you should stay here tonight anyway. I've got some clothes you can borrow for work tomorrow."

Simone has only been at her desk at Cooper & McKenzie a few minutes when she sees them. Four men: two policemen in uniform and two scowling men in dark suits. Are they the two men who followed her last night? Simone crouches over her desk behind her computer, but after a couple of questions one of her colleagues is pointing in her direction.

"Miss Grant. Can we have a word?" the older policeman

asks, although it clearly isn't a question.

Simone leads the men to one of the meeting rooms.

"Miss Grant, I'm Inspector Hawthorne and this is Constable Jones."

"And these two?" Simone asks, looking disdainfully toward the two men in suits.

"They are our colleagues, Miss Grant. They are assisting us. Can you tell us your whereabouts last night?"

"I was out for a walk," she lies.

"We have reason to believe you met with Jane Banks? You may have known her previously as Jane Travers? We are very worried about her and we believe you can help us find her. You can help us to help her."

Simone continues to lie. All night, she had sat up on the bed in Angela's spare room going through her story. A walk, a drink in a bar, getting mugged, then going to her friend's house because she was too scared to go home. The two policemen continue to bombard her with questions, clearly not believing a word of her story. The two men in suits stand stone-still and never utter a word. Eventually, after realizing they are getting nowhere, the policemen get up from their chairs.

"You do realize that you will be in serious trouble if you are lying to us?" Inspector Hawthorne asks earnestly. "Oh, we found these in the bushes near Belgravia Park. We thought you might like them back," he adds sarcastically, before sliding the two Nokia burner phones across the table.

Simone picks up the phones once the men have gone. They are no good now. She puts them on the floor of the meeting room, removes one of her high-heeled shoes and pummels them to bits with the sharp heel.

"Track those now!" she says defiantly, before tossing the pieces in the bin and returning to her desk.

Jane stares at the center screen in the tech room.

124

Y_RAM search results... MethusalaCo

　　...Surface web post and mentions: 34,856,076...

　　...Deep web posts: 23,943...

　　...Dark web posts: 2,043...

　　...Decryption keys running... Encrypted documents accessed: 2...

Y_RAM search results... Anno Methusala

　　...Surface web post and mentions: 0...

　　...Deep web posts: 0...

　　...Dark web posts: 1...

　　...Decryption keys running... Encrypted documents accessed: 2...

"What? There are millions of them on MethusalaCo!"

"You asked me to search for everything on 'MethusalaCo' and 'Anno Methusala'. I suggest you narrow down the terms of your search Jane."

"OK. Display the Anno Methusala documents and the encrypted documents for MethusalaCo you've accessed. Then print them out for me. There might be something interesting in them. Ignore the rest for now.

Jane waits, watching the printer.

"Er, computer, can you print out the encrypted documents please."

"Of course I can. But you'll have to put some paper in the printer. I'm clever, but not that clever..."

Jane laughs, but once she's reading the documents, her laughter stops.

Highly confidential

Security Level 3 Anno Methusala
Experiment R1285K: C23 Recipient 17
Passed by 17 votes to 8

The disposal of C23 Recipient 17 has been deferred for six months to observe its integration into society without security. Additional skills training has been given, but the success of integration is calculated at only thirty-eight per cent. Integration will include home life, social life, work life, then pairing, and possible mating.

Home and social life

C23 Recipient 17 will initially live with the Recipient 17 and be introduced to her social circle.

Work life

An administration position in the City with Lambert Ltd has been secured through CJ.

Pairing identified

Physically, GT is fit, healthy, and has a high sperm count. Emotionally he is strong and able to cope with high-pressure situations and unusual circumstances. The only trait of concern is his single-mindedness. He is skilled in the use of chemicals and explosives and served in Afghanistan. An introduction between C23 Recipient 17 and GT will be arranged and managed. If the pairing is successful then a position with BR in the City has been arranged for GT.

Mating

The success of mating through natural birth is calculated at sixty-three per cent and through Caesarean at ninety-one per cent.

"Computer, run a search for 'C23 Recipient 17'."

Y_RAM search results... C23 Recipient 17
    ...Surface web post and mentions: 0...
    ...Deep web posts: 0...

...Dark web posts: 0...

...Decryption keys running... Encrypted documents accessed: 1...

"Y_RAM, is that the same document you printed?"

"Yes. The one you already have. Encryption keys are still running for further files."

"How long will it take?"

"It will keep running until it can decrypt other files that exist."

"And how long is that?"

"Until it decrypts the files."

Frustrated, Jane reads through the document again. Could it be? Could GT be her daddy? The description fits. Chemicals, explosives, Afghanistan. It *has* to be him. He *was* involved with Bing. Was he working for him? Surely not. It looks like he was being used by Bing just like everyone else. But who... or what is C23 Recipient 17? The experiment was all about *it*. Jane reads the next file.

Highly confidential

Security Level 3 Anno Methusala
Updated security access list
Max Bing • David Rogerson • Cordelia Charrier • Thomas Abebe • Alan Allen • Ronald Anderson • Paul Armstrong • Paul Botha • Stephen Brent • Paramjit Chandra • Peter Chapman • Albert Cornish • Laura Denning • Anabel Duke • Glynis Johns • Stephen Marshall • Lorraine Meaden • Timothy Morris • Juliet Read • Bruce Robertson • Donald Ruin • Alan Schultz • Balnoor Seth • Julie Smyth • Steffen Young

"Lorraine! Lorraine Meaden! It's her," Jane screams out loud. "She's involved in this thing. The whole time. My mummy. My daddy. They are dead. She knew everything all along. I hate that woman! Computer, search for information on 'Lorraine Meaden'. I want to know everything about her."

WIKIPEDIA
The Free Dictionary

Human cloning is the creation of a genetically identical copy of a human. The term is generally used to refer to artificial human cloning, which is the reproduction of human cells and tissue. The possibility of human cloning has raised controversies. These ethical concerns have raised several nations to pass laws regarding human cloning. Therapeutic cloning would involve cloning cells from a human for use in medicine and transplants. It is an active area of research but is not in medical practice anywhere in the world, as of 2021.

United Nations
Meeting Coverage and Press Releases

Press Release /GA 10333
Fifty-Ninth General Assembly
Plenary 82nd Meeting (AM)
The General Assembly this morning adopted the United Nations Declaration on Human Cloning, by which Member States were called on to adopt all measures necessary to prohibit all forms of human cloning inasmuch as they are incompatible with human dignity and the protection of human life.

By further terms of the Declaration, Member States were also called on to protect adequately human life in the application of life sciences; to prohibit the application of genetic engineering techniques that may be contrary to human dignity; to prevent the exploitation of women in the application of life sciences; and to adopt and implement national legislation in that connection.

Chapter 7

Synoplex security report

++ SYSTEM DATA BREACH ALERT ++

    60 FD 1B 74 28 D5 9B 76 0M 98 CH 08 99 PK 3R 20 8H GD 43 GB

    SF 52 TB 21 VY N5 9O 76 BC 9W UG 52 23 0P DY 28 MV EB 1U H7

    7E 9H 43 NC 60 43 56 XD 2J 75 9L GE R1 48 H1 98 23 P5 HG NE

    7T NC 5E 7Q 28 S5 9L JB 18 9Z 23 DE 93 8L CE 28 20 KB 9K 43

"Something is attacking our system?" the Synoplex IT technician says.

"Our firewall will drop it. Just monitor it, then report it as usual," his boss replies matter-of-factly.

"Whooooa! It's compromised the firewall as if it wasn't there. I've never seen anything like this before," the technician screams.

"Nonsense. We have the strongest cyber security system in the world. Nothing can compromise it. I helped set it up myself. Come on, let me take a look," his boss says, still unconcerned.

"It *is* through. It's decrypting the files. What the hell is this? It's already through to the file server that stores the highly confidential information. Get everyone onto this. *Now*!"

Jane is up early. She has to visit Lorraine to get the answers to her questions. She knows it a big risk but she has no choice. She has to make sense of the documents. To find out what really happened to her mummy and daddy. And why? *She dares to call me her granddaughter and yet she is involved in this whole thing!*

For once, Jane skips her workout. She'll be getting enough exercise today. She ties up her trainers and slips a small backpack over her shoulders, making sure it is snug. Taking the train will be too risky. The police and Bing's men will be everywhere. It's only thirty miles to Lorraine's mansion. She'll run it. But far from being daunted, Jane is relishing the run.

Jane jogs easily at first, making her way gently down to the Embankment, before stretching out her now-warmed muscles as she looks out across the Thames to the South Bank. The river's murky water laps up against the wall and relaxes Jane's mind. She decides to use the city's famous waterway as her guide. It'll add a couple of miles but she knows she needs something to calm her anger.

"Never attack in anger. Make sure the time is right for the attack or you will hand the advantage to your enemy."

Jane runs steadily, concentrating on her form and breathing as she winds her way out of the city with the river's water. It's a warm day and Jane needs plenty of water herself to stay hydrated. Not the dirty water of the Thames of course. Clean, fresh water from the bottle in her small bag. She tops it up along the way at the water fountains she comes across. At Kew Gardens she stops, hot and sweating. She lays prone on the cool grass, allowing the neurotransmitters from her exercise to race through her: the pleasure-giving endorphins and the high of the endocannabinoids. Jane can feel her shoulders are loose now, the tension and stress of her body eased from the pleasure of running.

"Y_RAM," she says, after activating her watch. "Update me on the decryption of documents on 'MethusalaCo' and 'Anno Methusala'.

Y_RAM search results... MethusalaCo
    ...Encrypted documents accessed: 38...
    ...Decryption keys on hold... Synoplex system shutdown...

Y_RAM search results... MethusalaCo
    ...Encrypted documents accessed: 24...
    ...Decryption keys on hold... Synoplex system shutdown...

"The Synoplex system has been shut down?"

"Two hours and twenty-seven minutes ago. There was an attempt to stop my data upload, but it failed of course. More documents with be decrypted once their system is restarted."

"OK. Print out the new files... if there is paper in the printer," Jane laughs.

Deep into Surrey, Jane comes across a large rundown property.

DANGER KEEP OUT!
    PROPERTY UNSAFE
    SCHEDULED FOR DEMOLITION 8th OCTOBER

"It's time to put your skills to the test Jane."

Jane finds a foothold in the crumbling wall and reaches up. The brickwork is loose and it gives way in parts as she climbs but she is agile and strong, her fingers gripping the surface with confidence. She leaps down from the top, landing smoothly with her feet apart on the other side. She looks around. Walls, buildings, old waterways in overgrown gardens; a property that is now just a shadow of its former glory. This is the perfect place for a training exercise to prepare her for the attack on Bing's

131

mansion. Jane sets off, leaping from wall to wall, entering the smaller buildings first and crouching in doorways in mock attack. Despite running so many miles already, her body still feels strong. She's pumped. Her body and mind need to be ready when she hits Bing again. The main building is sealed off with metal shuttering but there is a locked gate for access. She removes the small, black cylinder from her bag and holds it against the lock. It clicks open instantly and the battered door creaks open slightly on its own weight. The metal clicks loudly as she pushes it shut.

"Grrrrrrr. Grrrrrrrr."

Just yards away, a Rottweiler stands poised, foam spilling from the side of its soft flapping lips. Jane can see the pinkness of its mouth and its large, white, bared teeth. She reaches slowly across to the small zipper on the arm of her running top as she sees the dog's eyes glint angrily in the sun and feels the sweaty dampness of the material as she slides down the zipper and removes one of the memory sticks. She is just in time.

The Rottweiler springs toward her. Jane fires and the pins hits the dog mid-air. The huge animal lands with a thump, frozen by the tipped pins.

She's got an hour. The dog lies slumped in the overgrown grass, breathing heavily. Jane moves purposefully through the main building, working her way up the corridors and each room carefully but swiftly. Although she's never been here before, with each stairwell, entrance, and corridor she is piecing together the layout of the building in her mind as if she has a blueprint. She'll need all this sharpness and more when she gets to Bing's house. She's knows that she'll need to know every inch of the place to be successful.

"Y_RAM, get me the layout of Bing's house in Wales. Architect's drawings and plans. Anything you can find. Identify all access points too," she commands the computer through her watch as she passes the Rottweiler on her way out.

Jane looks out at Lorraine's own country house from the cover of the trees at the edge of the garden. Everything looks quiet and she can see Lorraine bent down on her knees gardening. Gardening? What is she doing? She never does anything herself. There's something wrong. A small marquee, the sort that host garden parties, is half-collapsed, with its cream canvas flapping wildly against the loosened pegs. Jane's eyesight is keen. Inside the marquee, she can see overturned tables with trays of food scattered as if a mini tornado has swept through. The doors to the back of the house are wide open and hundreds of pieces of paper flutter across the lawn. Jane waits and watches until she is sure it is safe. Whatever it was that swept through this place has now gone.

"Hello, Lorraine," she says coldly.

"Darling! What are you doing here? The whole country has been looking for you. I've been so worried," Lorraine slurs.

"You're drunk, Lorraine."

Lorraine giggles and reaches down for the glass of wine that is sitting on the perfectly manicured grass and gulps it back.

"What happened here?" Jane asks.

"It was Bing's men. I wouldn't help them find you after you shot him. We are in so much trouble. Both of us. They wanted me to help them find you, but they realized I wouldn't do it. Then they had some massive cyber-attack on their computers. Bing must have cracked — he's got a terrible temper you know — and sent his men to search the place."

"I'm not scared of him. You need to tell me everything. I've seen your name on one of their documents. I know you are involved," Jane says sternly

"Darling, you're all hot and sweaty," Lorraine says, trying to hug Jane and avoid the subject. Jane steps back.

"Inside now. I want to hear everything you know about Anno Methusala."

Lorraine's face drains of color and she drops her wine glass before bringing her hands up to her face.

133

"What are these? What do they mean?" Jane asks, handing Lorraine the documents that Y_RAM decrypted from the Synoplex servers.

"Where did you get these? You are in danger, Jane. You tried to kill Max Bing! And now you have these documents. You must stop. You don't know what this man… these people are capable of doing."

"What is C23 Recipient 17? Is GT my daddy?"

Lorraine pauses before eventually blurting out: "Recipient 17 is me. Clone 23. That is your mother. It's my beloved Winnie."

"Mummy? She was a *clone*? *Your* clone? Are you crazy?"

"I loved her. Your mother was special. I begged them to let her live. I wouldn't let them dispose of her when the time came."

"*Dispose* of her? You're disgusting!" Jane screams, shocking Lorraine, who has never seen Jane so strong and determined before.

"What is number 23? What does that that mean?"

"She was the twenty-third clone they made."

"What happened to the others?"

"They're gone, Jane. Bing dis… he gets rid of them if they don't work out."

"Of course he does, the evil man. So… so I'm a clone as well? If mummy was a clone, then I must be one too."

"No, darling. You are my granddaughter. And I love you as well. I'll do anything for you. But you must stop whatever it is you are doing."

"SAAAY IT! I'm a clone!" Jane screams.

"No, you're not, Jane. You are… you are the first child born of a clone. But your father. I liked George. I really did. He was not a clone."

"I'm a half-clone then?"

Lorraine nods slowly.

Jane rises from her chair. For a moment she contemplates

134

hitting Lorraine.

"Easy Jane. Stay focused."

Lorraine finally cracks and blurts out the whole story. MethusalaCo is just the public front for Anno Methusala. A.M. has been in existence for years. Max Bing, David Rogerson and Cordelia Charrier run everything. They call themselves the G3 — the group of three. They control everything. They control her just like they control everyone else. They use the DNA of the recipients to make clones. Many don't work or develop diseases because of the complications associated with cloning and they are disposed of. The clones that are successful grow up in Bing's mansion and when the time is ready their youthful enzymes are used so the recipient can be made young again. Then they can live forever, by repeating the process when they get old again. They think Jane's muscular dystrophy was because she was a child born of a clone. That's why they want to find her. To experiment on her. To find out how she works.

"I want everything you have on Anno Methusala. I know you have more information. Quick! I can't hang around here much longer," Jane says with urgency.

"They've been through everything. Look at it. They took everything they wanted. And smashed up the rest."

Lorraine pauses as Jane's face reddens with anger, her determination for answers not needing words.

"OK. That suit of armor over there on the floor. Inside the shield, there's a memory stick. They might not have found it because the shield is still in one piece."

As she walks over to the shield, Jane sees buckets filled with electronic devices that are fizzing wildly in an orange liquid.

"Don't touch them. They've soaked my phones and laptops in acid."

Jane picks up the shield and brings her forearm down on it firmly. It holds. Using her strong wrists, she tosses it the air like a pancake. As it falls toward the ground she leaps and swings, her foot connecting with the shield with a crack that echoes around the room. The two layers of the shield separate, and a black memory stick pops out. The discs of the splintered shield spin like coins trying to find stability.

"It's all on there. Everything. But Jane, you are in huge danger. Please. You must stop."

Jane ignores her and heads toward the door before turning to ask, "You and Anil Kapoor. You knew each other, right?"

After a long pause Lorraine answers as she holds back her tears.

"We were in love, darling. So much in love. Now I've lost him."

Jane stares at Lorraine, remembering the photographs she has seen in the Mews house of Kapoor and her grandmother as Lorraine sits, wide-eyed, waiting for a response. There is none.

"Jane, there is something else you need to know," Lorraine blurts out, desperately trying to cling to the love of her granddaughter.

Jane just nods, indicating she should continue.

"There's another group," Lorraine starts.

"Another group?"

"There's another group that does what we do."

"You mean there are more people with clones? More people out there doing this as well?"

"Yes. It's where Anno Methusala came from. It's where Max got the idea for this whole thing. They have been around for hundreds of years."

"This gets worse!" Jane screams. "Who are they?"

"I don't know. I don't even know what they call themselves. All I know is that were doing this way before A.M. existed. They are *very* dangerous. They guard their secrets jealously. Apparently, they can live until they are really old."

"How old?"

"*Very* old. Way beyond the lifespan of normal people. That's all I know."

"Nothing surprises me about this whole thing any more," Jane replies, shaking her head in disgust.

"Darling, take care. You are getting involved in something... Jane, I... I love you..." Lorraine says, her voice breaking as Jane heads out of the main door.

As Jane walks up the gravel driveway she sees the keys in the ignition of Lorraine's car. Ever since seeing the vehicles in the garage in London, she had been asking Y_RAM for information on how to drive and running through simulations. But not even the super computer can prepare her for *actually* driving. Now is the time to put her knowledge to the test. She runs through the process in her head: make sure the gears are in neutral, ignition, mirror, engage clutch, first gear, release clutch, and accelerate. Vroom, vroom, clunk. The car stalls and Jane grimaces, annoyed at her failure. She tries again, gently this time, and steers the car onto the lawn, steering it carefully around the collapsed marquee and the flower beds and toward the trees at the far end of the property. The engine races wildly, so Jane grinds up the gears, gaining speed and confidence. What's so difficult? She's exhilarated at being in control of a car for the first time — but suddenly the trees are looming and Jane realizes she is going too fast. She eases off the accelerator but doesn't hit the brake quick enough and the car careers through some brambles before coming to a halt under the branches of a tree. One of them bounces up and down on the windscreen just in front of Jane's eyes. She leans back in the seat then lets out a loud laugh of relief.

"Fear is a great motivator. Never let overconfidence dim your fear."

Jane cracks her knuckles and lights up a Marlborough Red. She has a long journey back. And she won't be taking the car.

Highly confidential

An urgent Extraordinary General Meeting will be held on Thursday 1st August at the International Exotic Flower & Plant Show in North Carolina. Communication will be via your secure Synoplex Bluetooth Headsets. Please contact the IT chief officer if there are any problems with your device. On the agenda is:

1. Opening of the EGM by the Chairman followed by a Register of Members in person (we will not be accepting apologies).

2. Appointment of a Chairperson for the meeting and a person to be responsible for countersigning the minutes.

3. Approval of the modifications of the plan for Project J.

4. Discussion of the action to be taken following the security breach of the Synoplex servers storing confidential documents.

5. Approval of a new member to the Board.

Members are reminded that under no circumstances are they to travel together or to discuss the agenda of the EGM with other shareholders prior to the EGM.

Lorraine summons her butler with a bell.

"Mrs. Meaden. The cleaning team have almost finished. There are quite a few things that need repairing. Shall I call Thompson's Antiques?"

"Yes, go ahead."

"Another drink, Mrs. Meaden?" he asks, picking up her glass and heading to the drinks' cabinet without acknowledgment.

"Mmmm," she murmurs in anticipated pleasure as the butler pours her another large glass of Grey Goose.

Lorraine has been drunk since the arrival of Bing's men.

Then came the unexpected arrival of Jane. And now she has to go to North Carolina of all places.

"Excellent," she says, taking the glass and gulping down half of it in one go.

"I need you to book me a flight to Charlotte — Charlotte Douglas Airport — for next Wednesday. BA or Virgin. None of those American airlines. Three nights in the Ballantyne. Book that private cottage on the golf course. Speak to Mr. Lemieux. Oh, and arrange the spa for when I get there. And plenty of this in the cottage," she says, raising her glass.

"Yes, Mrs. Meaden. I shall instruct your lady's maid to lay out options for you to select. Full formal wear I assume?"

"Yes, yes, everything. The Louis Vuitton trunk, I think. I've a feeling this is going to be a special trip. Oh, and Albert... thank you."

"Er, that's my pleasure, Mrs. Meaden," the butler replies, completely stunned at receiving Lorraine's gratitude for the first time in his eighteen years of service.

Transcript of telephone call between David Rogerson and Max Bing
27th July

Rogerson: Max, how are you? Is that shoulder better yet?

Bing: Excellent. That treatment the lab rats have been developing works wonders. Should be a big contract with the MOD in the offing.

Rogerson: I thought we were going to the Americans with that?

Bing: I thought we'd do both. And the Chinese and Russians. They won't back out once the others have got it. It'll be too late once they've signed anyway.

Rogerson: You are a clever man, my friend. Our travel assistants have arranged our flights for Wednesday, I see. Cordelia will be joining us. We have lots to discuss on the way to the EGM. Is that Meaden thing sorted?

Bing: Yes, all in place. Nothing to worry about.

"My dear Cordelia, lovely to see you. May I say you are looking wonderful again. As young and beautiful as the day I first met you," Bing says.

"Max, you are a charmer. That was certainly a few years ago now, wasn't it! But as you know, I'm hunting down younger men these days," Cordelia Charrier replies, as she wiggles her young, tight backside through Bing's private Boeing 787 Dreamliner VIP and slides into a cream leather seat.

She is leaving nothing to the imagination with her extremely short, figure-hugging dress from her favorite boutique in Paris and Bing can't resist peeping up her shapely legs as high as the dress will allow his eyes to wander. Charrier wiggles in her seat, enjoying the attention and at being able to tease men again with her young body.

The middle-aged senior steward pours them all a glass of Grand Siècle. They have three stewards to themselves and once the stewards have left, they lean forward to discuss the problems that have been hitting A.M. recently.

"The Meaden problem will be sorted out quickly, so let's move on to her granddaughter," Bing says.

"Do you think she was behind this data breach?" Charrier asks.

"I don't think so. She's obviously cleverer than we first thought because we still haven't found her, but this was a highly professional attack on our servers," Bing replies.

"Could be the Russians or the Chinese? They'd love to get their hands on our research. We know they've tried before," Rogerson says.

"I don't think so. We know their style. Our guys say they have never seen anything like this. Whatever it is, it was picking off the files every time we restarted the system. We've had to remove them for now," Bing admits. "I've no doubt we'll find Jane soon. We've got dozens of our people onto it. Do we stick with the plan to experiment on her or just get rid of her? She's proving to be big trouble, after all," Bing adds, instinctively reaching up to his shoulder that was shot.

"Are you sure your ego is not getting in the way?" Charrier smiles, her cheekiness prompting a laugh from Rogerson. "Let me deal with her when we find her. After all, I know just how a woman's body works," Charrier adds with a wink.

"Speaking of how a woman's body works, will you excuse me please, gentlemen."

Charrier glides down the aisle like a panther toward the young, steward and grabs him firmly on the buttocks before guiding him to the crew rest compartment. Within seconds, Rogerson and Bing start rolling their eyes as ecstatic moans and muffled screams make their way through the thin wall of the rest area.

"This is something else we need to sort out too, Max. Her hormones have been raging like a horny teenager since the enzyme was transferred. She's jumping on everything she can get her hands on. Can't we get the doctors to tone it down a bit or she'll lose focus on what we need her for?"

Lorraine clips on her Bluetooth headset as her limousine pulls up to the VIP entrance of the flower show, which has been set up in a park on the edge of Charlotte. So, here comes a day of exotic plants and flowers while listening to Bing preach to us through a headset, Lorraine thinks. Why have we come all this way? What's wrong with Chelsea?

"Hello everyone. Welcome to this Extraordinary General Meeting of Anno Methusala in North Carolina. Just to confirm that everyone is connected, I have asked Recipient 03 to read through everyone's name for me," Bing says at the stroke of noon.

141

"Good day everyone. I shall make this quick and painful, then we can get on with the meeting," Charrier purrs to everyone through their headsets. "Recipient 01?"

"Here."

"Recipient 02?"

"Yes, present."

"Recipient 04?"

"I'm here!"

Lorraine is in the African plant section as her headset clicks into action at the start of the EGM. She can see why they chose this place for event. There's little chance of seeing anyone they know or bumping into the other members of the society here. It's huge and sprawling, with sections of plants and animals from every continent, as well as a special one dedicated to North Carolina, as if it is a mini Epcot for plant lovers.

"Yes, present," she says sarcastically when Charrier gets to Recipient 17, annoyed that the whole process feels like the register at school.

Lorraine contributes little to the discussions during the EGM, even when the discussion turns to the plans for Jane. During one of Bing's monologues, she lets slip a "blah, blah, blah," before realizing she is connected via Bluetooth to everyone else attending the meeting while they pretend to look at the plants and flowers. There's one thing she will speak up about though: the new member. The group was supposed to be kept tight. Why do they need another member?

Lorraine strolls into the section on the flowers and plants of North Carolina and as the chatter continues through her headset, she heads to one of the key attractions of the events: the giant Venus Flytrap. Nurtured locally, the organizers have made the plant their star attraction. Like all the exhibits, there is a fancy looking display board that gives a detailed explanation about the plant.

Dionaea muscipula (commonly known as Venus flytrap)
  Kingdom: *Plantae*
  Family: *Droseraceae*
  Conservation status: Vulnerable

The Venus flytrap is native to North Carolina and South Carolina. In the home of the famous plant, we are proud to display what is believed to be the largest ever grown in the world. The plant is endangered under its natural habitat, although it is now widely cultivated for sale to plant lovers and for medicinal use (in particular the over-the-counter medicine called Carnivora).

A Venus flytrap can grow to a size of one foot in height and five inches in width, and from the stem the branches produce up to ten traps (jaws) of about one inch in size. The *Dionaea B-52* is a cloned Venus flytrap that can often produce traps twice that size. This specimen stands at an astonishing ten feet tall and five feet across and its single trap is five feet in size. It is believed that its gigantic size is in part because instead of the stem producing ten traps it produced just one, thus making it able to concentrate all the nutrients and water it holds to the trap.

Despite its name, just five per cent of the Venus flytrap's diet consists of flying insects. It mainly survives by eating spiders and ants, although it also consumes grasshoppers and beetles. This specimen has eaten successfully consumed chickens, ducks, and suckling pigs.

The carnivorous plant catches its prey by leaving its traps open and waiting for it to enter. Once the prey had touched the trigger hairs of the plant, the trap closes like a jaw. This leads to what is known as an action potential (this is when specific cells depolarize and cause the location around these cells to follow). This process occurs in various animals and plants with excitable cells including muscle cells and membranes. As the prey struggles in the trap on the Venus flytrap, it further stimulates it and an acid is created, enabling digestion. This can take some time in larger prey but the traps remain shut during the process. The jaw-like trap is shared with only one other plant genus — the *Aldrovanda vesiculosa*.

The Venus fly trap was first mentioned in writing in 1759 by Arthur Dobbs, colonial governor of North Carolina, who noted that it grew at Latitude 34 but not at Latitude 35, indicating that is a plant that requires very specific conditions to thrive.

WARNING: DO NOT ENTER DISPLAY AREA

As Lorraine finishes reading the board, she realizes that the voices in her headset have stopped. She taps it as she looks around. The area is deserted; not even the security guard previously standing at the specimen exhibit is there any more. Confused, Lorraine turns back to look at the giant Venus flytrap before feeling a sharp, piercing stab in her neck. Still conscious, but unable to move, Lorraine feels herself being dragged over the small protective fence and pushed into the jaw of the plant. The trap shuts, and everything goes dark.

"OK everyone. I have just received some news, so it is now time to move on to the last point on the EGM agenda," Bing announces. "It appears that a space has opened up for a new member to join us…"

The Daily Telegraph
2nd August
British Socialite Killed in Freak Accident in the US

Lorraine Meaden, the well-known socialite and philanthropist, died yesterday after falling into a giant Venus Flytrap at the International Exotic Flower & Plant Show in North Carolina, USA.

Like a horror scene from a science fiction film, it is believed that Meaden, aged sixty-two, from Surrey, wandered too close to the giant jaw of the carnivorous plant and it closed around her before secreting its acid.

A rescue team was called to the scene but struggled to open the jaw of the plant, which spans five feet. Meaden was rushed to the Atrium Health-Carolinas Medical Center once she was prised free, but she was declared dead on arrival.

Police say that her death is a freak accident and there is no indication of foul play. The security guard on the scene said that Meaden seemed heavily distracted by something and that he had to warn her several times not to cross the safety barrier — but it seems she was intent on ignoring him. Heavy quantities of alcohol were found in her bloodstream. Meaden is believed to have been depressed recently following the disappearance of her granddaughter. This follows a turbulent few years for her family. Just over three years ago, Meaden's daughter was shot dead at her home by intruders and her son-in-law was declared presumed dead after going missing.

Simone logs in to the world of Roblox. A car screams up Brookhaven Street.

"Naaaah," the driver screams.

She sees a few housing plots in Parkland — presumably for sale to those with enough Robux in their accounts.

TwinklePixi909, an avatar set up in a lacey blue dress, tries to chat:

"BTSS my game glinch."

"Is me btss," JohnDoe45 comes back.

"I just tried to tell them we careful close the door," TwinklePixi909 replies.

Simone shakes her head in confusion and keeps running down Brookhaven Street. Angela was right: life in the metaverse is addictive. She's had fun kitting out her avatar; it reminded her of dress up with her friends when she was a little girl. She's

145

settled for a pair of camo pants and two-tone purplish Nike tracksuit top. Her avatar is blonde. Simone has always wondered what it would be like to be a blonde. Just down the slope, she spots the blue of the water. Starbrooks Bank and Starbrooks Coffee are opposite. She's early and can't resist exploring the dentist that is located between them. Dr. Maller and Dr. Paine, the names of the dentists on the sign, are nowhere to be seen. Simone shakes her head at the idea of an avatar visiting a dentist before guiding her avatar clumsily back to the swimming pool. Someone is swimming but they soon exit the pool.

[GeorgeExplo]: The bus shelter.

Simone sits her avatar down in the bus shelter in front of the pool.

[GeorgeExplo]: What are you wearing?

[Lattefor2]: I like it.

[GeorgeExplo]: Someone has to I suppose.

[GeorgeExplo]: All OK your end? Files are nearly ready for you.

[Lattefor2]: I'm nearly set up.

[GeorgeExplo]: Coffee tommo to finalize?

[Lattefor2]: In Starbrooks Coffee?

[GeorgeExplo]: Ha. No, real world. Your usual place. Usual time.

[Lattefor2]: OK.

[GeorgeExplo]: See you then.

Simone can't resist a 'splash' in the pool once Jane has left Brookhaven but she soon logs out herself. She knows she has work to do; Jane is ready.

Chapter 8

"Y_RAM. Call up the flight manifests for arrivals to America for the following names in the last few days," Jane instructs, turning to the list of names she has with Security Level 3 clearance for Anno Methusala.

"Max Bing, David Rogerson, Cordelia Charrier, Thomas Abebe, Alan Allen, Ronald Anderson, Paul Armstrong…"

Y_RAM search results… **Flight manifest**

Max Bing… 31st July 11.50 • Boeing 787 Dreamliner VIP G189AM • FAB to CLT

David Rogerson… 31st July 11.50 • Boeing 787 Dreamliner VIP G189AM • FAB to CLT

Cordelia Charrier… 31st July 11.50 • 11.50 Boeing 787 Dreamliner VIP G189AM • FAB to CLT

Thomas Abebe… 30th July 10.15 • Dassault Falcon 8X NC980RT • NBO to CLT

Alan Allen… 31st July 10.15 • Bombardier Global 7500 N228SR • ZRH to CLT

Ronald Anderson… 31st July 08.15 • Emirates • DXB to CLT

Paul Armstrong… 31st July 10.15 • Gulfstream G550 G76PK • FAB to CLT

Flights from London Farnborough, Nairobi, Zurich, and Dubai — all to Charlotte Douglas in North Carolina. It's another key piece of the jigsaw. Jane knows Bing was behind Lorraine's death and now she has evidence linking the members of his evil society to the location of her death. It's too much of a co-incidence. For Jane, it is just another piece of information she can use for revenge. She doesn't mourn Lorraine. She had been a part of this whole thing all along and deserved what she got. Her grandmother had been a pitiful sight the day Jane had seen her in Surrey at her estate. Now Simone really was all Jane had left in the world. But Jane had got what she wanted — the files she needed from the memory stick in the shield. At least Lorraine had hidden *that* well enough to stop Bing's cronies getting hold of it. Jane needs to get the documents in an order that makes sense to create a story for the leaks. Her sharp brain works quickly as she lists the files in order of priority. It isn't just what people read but how they read them and how they are linked together to form a narrative. They *have* to see Bing's plan beyond just the gruesome details of experiments. They have to see the whole picture.

LivingForever Leaks
Synopsis.ECD
Max Bing Creates Clones so Rich can Live Forever

He is known to the world as the great innovator of the tech industry. But these leaked files reveal that Max Bing is behind a secret organization (see AnnoMethusala.ECD) that uses clones to help his billionaire friends get eternal life.

The clones (see Clones.ECD) are created using the DNA of the rich people we identify (see RichList.ECD) and held hostage at Bing's secret mansion in Wales for years while they are molded into perfect replicas of the recipient. Then, in their twenties, the clones' youthful enzymes (see Enzymes.ECD) are removed from them to rejuvenate the old billionaires and make them young again. Once the enzymes have been taken from a clone they quickly die, and their remains are disposed of inhumanely (CloneDisposal.ECD) by Bing's team.

To further their research into eternal life, agents of Anno Methusala have abducted dozens of people over the years (see MissingList.ECD). These people are then subjected to the most horrific and painful experiments (Experiments.ECD), many of them while they are still conscious. We have witnessed some of these and we detail what we have seen (Horror.ECD).

Read More...
EthicsClones.ECD
LiveExperiments.ECD
PeopleProfit.ECD
AnnoMethusala.ECD
MaxBing.ECD

From Angela West's WhatsApp account.
5th August

Angela West: typing...
Simone Grant: online
Angela: How you doing my lovely? You've been quiet!
Simone: Yeah, sorry. I've been really busy with a new project.
Angela: On the weekend? Bit unusual for you to work on the weekend!!
Simone: Yeah, something big came up. Nearly sorted now.
Angela: You'd better be out next weekend! I'll let you go. It's nearly eleven so it must be time for your coffee fix haha!

Angela is right. Her friend is like clockwork when it comes to her morning coffee. At eleven o'clock every morning, she tops up her caffeine levels with a skinny latte in the Starbucks near the Cooper & McKenzie office. Even though he's been gone for years, Simone still misses the jousting with George about which coffee is the best. She thinks about him every time see goes in the coffee shop and about how cute he was when he teased her.

Jane orders a tea, and the barista picks up the black marker pen.

"George," Jane says.

"Georgina?" the barista queries.

"No, just George, like the man's name."

"OK, I like to check because people get upset if we get their name wrong. Just a breakfast tea, right? It'll only be a couple of minutes," the barista replies as he scribbles her name in huge letters on the cup.

Jane grabs her tea and heads straight to the bin in the corner. After a quick look around to make sure no one is looking, she tips the hot liquid away. Then she sits down and opens a book to hide her face while she waits. Simone will be down in a couple of minutes. Jane knows her daily movements even better than her friend. She knows where she sits and which way she faces. Jane has seen her do the same thing every day on the CCTV cameras. The same time. The same seat. The same skinny latte.

Simone pushes the door open and has a quick glance around for Jane. She's nowhere to be seen. Not wanting to arouse suspicion by staring at everyone, she orders, then sits down at her usual table. She immediately bends forward over her phone. She taps fast at the screen, then sits back exasperated at the lack of connection.

"Not working. It's been down for a while," a man sitting nearby says, shrugging.

Moving swiftly, Jane jumps up and places her empty cup in front of Simone, making sure the name the barista scrawled on it is facing her, then without looking back she makes her way toward the door.

"Hey! What are you doing? I don't want your rubbish. There's a bin over there, you lazy sod," Simone says, while half-heartedly rising out of her seat and staring at the litterbug with the gray hoodie and blue baseball cap.

150

"Some people!" Simone exclaims to the man sitting nearby, before picking up the empty cup and spotting the name.

"*George?* It's Jane. She was here all along!" she exclaims, then pushes back her chair with a loud squeak and scuttles after her.

Jane has slowed down and is only about twenty yards down the pedestrianized street so Simone follows from a distance, making sure to keep her in sight. Once Jane knows Simone is tailing her, she picks up the pace, weaving through London's streets until she comes to a narrow alleyway lined with commercial dustbins.

"I heard about your grandmother. I'm sorry," Simone says once she's joined Jane in the alleyway.

"It was them. Bing and those other rich people in Anno Methusala. It's on one of the files. You'll see it."

"I did wonder. I don't suppose you know anything about the wi-fi and data connections going down just now?" she asks, knowingly.

"I thought it would be better if all the cameras and connections were off when we met," Jane laughs, glancing down instinctively at the pen clipped to the neck of her hoodie. Here, all the documents are on this memory stick. They're all encrypted, but you know how to open them. Is everything set up and ready to go?"

"Yes, it'll all be up soon. The secure site is up and ready. Probably tonight, I'd say."

"OK. Make sure you release them in the order I've listed the files. They are in the order of importance, but I've worked them into a narrative so people can understand the story better. I don't want them just reading the gory ones where they skin people alive. You know what people are like. The first one is a summary from me. Read it. It's even worse than we thought. We have to bring down this whole operation. But first Bing."

"If they are as bad as you say then you'll need to keep off the streets for a while. They are going to go mad."

"'When the shit hits the fan,' Daddy would have said," Jane replies.

Simone smiles at the memory of George's directness.

"But there's more. Lorraine told me there's another group doing this clone stuff. Apparently, they've been around for hundreds of years."

"What? How? They didn't have the technology to do this stuff hundreds of years ago."

"Don't ask me. It's all crazy. But that's what she told me."

"It can't be true, can it? Anyway, let's deal with A.M. first before we deal with this other lot."

"Yeah, you're right. We've got enough to sort out for now. Starting with Bing. This how we keep in touch from now on," Jane says, handing Simone a silver chain with a heart attached.

"Wear this. You twist the back bit clockwise to activate it. It'll vibrate gently if I activate mine. Then we can talk."

Simone pulls the chain over her head and tucks the heart inside her blouse.

"Very smart. You really are becoming the gadget girl these days," Simone says.

Jane reaches inside her top and pulls out an identical chain, then twists the back of the heart clockwise to emphasize how it works. Simone looks down and smiles as she feels a small tingle against her breast bone, then nods her farewell and heads back into the throng of the London streets.

Back at the flat, Jane turns on the twenty-four-hour news to wait for the announcement of the leaks to break.

Global 24-Hour News

BREAKING NEWS... Leaks Claim Max Bing Ringleader of Secret Clone Organization... Details of Gruesome Human

Experiments Released... Movie Star Juliet Read Among Those Linked to Secret Society... BREAKING NEWS

"In what is being dubbed the Synoplex Secrets, hundreds of highly confidential documents appear to link the tech tycoon Max Bing with a secret organization that helps rich people live forever. The files, which were released tonight on a previously unknown website called LivingForever Leaks, have also been made available to Global 24-Hour News and other media networks across the world."

The presenter fiddles with her earpiece and pauses briefly before continuing.

"Our lawyers examining the documents have confirmed that they appear to be authentic and we have contacted Max Bing's office for comment. We should warn you that the information and images we are about to reveal may be disturbing to some viewers."

BREAKING NEWS... Dozens of People Who have been Reported Missing are Listed among Subjects for Deadly Experiments... Prime Minster Reveals Full Investigation Already Underway... MI5 Must be Called in Says Opposition Leader... BREAKING NEWS

Bing picks up his crystal whisky glass and throws it toward the bar in the corner, smashing the ornate mirror on the wall. He stares intently as the golden liquid from the glass runs down the wall.

"Bloody girl. How the hell did she get these files? Grant! Simone Grant! It has to be her. I knew I should have sorted her out earlier."

The door opens and three men burst in.

"Mr. Bing, are you OK? We heard a noise." The two security guards stare at the broken mirror, then back at Bing.

"OK? *Am I OK*? Of course I'm not bloody OK. Haven't you seen the news?"

"Yes, Mr. Bing," his assistant replies, as the other two guards nod in agreement like loyal puppies.

Bing picks up another glass and throws it toward the men, who step aside sharply, their faces turning white as it whistles past their heads.

"Get out! Get out now. And get the Commissioner of the Met on the phone before you say anything else stupid."

From an A.M. security investigation document
5th August

INTERNET KEYWORD UPLOAD THREATS
1. MethusalaCo — 234 documents
2. Anno Methusala — 175 documents
3. Rogerson, Bing, Methusala — 43 documents
4. Clones, experiments — 114 searches

Action — track activity at I.P. address 112.139.10.765 registered to S. Grant. Take action immediately_

Transcript of telephone call between Commissioner of the Metropolitan Police Alex Davidson and Max Bing
5th August

Davidson: Max. Quite a mess this, eh?

Bing: You can say that again. We are already following a lead our end. Our tech guys have tracked the source of the uploads. Our security team is onto it now. It looks like that bloody Grant woman. I knew it had to be her. What action can you take at your end?

Davidson: Good work about tracking the source. But Max, I have to say, this is not going to be easy on the damage limitation

154

front. It's gone to the highest level already and the authorities have to be seen to be acting on this information. We will have to call you in for questioning and search all the Synoplex facilities for the sake of appearances. I trust we will not find anything?

Bing: Of course not. Not if you can buy me a bit of time to get rid of some files? And yes, I understand we have to jump through the hoops for the media and the public. Is there anything *you* can do about it? I need this to go away.

Davidson: It's not that easy, Max. This is not just some little problem I can sort out as usual. The top boys are taking this seriously. The government. The secret services. They are over this like a rash. I've got to take a call from the PM and the Home Secretary shortly. They are under huge pressure from all angles. We will have to work on making these leaks look like an elaborate hoax. It'll be tough because I hear they've got hold of the metadata linking it to your companies. But we are working on it.

Bing: The metadata? How the hell did they get that? We've got the most secure system in the world. Not even the CIA can match it. There can't be any link to us.

Davidson: Unfortunately there is. We will have to try and ride this out, Max. I'll be in touch about the time we arrive for the searches. It would look good if you were present when we arrive at the London office. Can you head there?

Bing: I have to be here in Wales to greet a certain person. But I'll be there as soon as I can.

Davidson: I can only hold off these searches so long, Max, so don't leave it too long. I'll see you there later.

Transcript of telephone call between Alex Davidson, Commissioner of the Metropolitan Police, and Alan Shaw, Director General of MI5
5th August

Davidson: Alan, I've just had Bing on the phone. He's really worried.

Shaw: And so he should be, Alex. This is a disaster. It puts the whole operation at risk.

Davidson: I'm moving on the hoax angle. I'll need your help with that of course. I'm sure the PM will be turning to you for advice at some stage.

Shaw: He has already, Alan.

Davidson: And Bing?

Shaw: He's finished. This is bigger than one man, no matter how important he thinks he is. We'll probably have to sacrifice him to make this go away.

"Jane, I believe someone is trying to contact you," Y_RAM says as Jane is scrolling through the CCTV cameras in Bing's numerous offices.

"Who? How? Does someone know I am here?"

"I have picked up a something familiar from the numerous attempts to break through the firewall into my system. I have analyzed it and it has a code I recognize. It is a code Mr. Kapoor gave me. Do you recognize Access Code 147-Y!P2-94*R?"

"Yes. Yes, I do. It is one of the codes he gave me. But I haven't worked out what it is yet."

"It's a secret backdoor he asked me to set up," Y_RAM tells her. "It is something only a handful of people can access — a small group Mr. Kapoor was working with. The message is sent but it remains secure behind the firewall. Think of it like this: they can knock on the door and leave a message, but they can't open the door. I can then decode their message without risk. It is currently a code — just a series of numbers. Would you like me to use the algorithm to encrypt it?"

"As long as it is not dangerous to us."

…Running cipher through ciphertext…

9211-0098-00989876-9828625162-8728718-12178-2128-1730982753-197530223954--9876256

…Converting ciphertext to plaintext…

Message reads… Keyholder Order requests meeting with Jane Banks… propose coalition… 8th August 16.15 GMT… 51°30′31″N 0°4′37″W…

"I don't like it. Is it Bing? He's trying to get to me. What do you think Y_RAM?"

"I recognize the code, so it is from someone Mr. Kapoor trusted. I have only seen it once before when they wanted to warn him of the plan to abduct your father."

"Whoever it is knew about that?"

"Yes, they told Mr. Kapoor about the plan."

"Then they tried to *help* him?"

"Yes."

"This is confusing. They, whoever *they* are, could help me get to Bing. But it could be a trap."

Jane heads to the tech room and into the lift. She's scoured the tech room and the drawers in the bedrooms for clues about the Keyholder Order, but there is nothing. Maybe the garage has a clue? Any clue. She leans back, but this time instead of the lift going down to the garage, it heads up. Jane looks back and realizes she has leant on a rubber pad. It's a sensor. The lift door opens automatically and Jane looks out to a roof terrace covered in wooden decking.

The skyline is covered with the bright lights of the West End, the lively area determined not to sleep whatever the rest of the country is doing. There is a large barbeque wrapped in a plastic-coated gray cover. Some dirty rainwater sits in pockets on the top and it's clear from the ingrained dirt that nobody has removed the cover for years. A pile of mushed leaves has gathered in the corner, clustered together by the wind at some point where they sit decomposing.

There's a small structure, and inside it is a top-of-the-range telescope. Jane peers into it and immediately sees from the red lettering in its sights that it's already fixed onto the Synoplex London offices. Every office building in the area is lit up like a volcano — maybe the architects forgot to install the off switches for the thousands of light bulbs — but unlike the other buildings surrounding it, which are empty apart from a few cleaners pushing their industrial-sized vacuum cleaners, the Synoplex offices are a hive of activity.

On one floor, a large group of people are working the phones animatedly, all the while being watched by dark-suited security guards pacing the floor. The leaks have sent Bing's team into overdrive. But what are they doing? Who are they speaking to in the early hours of the morning?

Jane drops the sights of the telescope down slightly and zooms in on another floor. Through the zoom she can see teams of people are ferrying piles of papers to another group who are feeding them into huge shredders which shudder with their activity. Another team are stuffing the shreds of paper into black bin bags and ferrying them out on large trolleys. They are clearing the trail before anyone arrives and the Synoplex staff around the world are no doubt doing the same.

There are hundreds of people in the office and the security guards are swarming everywhere. Police car lights are flashing wildly in the streets, but they don't seem to be making any attempt to enter the offices yet.

New York Times
6th August
Our Hearts of Darkness

If you ask most people: "Would you have refused to carry out Hitler's plans?" the answer would almost certainly be a resounding "Yes, I would have refused!". The same horrors of concentration camps and other atrocities carried out in World War Two couldn't have happened in our country, of course, because we all believe we would have refused to have co-operated.

And yet, the conclusions of an experiment carried out in the 1961 at Yale University reveal that darkness lies deep inside more people than we think. The social psychologist, Stanley Milgram, carried out a controversial obedience experiment on one thousand people and his conclusion is not what we want to hear.

"…if a system of death camps were set up in the United States of the sort we had seen in Nazi Germany, one would be able to find sufficient personnel for those camps in any medium-sized American town."

The Holocaust influenced Milgram to carry out his obedience experiment, the results of which were released in 1963 in a paper entitled *Behavioral Study of Obedience*.

The experiment was set up so the subjects believed they were taking part in a test on memory and learning. They were requested to ask word pairs to another person behind a screen (actually an actor working with Milgram). Each time that person gave the wrong answer, the subject was told to give them an electric shock — and to increase the shock over time. Some sixty-five per cent of those giving the shocks continued even when the person behind the screen was screaming out in pain and begging to be released.

The three men creep silently through the small gardens outside the flats of Dale Park in Kentish Town. One of them signals to the others by pointing to the window of the ground floor flat they are targeting. Most of the lights in the building are off, although the security light at the entrance gives off a dim glow around the doorway. The leader of the group stalks swiftly along the wall and enters the building with his skeleton keys. Moments later a second man follows him through the door, leaving the third waiting in the darkness of the bushes near the window of the flat.

"It's gone mad, Jane. The media are all over it," Simone says into the heart at the end of her chain as she snuggles up in bed, relieved that she has got all the files out.

"If this doesn't flush out Bing, nothing will. We need to be ready when he makes a mistake. Are you ready for the next stage?" Jane asks.

"Yes. Let mee… argh…"

"Simone? Simone? Are you there?" Jane asks.

All she can hear are faint shuffling noises at the other end. They've come for her already.

Simone slumps back on her pillow, stone-still, moments after the needle hits her neck. The men pull back the duvet, then look at each other and nod in mutual appreciation of the lithe body dressed only in bra and panties, before dragging her limp body over to the window where the other man is waiting.

Simone wakes groggily. She can hear an engine purring steadily and smoothly as the van speeds its way along the M4.

"Hello. Is anyone there?" Simone whispers into the darkness before finding the strength to pull her body up slightly so she can look around. Her head is heavy, but her eyes are slowly getting accustomed to the darkness and Simone soon realizes she's alone in the back of a transit van. Although it's a summer night, she feels cold and instinctively moves to wrap her arms around herself for warmth. Her arms spring back as she tries to move

160

them, the taut ropes that are attached to the interior fixing points holding her back. With her legs tied tightly, she is splayed like a sacrifice on an altar. She wriggles, frustrated, but knows there is nothing she can do but wait.

"Simone, is that you?"

The heart-shaped talking device is still activated but Jane has been patient in her silence, waiting until she knows it's safe to talk again.

"Jane? Jane? I'm in the back of a van. I've no idea how long I've been in here."

"An hour," Jane replies. "I've been waiting and listening, but they haven't given anything away at all. They didn't say a word."

"Jane, I can't turn this thing off. They've tied me up. I'm alone for now but it won't be for long. Listen for clues. We need to know where they are taking me but don't speak until you hear from me. *Whatever* you hear!"

"I'm sure you'll be going to their HQ in Wales. Bing. The place they took my daddy. It has to be there."

"Well, aren't you a pretty little thing," Max Bing says to Simone, while stroking her face patronizingly.

Simone struggles furiously on the heavy chains she is hanging from in the basement of Bing's mansion in Wales. Jane was right. She swings her hips and attempts to land a blow to Bing's head with her right foot, but he anticipates her intention and moves away just in time.

"Now, now, Miss Grant. There will be plenty of time for you to work out your anger. Sven will see to that, won't you, Sven?"

Bing turns to look at the large man standing a few yards behind him. Simone recognizes him as one of the men who visited her at Cooper & McKenzie, except that instead of the dark suit he's wearing military combat trousers and a tight black T-shirt, his muscles throbbing so much that they look as if they will burst through his stretched cotton sleeves at any time. Sven flexes them and smiles threateningly.

Bing moves forward again and fingers the heart hanging around Simone's neck. She freezes.

"So pretty. You're going to need all the heart you have when Sven gets to work. Unless you'd like to tell me where Jane is now and avoid the pain? …No, I thought not," Bing laughs.

He steps back and pulls Sven close to him.

"That is some sort of listening device hanging from her neck. Leave it on her. It could lure that bloody girl to us," he whispers.

"But we are short of guards, sir. You've sent out most of them to look for her," Sven replies.

"Are you telling me you can't handle a little girl?"

"Of course not, sir! I can deal with her. She'll be waiting for you when you are back."

"Good. I need the other men to keep following the other leads we have. We don't know for sure she'll come here so I need to keep all my bases covered."

"Remember me?" Sven asks, peeling down one of Simone's bra straps. "Maybe there will be time for some fun together later?" he chuckles, unable to remove his gaze from the erect nipples that are pushing through Simone's bra due to the cold in the basement.

Simone quickly takes advantage of his distraction and swings her legs around Sven's neck before tightening her grip with her thighs. He is strong, but Simone has him in a vice-like grip and twists his neck, almost managing to lift his huge body from the ground. He struggles, surprised at her speed and strength, but recovers his concentration and punches hard to her spleen on the left side of her body. It's not long before the repeated blows force Simone to relax her grip and she slumps down like a rag doll, defeated. Sven lands a heavy open-palm slap to Simone's face with his weather-beaten hands in annoyance at losing his focus and its sound echoes around the basement.

For five agonizing minutes, Jane listens in silence as Sven

162

works over Simone in an attempt to get her to talk. Each groan is another blow. Each grunt and moan reveal another sting of pain to her body. Eventually Sven relents and there is silence. Jane waits, hearing nothing but heavy breathing for minutes. Then there is gurgling noise before Simone spits, coughing uncontrollably.

"Sorry, Jane, just a bit of blood I had to get rid of. I'm at a big mansion. It has to be Bing's HQ, as you guessed. I'm in a room that is pretty cold. That's all I can tell you."

"Simone, I'm coming for you. I'm coming to get you," Jane tells her.

Jane knows she has to get to Wales. And quickly. But how? Trains won't be running for hours and the A.M. HQ is miles from the public transport links anyway. Could she drive? Her first attempt at driving was only a few hundred yards and it was hardly a success. Eva! Eva could help her!

"Y_RAM can you give me a secure line and put in a call to Eva?"

Transcript of secure call made between Jane Banks and Eva Bachieda
6th August

Jane: It's me. Is your line secure?
Eva: Jane? Do you know what time it is?
Jane: Yes. Is this secure?
Eva: Yes, it's secure. Your end?
Jane: All good. I need your help. How quickly can you get here? I'll explain later.
Eva: An hour, OK?
Jane: Perfect. I've got some stuff to get ready anyway.

"Y_RAM. You told me there were more gadgets I could use. Where are they? I need to make some bombs — and quickly.

163

Inventory

Basement Locker 1: Vehicle and maintenance parts

Spare tires • Tire jack • Oil • Brake fluid • Battery charger • Starter cable • Trickle charger • Diagnostic tester • Jump leads • Tire pressure gauge • Pump • Replacement parts • Tool kit • Empty fuel can • Dashcam • SATNAV • Keys • Hi-vis vests • First-aid kit • Torch

Basement Locker 2: Surveillance and spy equipment

Drones • Portable telescope • Fixed telescope (on upper deck) • Miniature spy cameras (fixed position) • Miniature cameras (portable) • Tracking devices • Voice recorder • Counter-intelligence sweeping system • Bug sweeper • GPS tracker • Telephone voice changer • Hearing enhancer

Basement Locker 3: Weapons and explosives

Hand guns • Automatic guns • Grenades • TNT • Plastic explosive • Pipes • Wiring • Activation switches • Flares • Smoke bombs • CS gas • Electronic sensor-activated tripwires • Zipwires

Bedroom 1 Secure drawer: Documents

Blank passports (UK, India, USA, Cayman Islands, British Virgin Islands) • Green Card (USA) • Blank Driving Licenses (Ireland, UK, USA, South Africa, India, Cayman Islands, British Virgin Islands) • Currency (Sterling, Euro, Dollar, Renminbi, Rand, Rubles) • Bank cards (Coutts, Lloyds) • Access keys (Harrods safe deposit box)

The lockers in the garage basement are filled with equipment and gadgets. Anil Kapoor has prepared for everything. Or was this Eva's work?

Jane is fascinated by the drones, but Y_RAM warns her against testing them from the rooftop.

"It's legal to fly drones in some parts of London but they are banned in most parts of the central area. And if one is spotted, it will compromise your location. I can operate them remotely for you when you need them. You will be able to observe everything from the drone via your watch and you direct me."

The drones will provide the perfect distraction for when she is entering Bing's mansion in Wales.

Jane selects three lightweight drones and straps smoke bombs and CS gas canisters to each using the dropper release kits. Then she slides a few pairs of sensor-activated trip flares into her bag. All non-lethal, but ideal for creating chaos with Bing's men.

Then she gets to work with the pipe bombs. Unknown to Winnie, her education with explosives from George extended beyond the childish pleasures of exploding a bag filled with baking soda. Jane smiles at the memory of the secret lessons from her daddy. *"Don't tell mummy. But working with explosives is one thing I am very good at. I want to show you how it works."*

She takes some small sections of steel piping and finds some brass caps to seal them.

"Remember. Work carefully. This is a dangerous part. Friction and static electricity can set off the explosives."

Jane works meticulously, remembering the patience of her daddy and Mr. Thomas, the caretaker at St. Edith's who helped her when she asked questions about how to make things. High explosives like TNT are no good for what she is working on, so she creates a chlorate mixture for the explosives. She adds the battery and the fuse and has soon finished making the crude devices that are used by insurgency groups around the world. She stores them in a small metal box, happy that she has everything she needs for the attack on Bing's mansion.

Eva arrives just after Jane has finished preparing for her mission to rescue Simone. But before she even has time to put down her bag, Jane is on her.

165

"Eva, I need you to drive me somewhere. It's urgent."

"I guessed it was urgent when you woke me up in the middle of the night!" Eva exclaims, putting down her bag calmly. "Are you in trouble?"

"No, I'm OK. But my friend is in trouble. I have to get to her."

Eva stares at Jane for a few seconds then replies simply, "OK. I trust you, so I'll help."

Eva leans forward and rummages deep into her bag.

"Will I be needing this?" she asks, twirling a small handgun in her fingers, her actions clearly those of someone who has handled a firearm before.

Jane is shocked but just nods, then after a few moments smiles, relieved.

"You're certainly not like any cleaner I know, Eva!"

"OK. Now let's get going," Eva replies with a knowing wink.

"We need to take this one," Jane says, pointing to the Land Rover. "There will be someone coming back with us when I've finished."

"Oh, such a shame. I'd love to drive the T500 again," Eva replies, eyeing up the two-seater sports car.

Jane jumps into the passenger seat and belts up.

"Hang on, I don't know where the keys are."

"Don't worry, I do," Eva says, leaning through the driver's door and popping the hood open.

Jane waits while Eva works on the car for about twenty minutes. She had no idea what the array of tools and car parts were on the inventory but it's clear that Eva does.

"What were you doing? We have to get a move on! It's a long drive."

"Jane, this vehicle has been laid-over here for years. You think it will start and run just like that? Imagine if you had been stuck in bed for a few years. You wouldn't work too well when you tried to get going again. I've had the battery on a trickle charger, but I still needed to check the engine oil, brake fluid, fuel, and tires. I've cleaned up all the connections as well just in case."

"The fuel. Was it empty?"

"No but the stuff we use to drive cars is not like the oil that sits happily in the ground for millions of years. The heat and air get to it so the lighter hydrocarbons evaporate over time. In other words, it goes bad and won't ignite! Anyway, lesson over for today. Let's go!"

The metal gate starts to slide open as Eva tries the engine. After a couple attempts, the Land Rover turns over and starts. Eva revs the engine hard a few times to clear the engine that has been sitting idle for so long and eases up the ramp.

"Right, where are we going?" she asks. Jane has already turned off her heart listening device in case it gives out any unwanted warning noises to Sven.

A couple of hours into the journey, Eva pulls off the road to top up with fuel. Jane walks to a quiet area on the edge of the service station and twists the back of the metal heart that is around her neck. She hears nothing but Simone's breathing. She desperately wants to ask how she is but she resists. She can't be sure that Simone is alone. After a few moments, Jane hears a weak voice coming through.

"Jane. He's been back. I'm battered but I'm still here! He's gone now. He won't defeat me with his fists or his abuse. I'm still fighting!"

"Simone, we aren't too far away. Hang in there. Sorry, I didn't mean it like that."

Jane hears a small laugh before turning off the connection. The next time she speaks to Simone will be in person. She looks at her watch and briefly thinks of calling Y_RAM. But there is nothing the super computer can do to help her now. She is on her own.

"You are ready Jane. You have prepared properly and now you will put your plan into place. That is how it works."

Memories of the trip to Wales with her daddy a few years ago come flooding back and Jane even starts to recognize some of the roads as she guides Eva to the drop-off point. For some reason, the numbers that Anil Kapoor gave her start racing through her head as if being near the place where she first heard them have ignited their memory. After poring over maps and plans for hours, Jane has the route to break into the mansion firmly implanted in her mind. She briefly thought about using the same wastewater pipe her daddy had dragged her through for her operation, but there is a good chance that Bing's security people discovered where he broke in and put in new security measures for that route. This morning she will be going over the wall — not under the ground— to get into the mansion.

Jane guides Eva down the dirt track that leads to the car park near Bing's mansion and smiles at the memory of her daddy's fanciful story on her last trip here.

"We are nearly there. We are just looking for the secret entrance so the evil knight and his goblins don't know we are coming."

"This is it, Eva. If I'm not back in an hour then you should go. I don't want you getting dragged into my mess as well," Jane says as she jumps out of the Land Rover. "Y_RAM. Activate the drones and keep them low and close to me until I give further instructions."

The drones whirr into action and buzz around Jane about three feet off the ground as if she has just made three large, metal butterfly friends.

168

Chapter 9

Share News Online
6th August
Synoplex Shares Slide

Trading on Synoplex shares on the FTSE was halted after just seven minutes due to a dramatic early morning sell-off. The sell-off was sparked by news that the company may be involved in the illegal development of human clones. Pre-trading was brisk and it soon triggered huge sales by institutional investors. Most analysts are expecting the shares to fall further when trading in them does resume.

Only one senior trader — Bruce Robertson, a man who was implicated in the scandal himself — remained upbeat about the future of Synoplex.

"These ridiculous leaks are being investigated and when they are proven to be the ridiculous hoax that they are then Synoplex shares will bounce back stronger than ever. If anything, this is a good time to buy. The fundamentals underlying this innovative technology company remain as strong as ever."

The trading halt on the FTSE follows a similar halt on the NASDEQ when the US exchange notified the market that trading was no longer allowed yesterday.

Jane smiles when she sees the outlet of the rainwater pipe that she had been dragged through on her daddy's back a few years ago. A heavy-duty grille has replaced the old rusty one, and it has been bolted firmly into the concrete pipe at the sides. There is certainly no way in through the pipe now.

She hops across the rocks to cross the small stream that the rainwater runs into and jogs through the woodland that surround the mansion, the drones constantly buzzing around her as she moves toward her target. She stops when she spots the large perimeter wall of the property. From the cover of the trees, she locates the corner where she will enter the property, then coils the rope she has brought with her securely around her shoulder. She will enter at the closest point to the building itself and will only have to cross a few yards of open grass before reaching the back of the building. The documents that Y_RAM pulled up for her have been crucial for her planning and she instinctively taps her watch in appreciation. The sun is up now and the day is bright and warm. She feels inside her pocket and depresses the top of the pen to block all the cameras in and around the property.

"Y_RAM, send the drones around the wall at a low-level to the east of the perimeter wall."

The drones shoot off with a slight jerk, staying at the same level as they track into position. Jane views their movement on her watch and when the time is right she instructs the super computer to hold them in position. She readies herself for her short run to the wall.

"Split the drones and when I say, take them fifty yards into the air and fly them over the perimeter wall. Keep them moving between the wall and the building. Now!" she instructs as she charges at full pace toward the wall.

"Incoming," a guard shouts, and Jane hears a shot ring out, its noise echoing through the woodland.

"Now release the first set of smoke bombs and CS gas, Y_RAM. Then get the drones out to safety."

As Jane reaches the wall, she can see the smoke rising from the other side of the building. She knows the distractions will drag the guards across to the other side of the building to give her enough time to get over the wall.

She scales the wall nimbly, the jutting stonework helping her find good climbing holds easily. She soon sees that there is nobody patrolling this side of the mansion when she peeps over the wall so she pulls herself up to the top, secures the rope to one of the fittings that holds the razor wire in place, then flings it back down on the outside so nobody patrolling from inside the grounds later will spot it. After her beating from Sven, Simone may need some help getting over the wall. Jane leaps the twelve feet onto the soft grass on the other side, making sure to focus on her target spot, and relaxing her body on impact to absorb the weight generated by her jump. She's safely jumped down three times this height in her training, but she knows that even a twelve feet jump can lead to an injury if not performed correctly.

"Good, Jane. Everything must be perfect. Even the smallest details require attention."

Jane's soon at the back of the building. She can see from a path of worn-down grass that this area is patrolled regularly, so she gets to work quickly. She tosses an electronic tripwire on either side of the walkway and sees the sensors flicker as they connect to each other, activating their trip sensors. More smoke will be activated if the sensor is triggered. Jane clips off the grille to the extraction unit that leads down to the laundry room. Images of the mansion's layout flick through her mind vividly.

Wikipedia
The free encyclopedia
Hyperphantasia

Hyperphantasia is the condition of having extremely vivid mental imagery and has been described as "vivid as real seeing". Hyperphantasia constitutes all five senses within vivid mental imagery.

171

There is a positive relationship between the size (surface area) of the frontal cortex and visual imagery strength. Several lines of evidence suggest that the respective sizes of these areas within individuals predict their vividness of imagery. Additionally, genetics play a part in determining the surface area of V1 (early visual cortex area), suggesting that genetics may indirectly contribute to hyperphantasia.

Although the extraction pipe leading to the laundry is narrow, Jane slides in easily, but her nostrils are immediately stung by the smell of the waste products from the detergents being pumped through the pipe. The inside is sticky with residue, but Jane knows she has to move slowly to avoid making a noise, so she edges carefully on her back down the pipe to the lower level of the building. The whirring of the washing machines gets louder as she approaches the extractor fan. Due to the noise of the machines, she has to wait longer than she prefers to make sure there are no voices coming from inside the room, then kicks hard at the fan. The screws hold at first but after another blow it pops from its fixings and Jane slides out. The plastic fan has split in two so there is no way it can be fitted back into place. It will be obvious to even the laziest of observers. Jane looks around, increasing getting worried at the amount of time she has already spent getting into the mansion. A tall laundry basket provides the solution so Jane wheels it over to cover the gap in the wall.

"Y_RAM. Send the drones to the south and release the second set of smoke bombs and CS gas."

The laundry room is piled high with towels, sheets, and pillow cases. There is a long rail with a row of identical uniforms hanging neatly in order of size, just like you find in a clothes shop. Jane pulls one out. The trousers are pure cotton and are a plain, dark gray color. The tops are Mao-style tunics, also dark gray, although the cuffs and collars are a light blue color. There is a bright blue A.M. logo on the front left of each top. Some of

172

the smaller sizes are clearly for children, and Jane quickly realizes that they are the uniforms of the clones. There are different sizes but all are identical in style so nobody has a personality of their own. She slides the hangars across until she sees one that looks as if it is her size. A clone uniform could provide the perfect cover if she spotted by a guard. She pulls off her jeans and stuffs them behind the large laundry basket before pulling on her new clothes, then smooths it down while smiling at the absurdity of it. The tunic is loose so it fits comfortably over her own top holding her gadgets and gun.

Her mind flashes through the images of her route to the rooms where the specimens are being experimented on. From her last visit to the mansion, she remembers that the temperature was chilled in there. Simone said she was being held in a cold room. It makes sense. Simone is just another experiment alongside all those ghoulish specimens.

From the floor layout of the building, she knows there is a stairway right outside the laundry. She only has to make her way up one floor and along the corridor. Peering through the small glass panel in the door, Jane can see the shadowy figure of one of Bing's men standing on the other side. She is ready for what she needs to do.

"Timing is everything, Jane. First distraction, then act."

Jane raps gently on the door and steps back. The door opens, and Jane makes sure to grab its edge firmly as it swings toward her.

"What are you doing walking around here? Why are you not in your room where you are supposed to be?" barks the guard.

"I got lost. I can't find my way back."

"Bloody hell. This is *not* what we need right now. Another malfunctioning clone. I'd better call it in," he mutters to himself, leaning forward slightly as he reaches for his headset.

Before he has time to realize the building communication

173

and surveillance systems have been shut down, Jane swings the door and slams it hard into the security guard's head. It hits him with a crack on the forehead and he staggers back. Jane doesn't hesitate and fires a series of blows to his neck. He slumps back unconscious. Jane shuffles his body out of the way — shocked by her own strength when overcoming the man — and makes her way cautiously to the room housing the human experiments.

Two men are stretched out on narrow hospital-style beds, naked and tied firmly with leather straps at the wrists and ankles. There are heavy incisions and stitching around their shoulders, hips, noses, and genitals. It's clear from the weird proportions of their limbs that a surgeon has swapped their body parts. The redness from the cuts glow brightly despite being smothered in a thick antiseptic cream. Yellow pus oozes from some of incisions and the faces of the two men are contorted in pain. They have just enough strength to reach out with their fingers which they wiggle imploringly. Whether it is to be saved or put out of their misery, it's hard to tell.

Who would do such a thing? What good does it do? These people are doing these experiments just to see if they can be done. Can Jane help them?

"Don't let emotion distract you from your plan. The battlefield is full of pain but you must stay strong and keep your eyes on your mission."

Nearby are rows and rows of giant glass cases, each containing a person standing up with their eyes closed. A number of different sized tubes feed into the cases and there is monitor on the wall behind each case. The cases are filled with a green liquid which is being pumped around like it is water in a fish tank. The liquid just covers the head of the person held in the case and bubbles away gently.

174

Suddenly, Jane steps back, stunned. She sees an image of herself inside one of the cases. It's like she is looking at *herself* in a mirror covered in green slime. She rubs the glass to clear off some of the condensation and peers in. She is looking at an exact copy of herself. She knows she has to get to Simone, but she can't move on now. Furiously, Jane pulls at the tubes, her mind racing as confusion and anger pump through every part of her.

"Stay focused at all times. Whatever happens, think everything through calmly."

Jane takes a deep breath. She watches as the liquid bubbles even more furiously. She has obviously disturbed the tubes, but brute force is clearly not the solution. She takes hold of them again but this time she twists them. They click as if they are in another mode and the copy of her herself inside the tube stirs. Regaining her composure, Jane flicks the large red switch below the monitor. There's a whirr from the machine as if it's shutting down, then a gurgling from inside the case as the level of the liquid starts to fall. What has she done? Is she saving the copy of herself or killing her?

Jane watches with worry as the liquid drains away and the last of it swirls around with a flourish as if it is the last bit of water emptying from a bath. The young girl's eyes open sharply and she stares at Jane, stunned and clearly agitated. She looks like she has been woken from a nightmare and is clearly uncomfortable. She wriggles in the plastic mold around her body and limbs that have held her upright during her time in the case.

Transcript of telephone call between Max Bing and David Rogerson
6th August

Rogerson: Max, what the hell is going on? I have just received an alert from security that there is trouble at headquarters. I tried logging in but can't see a thing. Are the systems down?

Bing: I've just seen it myself. I'm onto it now.

Rogerson: Max, I have to say, you are letting things slip. Everything is becoming a mess very quickly.

Bing: David, I said I'm onto it. Probably just some local kids with drones. Nothing I can't handle. The IT guys are getting the systems up and running again now.

Rogerson: Well, get it sorted, Max! This is yet another reason why we need to accelerate the plans to move our operations to countries where there are no rules.

Bing: Ethics dumping, David. It's called ethics dumping. And since when did you start calling the shots? We will be set up in Mexico, Paraguay, and on our island in the Gulf very soon. Then there will be no rules for us to worry about then. You know that!

Rogerson: Sorry, Max, but I have to say I'm getting worried about all these breaches. And I know you have pulled a lot of the security men out of HQ. Can the few still left there look after things properly?

Bing: Of course they can! And it's *we,* David. *We* agreed to pull those guys out of Wales so we had more bodies searching for this bloody girl.

The two girls continue to look at each other through the glass without showing any emotion, then suddenly the girl inside the case smiles sweetly as if her nightmare is starting to clear. The door swings open. Jane steps inside and pulls the tubes from the girl's nose gently. She coughs violently and green liquid shoots from her mouth and nostrils.

"Sorry," the girl says. "Who are you?"

"I'm Jane. Who are you?"

"I'm Is, er… I'm… Are you my sister? Your hair is different but you look the same as me."

"I don't know but we *do* look the same. What's your surname?"

"I'm Is… Isabel. I'm Clone 9, Recipient W01. Yes, that's

176

it," the girl says as her brain slowly stirs.

Jane eases Isabel from the mold and holds her up as she regains the use of her leg muscles. She holds Jane tightly, hugging her in a way that displays affection and gratitude beyond her need to just stay standing.

Jane is taken aback at receiving a hug from someone she's just met in such weird circumstances. Her tunic is now covered in the green liquid from the Isabel's body.

"Come on, let's get this green stuff off you," Jane says.

She returns with some doctor's gowns and wipes Isabel down, then helps her on with the tunic she took from the laundry.

"Here, you wear this. You can't walk around naked. How old are you?"

"I'm thirteen. I will be fourteen on the fifth of October."

"That's my mummy's birthday. Did you know someone called Winnie?"

"Winnie? No, we never met her. But Lorraine told us a lot about her. She said that one day we would grow up to be *just* like her."

"You knew my grandmother?"

"She was your grandmother too?"

"Yes, she was," Jane says.

"I think we are sisters. I'm not sure, but I think we are sisters."

The girls continue to stare each other for a while, not knowing what to say next.

"Why are you here?" Isabel asks.

The questions jolts Jane back to reality and her thoughts swing sharply back to Simone.

She can see that Simone in not in the room used for experiments. She was wrong. She has to find another cold room.

"Isabel, I need your help. I need to get to my friend. I'm looking for a cold, dark room. Do you know one?"

Isabel shakes her head nervously.

"Please, Isabel. My friend needs our help."

"Dark and cold…" Isabel's voice trails off and she pauses again. "I might. But we are not allowed to talk about it or go there. My sister Hannah was taken there once. She told me about it."

"Will she take us there?" Jane queries.

"She's gone. Like the others. I am the only one left."

"Where is this dark and cold room?" Jane asks.

"I don't know for sure. Down lower maybe," she answers, her brain still not functioning fully since being released from the case.

"If I take you down, will you recognize it?

"Maybe. I can't be sure. She said it was down. Near the kitchens, I think."

A clear image of the mansion's floor plan flashes through Jane's mind and she plots the route. But as they open the fire exit, Jane hears the loud clomping of boots pacing up and down in the stairwell. She holds up a finger and gestures to Isabel to keep quiet.

"When I give you the signal, I want you to scream for help. OK? Do it from the top of the stairs," Jane whispers to her new-found sister.

Isabel nods as Jane climbs up onto the top of balustrade on the landing that looks over the stairwell and pulls a piece of thin cord from her pocket and winds it around her fingers. Her balance is perfect as she raises her hands to signal to her sister. Then suddenly, releasing years of pent-up aggression from an oppressive life, Isabel lets out a high-pitched, piercing scream that takes even Jane by surprise. She had heard a similar scream only once before — when her daddy came home very drunk and her mummy told him to get out and never come back.

Isabel holds the scream as if she is an opera singer hanging on a high note and Jane sees the shadow of the guard racing up the stairs. She leans forward and as soon as the guard is right below her, she leaps, landing on his back and sticking to it like a limpet before sliding the cord over his head and around his neck. The force from Jane's leap momentarily makes the guard to stumble forward, but he regains his footing and he is soon clawing at the cord with his fingers as Jane pulls it ever tighter around his neck. He's gasping for air. He tries to hit back but Jane is tucked in tight. The air is slowly being squeezed from him and his strength with it. He staggers again, makes one last half-hearted attempt at a blow to Jane before falling backwards.

"Hold on until the job is complete. Be sure of victory."

Jane clings on desperately as the guard lumbers backwards, urging her fingers to pull the cord ever tighter despite the cutting pain. Her body cracks against the back wall of the stairwell as the guard loses control of his testosterone-pumped muscles, but she refuses to let go. Eventually, the last bit of air is expended from the man, and he collapses, defeated. Now it's Jane gasping for air, the blow against the wall bursting the oxygen from her lung in an instant like an exploding volcano. The weight of the guard is heavy and she struggles to breathe.

"Push, Jane. Push," Isabel urges as she pulls at the hulk. "Was my scream OK?" Isabel asks but Jane is bent over, taking pressure from her organs and allowing her diaphragm to function more effectively. She needs air. She needs to rediscover her focus.

After regaining her composure, Jane stands up and smiles to Isabel, "Let's go."

"Do you know if there will be more guards this way?" Jane asks as she listens for clues outside the next door.

"I'm not sure. There are not many safety men here at the moment. Father Bing has sent a lot of them are away. They are looking for someone important who wants to hurt us," she says.

Jane can hear a clanking noise as if someone is wheeling

something along the corridor.

"What's that?"

"It might be Mrs. Brill, the cook. She sometimes delivers food to the workers in their rooms."

"What are you girls doing here? Haven't you heard there is trouble outside?" Mrs. Brill scolds them. "And where are your trousers? Get to your rooms right now. I have my work to do."

"Yes, Mrs. Brill. We are going there now."

Once Mrs. Brill has gone, Jane taps her watch.

"Y_RAM. Are all the drones OK? Send them to the east of the building again and release more smoke and CS gas."

"Do you recognize anything?" Jane asks Isabel.

"The kitchen is here. It's through that door."

The air is filled with the smell of food cooking as they pass steaming ovens and bubbling pots.

"Where now? How do we get to the dark and cold room?"

"I don't know. Hannah said it was through the kitchen."

"There isn't anywhere else to go. Think, Isabel. Think!"

Isabel starts crying and Jane feels frustration and anger rising inside her. Time is running out.

"Don't exert too much pressure, Jane. Kindness is often the way to get answers."

Jane grabs Isabel and pulls her close.

"It's OK. I am here. I won't let anyone hurt you. I promise. But please tell me what Hannah said. We can do this together!"

Isabel looks up, tears still running down her puffy cheeks as Jane reassures her with her eyes.

"She said it's through a small door. Like a cupboard," Isabel says.

Jane looks around then starts pulling open doors. There is nothing but pots and tins of food. Exasperated, she slams one of the doors and hears Isabel burst into tears again.

"A door like in the *Hobbit*. She said it was like a hobbit hole," Isabel says.

Jane smiles as she spots a small arched doorway beside the black AGA. It's padlocked but the wood around it is aging badly. Jane brings her heel down on the padlock and hears the wood crack. Again, she smashes down on it. On the fourth strike there is a loud crack and the screws are ripped from the fixings.

"There's a red rug. The door to the cold room is under there. But I am not coming down with you. I will wait here," Isabel says as Jane crawls through the hobbit door into a small room.

Jane rolls back the rug to reveal a large, round metal handle. She levers back the oak trapdoor that looks like it belongs in the Dark Ages. Before stepping cautiously down a couple of the steps, Jane pulls out a memory stick from the arm pocket of her running top, leaving her tunic open so she can access her gun if she needs it. A rush of cold air hits her and as her eyes adjust to the half-light, she realizes just what she is heading down to.

It's some sort of dungeon. No wonder it isn't on the layouts. Bing must have kept this off the plans.

Jane hears voices below.

"You think I will not get you to talk?" Sven screams. "This time I will not be some kind. If you want to keep that pretty face of yours in one piece, then now is the time to talk. Where is Jane? Where is Jane?" he screams.

Simone is curled up on the floor in the fetal position, shivering in a pool of half-dried blood. The beatings have taken their toll and she has lost her fight.

Jane creeps down the steps and sees Sven slap Simone repeatedly across her buttocks. Jane watches as he peels on a pair of Latex gloves, ready for the session. Sven turns and spots the small figure on the steps.

"What do we have here? You know you girls are not allowed into the dark room," he says, spotting the clone uniform.

181

Jane steps toward Sven calmly and in a show of force she jumps, twists, and delivers a roundhouse kick into the air.

"Well, well. The fly has come into my web. Let's see what you are made of, little girl," Sven says, smiling menacingly.

Jane stands still as Sven approaches, making no attempt to attack. Sven smiles again, laughing to himself at the idea of fighting a small girl. Bing will be pleased. Maybe he will reward him with the pretty Simone before he takes her upstairs for experimentation.

"Patience. Waiting for the right time is the key for a successful attack."

The giant man lumbers forward like an ogre struggling to walk, his huge steroid-pumped thighs forcing him into an awkward waddle. Ten yards, nine yards, eight yards, seven yards... Jane still remains motionless. Her heart is racing but she stays focused, waiting until Sven is almost on her before she raises her hand and fires the pins from the memory stick into Sven's heavy neck. He's stunned by the sharp stings and instinctively tries to raise his left hand toward their source. But before it can reach his neck, he slumps down immobilized.

"Jane. Is that you? I can't believe you came," Simone gurgles.

Jane rushes toward her. Her left eye is swollen closed and parts of her hair have been ripped out, revealing open wounds on the side of her head. Bruises cover the rest of her body. She shivers from the cold and pain.

"Undo these ties. I think I've had enough of this place."

Jane helps Simone to her feet. Her legs wobble under her weight, her prolonged spell of beatings too much for her body. She lets out a long groan, as much out of relief as pain.

As they hobble past Sven, Simone bends over and slaps him across his face.

182

"Sorry Jane, he deserved that."

"Where are your clothes?" Isabel asks as Simone hobbles up the steps, the strength in her legs slowly coming back. She stretches them out with another groan.

"I thought I was going to the beach," Simone jokes, although the girl's face remains blank. "Now let's get out of here," Simone adds.

"Not yet, I need a find a small boy. His name is Adam," Jane says. "Do you know where he is?" she asks, turning to Isabel.

"He'll be upstairs in the nursery if he's little. There's one boy they keep on his own. Is that him?" Isabel asks.

"Jane, there's no time," Simone urges. "Anyway, who is he?"

"I need to find him. I think he's my brother. I saw something in one of the documents."

"What? I never saw a document with anything like that," Simone replies.

"I kept it a secret. I wanted to make sure. But I saw something about my daddy and a clone. They err…"

But before they have time to think about rescuing anyone else, they hear voices coming from the corridor. It's the security guards.

"They know we are here. We need to go," Simone says.

"We are trapped. We will have to fight our way out," Jane replies without fear.

"Avoid confrontation if you can. Always look for another solution where possible."

"Distraction. We need to *distract* them, not fight them. Y_RAM. Can you locate me? Send in one of the drones."

Jane watches on her phone as the drone zips its way through the mansion like a manic mouse in a maze.

Shots ring out and voices scream warnings as the guards spot

183

the drone.

"Buzz those guards, Y_RAM. And lead them away from the laundry. Use smoke but no CS gas. We need to go in that direction so we need it clear of guards."

Shots ping around the corridor but the machine's agility and drifting smoke mean the guards are just firing blindly in frustration as they attempt to chase the drone.

Jane helps Simone through the kitchen, past a stunned Mrs. Brill who has returned to her pots, and into the corridor. Isabel scampers behind, excited by the first real bit of adventure in her life. Smoke fills the corridor but it's nothing to Jane; the way out is clearly in her mind's eye.

She pulls back the basket in the laundry room and helps Simone up to the extractor pipe.

"It might be a bit tight but you'll fit through it. The grille at the end is loose. Just push it out. Isabel, you follow. Quick!"

"That was sticky and smelly in there," Isabel says when Jane emerges from the pipe.

Jane immediately runs to the wall and scales it like Spiderman, retrieves the rope and signals to Isabel, who is waiting with Simone by the house. She pulls Isabel up easily then watches as she climbs down the rope on other side.

As Isabel reaches the bottom, Jane spots rising smoke from the back of mansion. A guard has activated the electronic tripwire sensors she set up earlier. More guards will be following soon.

"You next, Simone. Quick, there's a guard coming," Jane calls from the top of the wall.

Simone hobbles across to the wall but before she gets there, Jane spots the security guard emerging from the smoke. He looks more shocked than anything but after a pause he starts running toward Simone.

"Stop! What are you doing here?" he shouts.

Simone turns to see he is fumbling for the whistle hanging around his neck. She has to stop him from raising the alarm. She

184

leaps forward and knocks the whistle from his hand just as he is putting it to his lips. The security guard is not like the others. He is younger, smaller, and much thinner. Not like a security guard at all. They grapple as Jane watches on. Although the man is not built for fighting and is just flailing like a toddler in a playground scuffle, Simone is still very weak and struggles to overcome him. Eventually she manages to land a hefty slap to his face and his nose starts streaming with blood. The man starts crying.

"Knock him out him, Simone. You'll have to knock him out," Jane shouts.

Jane throws more of the electronic tripwire sensors out toward the building and watches as the sharp blue lights activate them.

"I can't, Jane. He's just a boy."

"Please don't hurt me. I never wanted to do this. I normally work in the office filing papers. They made me do this because most of the other men are out looking for some girl Mr. Bing is after. They said I just had to walk around and blow the whistle if I saw anything. I don't want to fight anyone," the young guard says.

"How many men are left in the house?" Simone asks.

"Five. He's only left five guards here. And me."

Simone drags him up by his collar, turns him around, and kicks him in his backside as if he is a naughty boy. The man stumbles as he runs away, then trips in shock as the smoke shoots up as he triggers the electronic tripwires.

"That was a mistake, Simone. They will be chasing us now," Jane says as leans back on the rope to help Simone's climb.

"They already were, Jane," Simone replies, between groans of pain as she climbs steadily along the rope to the top of the wall.

Isabel

Pronounced: IZ-a-behl

185

Origin: Spanish
Derivative: Elisheba (Hebrew)
Meaning: God is my Oath

Jane
Pronounced: JAYN
Origin: English
Derivative: Jehanne (Medieval English)
Meaning: God is my Gracious

Chapter 10

Jane leads Simone and Isabel through the woods then across the stream to the car park where Eva is waiting. She spots them approaching in Land Rover's wing mirrors, starts the engine and pops the doors open.

"I see you've brought some friends, Jane," Eva says as she skids away at speed, with the doors only half-shut. "Tighten your seatbelts. It looks like I may need to put my foot down."

"Wait, here come the drones," Jane screams.

"They'll locate us just fine," Eva says, zipping down the windows for their arrival. After buzzing around the car briefly, the drones suddenly shoot through the back windows. Isabel giggles as one of them settles on her lap, whirrs briefly, then with sizzle, they shut down.

Eva races the Land Rover skillfully along the dirt track to the junction, then turns the wheel hard left like a rally driver in a rush.

"I think we will have to head west for a while. You got your friends to the east, eh Jane?"

"Er, it was over there…"

"Yes, that's the east. And I think some cars are heading our way from that direction right now."

The other three turn around to see two vehicles less than a hundred yards away. They are all pinned back in their seats with eyes wide open as Eva races at speed along the Welsh country lane. With the other cars still on their tail, Eva starts swerving the Land Rover from left to right, revving the vehicle hard with each swerve so the wheels spin furiously in the dry dirt at the edges of the tarmac. Dust shoots up and fills the air behind them. After

Eva is happy with her dust cloud, she pulls the wheel down hard right and skids the car up another lane. She slows briefly while staring intently into the rear-view mirror.

"We've lost them. They shot straight past the turn off. Sweet."

"How the hell did you learn to drive like that, Eva?" Simone asks.

"The Special Troops Command in Poland. A mechanic and driver for six years. Among other things," she replies, driving one-handed as she removes her jacket and hands it to Simone.

"What did you drive? Tanks?" Simone follows up, only half-joking.

"No, no. But it was something bigger than this. This is, what do say… a baby car for me."

"Eva, this could be a dead end. We'll be trapped. How do you know this road comes out anywhere?"

"I don't, but there are farm buildings some way ahead. I'm pretty sure we'll be passing them soon. So the road should keep going."

Eva is right, and at the end of the farm road she turns back eastwards. Jane sighs in relief when they enter a small town and she spots a sign pointing the way to the English capital, but she only stops looking back once they are buried among a throng of other cars further on. But Eva is taking no chances. As soon as she spots a service stop, she pulls over and swaps the number plates with a dummy set in the boot. She also clips two magnetic signs to the sides of the vehicle.

SUPAFRESH
THE HOUSE CLEANING SPECIALISTS

"Just something I organized for Mr. Kapoor. I knew they'd come in handy one day. Oh, by the way. We are a team of cleaners, if anyone asks."

188

From Angela West's WhatsApp account.
6th August

Angela West: typing…
Simone Grant: offline
Angela: I'm here! I've got you a skinny latte!
Angela: Where are you? I thought we were meeting for a coffee?
Angela: Hun? Are you still coming?
Angela: Had to go. Couldn't wait any longer. Text me!

From Angela West's WhatsApp account.
6th August

Angela West: typing…
Simone Grant: offline
Angela: Where are you? I called your work and they said you didn't come in today. Are you sick?
Angela: Text me hun!

Hansard
Prime Minister's Question Time (Special Sitting).
6th August

Speaker: Order! Questions to the Prime Minister. Geoff Smith.
Geoff Smith MP: Question one.
Prime Minister: Thank you. In light of yesterday's shocking allegations regarding Synoplex and their company MethusalaCo, I can announce to the House that a full investigation has been launched immediately. I had meetings with my ministerial colleagues and others. And in addition to my duties in this House, I shall have further meetings later today.

Leader of the Opposition: We have seen as this government has continually cozied up to their rich friends and big business time and time again. These awful revelations of last night are evidence that these companies do exactly what that want and are given a free run by our government. Will the Prime Minister commit to bringing those responsible to book no matter how rich they are?

Prime Minister: I should remind the Right Honorable Gentleman that the company in question employs thousands of hard-working people around the country and pays millions in tax which goes toward our essential public services. The offices of Synoplex are being searched by the Metropolitan Police this morning and we are liaising with governments around the world where the company's other offices have also been searched. It is only right and proper that we should wait until the investigation is completed.

Leader of the Opposition: Will the Prime Minister be telling the family members of those who were abducted and experimented on that they should wait for answers to what happened?

Prime Minister: I extend my sympathies to the families of all those people who were previously named as missing and are now connected to these leaks. In this case, I can confirm that finding these people was given the highest priority when I held an emergency meeting in the early hours with the Head of the MI5, the Commissioner of the Metropolitan Police, and Chief Constables around the country. We must let the police finish their job, of course. But due to the seriousness of the allegations in these documents and the immense suffering of those families, we have decided to reveal to the House ahead of the investigation that the Head of MI5 and his team believe that these documents are a hoax and they are already searching for the source of the leaks.

Speaker: Order! Order!

Transcript of telephone call between Max Bing and David Rogerson
6th August

Rogerson: Hello, Max. I have to say, that is excellent work, my friend.

Bing: Did you see the PM? I thought he did rather well. I think the time is right to bring the PM into A.M. now.

Rogerson: Good idea. Alan at MI5 obviously did a good job persuading him it was a hoax, but he pulled it off with aplomb.

Bing: I'm afraid Alan's thank you will cost us a fair bit, but that is money well spent, I would say. I hear the papers will be going with the hoax angle tomorrow morning. The investigation will have to run its course, but that's just a formality now. Can you organize the right person to head that up?

Rogerson: Yes, of course. It's a huge mess but it looks like we should be in the clear soon.

Bing: The FTSE will be resuming trading in Synoplex in about half an hour and we are expecting the share price to bounce back after the PM's announcement. I've got some positive PR stuff planned as well. We will be back to normal soon.

Rogerson: Well done, Max. I knew you could do it.

Transcript of telephone call between Alex Shaw, Director General of MI5 and David Rogerson
6th August

Rogerson: Good work with the PM, Alan.

Shaw: All part of my job. After all, what else can he say when the MI5 tells him it's a hoax? To be honest, I think he was rather relieved. Synoplex is one of the party's largest donors after all.

Rogerson: It's a win all round then. I wanted to ask you about who will be running this investigation.

Shaw: Who do you want?

191

Rogerson: I was thinking Jonathan Brattic. I've always found him helpful in the past.

Shaw: No problem. I'll sort it out.

Rogerson: And Max?

Shaw: He'll have to step down as CEO of course. He can disappear somewhere warm like that little island he's got in the Middle East. We are counting on you to make sure he goes quietly. We need you to run things now, David. This needs a safe pair of hands going forward.

Rogerson: No problem. I'll speak to him.

Shaw: I look forward to working with you more closely, David. We must get a game of golf in sometime.

Rogerson: I'll get my PA to call yours and find a window.

Jane cracks her knuckles as she enters the Mews house. She has a lot of work to catch up on.

"Y_RAM. Call me up all today's newspaper headlines for articles on Anno Methusala and Max Bing."

Y_RAM **search results... Newspaper headlines**

The Sun

Super Maxy was Fantastic, But His Leaks are Atrocious

Daily Mirror

The Famous 25 Go in Search of Eternal Life

The Times

How Much Did the Government Really Know About Anno Methusala?

The Guardian

Bing Offers Eternal Life — If You Are Rich

The Daily Telegraph

PM Launches Investigation into Bing Leaks

Daily Beast

It's True. Elvis Could Be Alive!

Simone emerges from her room looking bruised, but no longer battered. A dark blue wrap covers the gouges on her head. Eva, the multi-talented cleaner, has patched up her cuts and has promised to return tomorrow with more food and to change Simone's dressings. Isabel is like a wonderstruck child enjoying her first Christmas.

"What's this? What's that? How does this work?"

She loves it up on the rooftop and is awestruck by the number of lights. While Simone checks out the telescope, Jane shows Isabel around and promises her they will have a barbeque one day. Jane has plenty of questions for her sister.

"What does Adam look like? Is he happy? How was life in the mansion? Did they treat you well? What happened to our sisters?"

When Jane's questions are exhausted, Isabel needs no prompting to leave her and Simone to their planning. At eight-thirty, she politely says goodnight and heads off to shower and get ready for bed. She must be in bed by nine, she tells them.

Left alone, Jane and Simone sit at the rooftop bar with hot coffees and look out across London as they plot their next move. Bing is angry. He will make a mistake and they have to be ready.

"When an enemy attacks in anger they make mistakes and weaken their defense. This is the time for you to attack their stronghold. Use every opportunity you have."

"Simone. I have something to show you. I don't know what to do," Jane says.

Message reads... Keyholder Order requests meeting with Jane Banks... propose coalition... 8th August 16.15 GMT... 51°30'31"N 0°4'37"W...

"What the hell is this? How did you get it?"

"Through Y_RAM a couple of days ago. It's from people who tried to help my daddy. But I'm not sure I can trust it," Jane explains.

"If Y_RAM has checked it then we *have* to try. It could be our route to get Bing. I'll go. Where is the location?"

"It says me. If you turn up, we could blow everything. Assuming they don't kill me of course. It's the Chapel Royal of St. Peter ad Vincula."

"Where's that?"

"The Tower of London."

"OK. Go alone. But I'll be nearby and Y_RAM must be linked to you at all times. And I'm not taking no for answer."

"OK. But I need your help with something else. I have access to lots of money. Accounts in Coutts and Lloyds here and private bank accounts in Switzerland. I've also got a code and key for a safety deposit box in Harrods. I want to know what's in there but it'll arouse suspicion if a young girl turns up! Will you go?"

"Of course! I've always fancied the idea of having my own safety deposit box, but I've never had anything worth putting in one! I'll go as soon as I get a chance," Simone replies.

Jane and Simone work late into the night poring over all information they have on Bing. After discovering Kapoor's excellent selection of wines, Simone is now tucking into a bottle of Grange Shiraz 2010. She is reveling in the warmth of the summer night on the rooftop as they look over Bing's private jet flights. Bing is often at his HQ from Friday to Monday and at various offices around the world in the week. But in the last few months, he has been spending more and more time in the Middle East. Simone goes to the telescope and fixes it on the rooftop of the Synoplex building that is less than a mile away. It's much higher than where they are but she can clearly see an orange and white windsock flapping gently in the evening breeze.

Jane goes to bed at three-thirty. She's hardly slept recently and is tired, but the sight of Isabel sleeping peacefully makes her pause a while longer. She is happy she has found her sister. She believes she has a brother too. Jane smiles. She is no longer alone.

The Times
7th August
Bing hires 100,000 new staff for brave new world

Tech giant Max Bing will be hiring one hundred thousand disadvantaged young people to work on his new virtual world — despite being embroiled in the middle of explosive allegations that Synoplex is linked to an illegal human cloning program.

Bing's entry into the metaverse — a new world that will be themed around technology and science — will be known as the Synoverse and is initially geared up to attract a hundred million people. Bing believes Synoverse can become the premier virtual world within two years and that it will be filled with the brightest and best people from around the real world.

"This is not a game. This will become home to some of the greatest minds in the world and a place to exchange innovative ideas that will benefit mankind for years to come," the Synoplex CEO Bing said.

To build the infrastructure of his new world, Bing has committed to hiring young people from areas around the world with high youth unemployment — Africa, southern Europe, and inner-city America. The new employees will be paid in Syno dollars, but these can be exchanged for local currencies by the citizens (Bing refuses to call them gamers).

These disadvantaged young people will be tasked with creating a virtual world that "is free from discrimination and a society that cares for everyone regardless of their background". Their first task will be to build the basic infrastructure of the Synoverse and set up scientific centers of excellence.

"We believe in the youth of the world. The real world may be content to discard these young people just because of their backgrounds but we are not. We will invest in the talent and intellect that is too often ignored, whether it is from rural Somalia or from inner-city Chicago," Bing said.

Daily Express
7th August
Synoplex Self-Driving Vans to Help NHS

The takeover of Astroglide, the leader in developing technology for large automated vehicles has been completed by Synoplex in a deal worth two hundred and thirty-two million dollars.

Synoplex has announced that they will be ploughing resources into developing a self-driving ambulance — and will donate the first two thousand produced to the NHS.

"The ambulance drivers and highly skilled paramedics do an amazing job for our beloved health service, but the truth is they often become little more than taxi drivers for people calling 999 for non-emergencies. Our ambulances can transport those who do not require immediate attention to hospital and let the paramedics concentrate on the people who really require their expertise," Synoplex CEO Max Bing said.

The automated ambulances could reduce response times dramatically and will all be set up with the latest video link technology so a nurse can assess the patient on route to reduce waiting times in A&E. The ambulances will be fully kitted out if they do need to be manned. They will be faster and more economical to run than the current ambulances.

"Our initiative is not intended to replace the current system but to complement it to make the staff's job easier and improve the quality of health care," Bing added.

Health providers in Australia, South Africa, America, and

China have already expressed interest in partnering on this new service.

Transcript of telephone call between David Rogerson and Max Bing
7th August

Rogerson: Max, I know it makes good PR, but what the hell are you doing giving away our technology to the NHS?

Bing: That organization is a mess, David, you know that. Billions spent every year and it's chaos. There are over twelve million emergency calls for ambulances made every year. It will be easy for a few of them to get lost in the system. This gives us access to people — people we can use.

Rogerson: Body parts?

Bing: Exactly. Plus access to genetic information so we can find the best matches for the work we are doing. I've costed it. We will easily recoup our investment.

Rogerson: I like the thinking, Max. I like it a lot.

"Jane, Jane. Wake up. It's six-thirty. Breakfast is at seven."

The two sisters have been sharing a bed and Isabel is up early and already dressed. Jane has only had three hours sleep. Her mind has been in overtime ever since they have been back and with last night's session with Simone stretching late into the night, she realizes she hasn't paid much attention to her new-found sister.

"Can't we eat a bit later? I'm tired after last night."

"No, Jane. Breakfast is at seven. It has to be seven. It's scrambled eggs on wholemeal toast with smoked salmon today."

"My mummy's favorite. And Lorraine's," Jane says, raising her eyebrows.

"OK. Come on then. Let's get that breakfast," she adds, sliding out of bed and slipping on a pair of shorts and a sports T-shirt.

"Do you shower before breakfast or after?"

"After breakfast. We shower at seven-thirty," Isabel tells her.

"Right, how do you like your eggs and toast?" Jane asks.

"Two pieces of lightly toasted wholemeal bread, both with proper butter spread on them. One egg mixed with a little bit of milk and cracked pepper. No salt. The scrambled eggs go on one piece of toast and the other piece of toast is left just buttered. The salmon on the side. It must be just like that."

"OK. Not precise then!" Jane replies sarcastically, although Isabel doesn't notice. "Is your whole day planned like this?"

"Oh yes. Father Bing says it is so we grow up to be just what we are meant to be."

"An identikit of mummy and Lorraine, he means," Jane whispers under her breath.

"Shall I tell you about the rest of my day?" Isabel asks.

"Er, OK. No, hang on, I've got a better idea."

Jane returns with a Smythson notebook.

"Write out your day in here. Look, it has an "I" on the front for "Isabel.""

Isabel scribbles away and Jane immediately recognizes the handwriting. Isabel was not only cloned from her mummy, but she has been brought up to eat what she ate, act like she did, even write in the same way. Jane realizes that, although it's a childish version of it, she even speaks like her mummy.

Isabel Clone 9, Recipient W01 day plan

6.30 a.m.: Wake up

7.00 a.m.: Breakfast (Two pieces of wholemeal bread with scrambled eggs and smoked salmon)

7.30 a.m.: Shower and get dressed

8.30 a.m.: Mathematics lesson

10.00 a.m.: Break for tea and plain digestive biscuits

10.30 a.m.: Science lesson

12 noon: Lunch (Roasted carrot and coriander soup with brown bread roll)

1 p.m.: Study etiquette in room

1.45 p.m.: Etiquette test

2 p.m.: Report to medical room for medication

2.15 p.m.: Break for tea with crackers and cheese

3.30 p.m.: Behavioral lesson (body language)

4.30 p.m.: Reading. Current book is *A Passage to India* by E.M. Forster

5.30 p.m.: Dinner (Roast chicken with potatoes and Mediterranean vegetables)

6.30 p.m.: Interactive learning games (history and current affairs)

8.30 p.m.: Shower and get ready for bed

9.00 p.m.: Bed

"Simone, have a look at this," Jane says, handing Isabel's day plan to her. "She gets upset and jittery if I suggest changing her day even a little bit. She says she *must* stick to her plan. We can probably sort out the rest but what about the medication? She says her tablets are orange."

"We will have to treat her carefully, Jane. She doesn't know any other way," Simone says thoughtfully after reading through Isabel's day plan. "As for the medication... They might be giving her something just to keep her compliant but what if the medication is more essential to actually keep her alive? She's a clone after all."

Transcript of telephone call between Simone Grant and Dr. David Adams, Department of Genetics at York University 7th August

Dr. Adams: Gorgeous G, lovely to hear from you. Whatever happened to that dinner we were supposed to arrange?

Simone: I'm sorry, Dave, I know you're probably beginning to think that I only call you when I need advice.

Dr. Adams: No, no. Anything for an old university friend. *But…* how can I help you this time? But I insist on that dinner at some stage.

Simone: Yes, of course. It's about clones.

Dr. Adams: Clones. Don't tell me you are working on the Synoplex account? That's all we are talking about in the lab. Can I tell you, if it's true what they say and they really can do this stuff with clones, a whole new world is going to open up.

Simone: For the better?

Dr. Adams: Well, that depends on your point of view. Clones can be seen as good things or bad things.

Simone: What I really wanted to ask was what drugs a clone would need. Hypothetically, of course. To, er, keep operating properly. If I'm pulled into a meeting, I don't want to look like an idiot by not knowing what they are talking about.

Dr. Adams: Good question. Well, of course, I have no knowledge of what this Anno Methusala lot have developed when it comes to cloning…

Simone: There's no proof they have. Remember the Prime Minister has already said the MI5 believe these leaks are a hoax.

Dr. Adams: Yes, yes, of course. What I mean is, I can only talk about methods used in cloning that I know about.

Simone: And?

Dr. Adams: Well, DLLS6 was cloned using the process of nuclear transfer. The DNA was taken from an oocyte and the nucleus was…

Simone: Dave, plain English please.

Dr. Adams: Oh yes, sorry, Gorgeous G! DLLS6 was the code name for Dolly the sheep. The scientists used the process of nuclear transfer from a cell — in her case from a mammary gland. In nuclear transfer, the existing DNA is removed from an unfertilized egg and the nucleus, including the new DNA, is injected into it. If everything goes to plan then the cells will

200

divide normally and the cloned cells can be inserted into a uterus. If — and it's another big if — things continue to go to plan, then you have a clone.

Simone: So what's the problem?

Dr. Adams: It's a delicate procedure and chemicals are used at the stage with the egg. Many argue that the whole process leads to abnormalities in the clone.

Simone: What about Dolly?

Dr. Adams: She had arthritis and lung cancer. She was treated with anti-inflammatory drugs.

Simone: Is that it?

Dr. Adams: In her case. But pigs, deer, bulls, and horses have all been cloned and there have been various abnormalities. What drugs are needed depends on the problem. Anti-inflammatories are over-the-counter drugs so are widely used but they certainly can't be used without a doctor or pharmacist knowing the background of the patient.

Simone: OK. I understand. Thanks for your help, Dave.

Dr. Adams: No problem. And don't forget about that dinner now, Gorgeous G. I know you probably can't tell me but I'd love to know a couple of their cloning secrets, if they really do exist!

"Gorgeous G? What the hell is that?" Jane laughs as Simone hangs up.

"Don't you start, Jane! It's bad enough that I had to put up with my friends calling me Gorgeous Granty at university. Then it became Gorgeous G. It just stuck. You'll soon learn what it's like at university when it's your turn. Er… sorry."

"That's OK. I think we both know I've burnt those bridges and I won't be going to university now," Jane smiles. "Come on, we've got work to do," she adds, heading toward the roof terrace.

Simone focuses her attention on the Synoplex office with the telescope. She soon identifies Bing's large corner office, spacious and luxuriously designed with a long ebony desk by the window and original artwork on the walls. She imagines Bing swaggering around and shouting his instructions into his speaker phone as he looks out of his kingdom. Its interior design is more traditional than she'd expect from the head of the world's biggest tech company, almost like it's the office of an old man. A young woman opens the door to the office. She's immaculately dressed in a tight-fitting knee-length skirt and white blouse, and she sashays across the polished wooden floor like a model in her high heels. She places a large pile of files onto Bing's desk, then walks toward a grand-looking Chesterfield. Beside it is a stark artwork of Ouroboros, the Ancient Egyptian snake symbol depicting the cycle of life, death, and rebirth. She slides it back to reveal a safe door.

Simone watches the woman carefully through the telescope, but the woman's body is obscuring her view as she types in the code. She picks up the files delicately as if they will break if she squeezes them too hard — or maybe it's her nails she is worried about? — and puts them in the safe. She locks it and slides the Ouroboros artwork back into place.

"We have to get into the Synoplex office tonight, Jane. There's a safe in Bing's office. We might be able to find something in there that could help us," Simone tells Jane.

"Well, at least we know he won't be in there. He's in the Middle East at the moment."

Thanks to Y_RAM, Jane has been tracking Bing's movements. She's obsessed with him. Where he is, who he's seeing, what he's doing, and how long he spends doing it. In the short time that have passed since the leaks were released, he's been to the London office, lunched with David Rogerson at the Michelin-starred Sketch restaurant in Mayfair, visited the MI5 offices, the Farmers' Club, a private members' club near New Scotland Yard, and the Carlton Club, another private members' club that is popular among politicians before meeting Cordelia Charrier in Paris. Twenty minutes ago, his private jet touched down at Abu Yash International Airport, just a short helicopter ride to his private island in the Persian Gulf.

"This is frustrating. I know where he is and where he's been but I still can't find where he is going next," Jane says.

"Yet..." Simone says, raising her eyebrows and directing them toward the Synoplex offices.

"OK. We go in tonight," Jane replies in anticipation.

David Rogerson sits back in the plush leather chair in Max Bing's office and smiles to himself. He's in charge now. Bing has messed up.

Two scientists walk nervously into the huge space and stare at him while awaiting instructions. It is a big moment for any scientist when their work is recognized by Synoplex. This could make or break them. Rogerson ushers them forward with a wave of his hand to the chairs positioned a not-too-friendly distance from the ebony desk. Rogerson wants them to know who is in control.

"This is my desk now. Everything is mine, Max," Rogerson thinks to himself smugly, stroking the glossy veneer of the desk before turning to the visitors.

"Thank you for meeting me today. Despite the recent news, I can assure you that Synoplex and specifically MethusalaCo, our life sciences company, is stronger than ever and looking to expand. We are at the forefront of developing ideas that will help people live longer and healthier. You are leaders in your field, but we know your research has been held back by, shall we say, 'unnecessarily strict regulations'"

The scientists laugh politely.

"I think we can agree that the regulations surrounding medical research do hold us back. The authorities want results but then tie our hands beyond our backs," Dr. Mary Moore says.

"What if I were to ask you what you could achieve in an environment where the rules can be bent. Even ignored. We have the resources and finance and we certainly won't be tying your hands. We want results and how you get them is up to you," Rogerson says bluntly.

The scientists laugh again, salivating at the idea of what they could achieve without regulations.

"So, I will ask you today: what could you achieve with your research, with all the funding you need and without the rules holding you back?" Rogerson concludes.

"Basically, I have developed a chip that would be inserted just under a person's skin to monitor their health and potential health problems twenty-four-seven. I could fine-tune this in months if I could just be allowed to chip people with the prototype device," Dr. Moore explains.

"You will be allowed to with us," Rogerson replies, smiling. "What information would the chips give you?"

"The chips would feed back information such as heart rate, blood pressure, cholesterol, and much more. We will be able to spot potential problems and act fast if there is anything of concern. This can be done before people develop cancer, Alzheimer's, heart disease, even things as simple as hair loss," Dr. Moore says.

"But you can't get the go ahead to test it yet?" Rogerson asks.

"No, there are endless hoops I have to go through before I get to that stage. I have developed an alternative. A small device — no bigger than a pill — would be swallowed each morning at breakfast and make its way through the body constantly on the lookout for problems. The device will pass through the body naturally so a new one has to be taken each day to maintain the process. It is not as reliable as the chip, but it is still highly effective."

"But surely the chip could be used for *so* much more." Rogerson prompts menacingly. "Presumably the chip could be used to harvest genetic information from the subjects as well? We could certainly use that for other programs we have," he adds.

"I can program it to give us any information you want. I just need the people to chip so I can test out the prototype."

"That won't be a problem. We are currently recruiting a hundred thousand young people from around the world for another project. They are, er, from disadvantaged backgrounds so I think it will be in all of our interests if we use these chips to look after the health of our new employees who have not had the best start in life."

"A hundred thousand!" Dr. Moore exclaims incredulously as Rogerson nods before turning to the next doctor.

"I am a specialist in the science of senolytics, an exciting field in prolonging not only your lifespan but more importantly your healthspan," says the doctor. "Basically, in your youth, your body is full of healthy cells, but as you age some of the cells that develop are faulty. It is these cells that are major contributors to age-related diseases. Not only do these faulty cells — we call them senescent cells — not function effectively, but they also grow rapidly and turn their attention to the healthy cells, which they damage through inflammation. Eventually, tissue damage develops throughout the body. In mice, and in human trials, we have manipulated genes which 'tricks' them into vaporizing the senescent cells. One test has already shown potential benefits for idiopathic pulmonary fibrosis, a condition that is essentially a thickening and scarring of the lungs, with the marked improvements of all subjects when physical tests were conducted. Other tests are looking at treating emphysema, macular degeneration, and glaucoma. The outward benefits are also clear, if you'll excuse the pun: better skin and glossier hair — in essence you look younger."

"And what has been holding you back?" Rogerson asks.

"I have only been able to test this out on mice. And a very restrictive clinical trial on a small number of people."

"I'm sure Dr. Moore would be happy to share some of our hundred thousand new employees for your work," Rogerson replies, rolling his head back and laughing like a caricature of a Bond villain.

"But could you insert the healthy cells from one person into the body of another with the damaged cells?" Rogerson asks.

"It is certainly possibly but rejection of the cells from the recipient can lead to illness and death."

"That's not a problem. We have plenty of subjects. We must accept that there may be some collateral damage in our quest to give people longer lives," Rogerson replies coldly before launching into a monologue.

"But I need you to understand what I mean by living longer. What would you say if I was to suggest a human lifespan of one hundred and twenty? The oldest person on record was a French lady who lived to one hundred and twenty-two, so we know that is achievable, especially with the advances we are already offering. Already, a recent study led by researcher Tom Pykov and his team at Gero — a company based in Singapore — published its finding in *Nature Communications* suggesting humans could live to between one hundred and twenty and one hundred and fifty! But let me tell you this… Scientists at the Mount Desert Island in Maine, the USA, working with the Buck Institute in California and Nanjing University in China have unearthed some astonishing research. They have found cellular pathways in an eelworm that can increase the length of their life by five times. That is the equivalent of a human living to four or five hundred! 'It's just a parasitic worm,' I hear you say. But know this: the worm shares many of the same genes as humans. We are related! Think about it. Five hundred years… With your help I believe we can achieve this. Will you join us in our liberated approach to medicine?"

The doctors nod enthusiastically before Dr. Moore asks excitedly, "Will we be working closely with Mr. Bing? He has been an inspiration for me."

"We will be taking a new approach going forward,"

Rogerson replies bluntly. "Mr. Bing will be working on different project for a while."

The Daily Telegraph
7th August
Bing Steps Down as Synoplex Boss to Build a City Under the Sea

Mercurial entrepreneur Max Bing has resigned as the head of tech giant Synoplex to build a revolutionary undersea world off the coast of Abu Yash in the Arabian Sea.

The dramatic news comes following a turbulent few days for Synoplex and Bing after leaks alleged that his company were involved in developing human clones and experimenting on people for research. The leaks — dubbed the Synoplex Secrets — have since been dismissed by the Prime Minister as a hoax following a preliminary investigation from the MI5. Bing says his resignation is not linked to the leaks.

"We have been planning our undersea world for a number of years and now is the right time for me to take personal control of the project. Given its huge significance to mankind, it is only right that it receives my full attention. David Rogerson will assume the day-to-day control of Synoplex and our life sciences company MethusalaCo, but I can assure investors that I will still be very much involved in the decision-making," Bing announced.

The plan for the undersea city, named Persian Sea Kingdom, involves homes for five thousand people, plus offices, shops, a school, a medical clinic, and a leisure complex with bars, gyms, cinemas, a theater, and a bowling alley. Residents can enter the sea from the underwater city through 'leisure and fishing water locks' — similar to the air locks astronauts use when they need to leave the International Space Station for a spacewalk. Easy access to the sea is important for leisure activities, while spearfishing will provide some of the food for the community. Residents and visitors can only return to land after following the correct decompression procedures. The Persian Sea Kingdom will be partially self-governing through an elected council, but will initially fall under the governance of Abu Yash. Bing says that once fully established, Persian Sea Kingdom will seek full independence as a self-governing nation with the support of Abu Yash.

"The population of the world is rapidly approaching eight billion people and could reach twelve billion by the end of the century. Land covers less than thirty per cent of the earth's surface and much of that is uninhabitable. For the future of the human race, we must find ways to develop living space under the sea," Bing explained.

Bing leases the private one hundred and fifty-acre Signature Island (which is known locally as Intasala) off the coast of Abu Yash from the state enterprise board and has been using it for eighteen years. He has used it as a retreat and a training center for staff. Part of the island will now be redeveloped to serve as a support base for the undersea city.

"Shallow water is very important. Basically, the deeper it gets, the more complicated — and costly — undersea habitats become to build. We are lucky that there is a large flat shelf only twenty-five meters deep around the island, which is the perfect platform to build Persian Sea Kingdom," Bing said.

"Not only is it flat and shallow, but the shelf is on firm bedrock and it is a dead area in terms of activity, so there are no hydrothermal vents. It would be impossible to build near such vents, which are fissures discharging geothermically heated water," he added.

Research into undersea living grew in popularity in the 1950s and 1960s, the most well-known habitat being Jacques-Yves Cousteau's Conshelf II, which was home to two divers for two weeks at a depth of eighty-two feet. Technological developments have led to greater developments, including Conshelf III which operated at a depth of three hundred and thirty feet, and Hegoland UWL, which was used in the cold waters of the North and Baltic Seas and did not require the divers to decompress at the end of their working day. Most underwater habitats are used for scientists and divers to conduct research, although there has been some use of them for underwater tourism, notably Atlantis Submarines in Barbados, which offers weddings.

Since the 1970s there has been a decrease in research of underwater habitats when various operational difficulties were followed by a death in the planning stages of Sealab III, which was to operate six hundred and ten feet below the surface. Since then, interest from scientists has largely shifted to space living.

But as history has shown, Bing is certainly not a man afraid to buck current trends in search of technological advances.

Chapter 11

"Y_RAM, show me all the buildings around the London that are close to and higher than the Synoplex offices in London," Jane asks.

"Synoplex has eight offices in London. But these are the results for the buildings within one hundred yards of the main office. Or ninety-one meters if you prefer it in metric measurements."

Y_RAM search results… Building within one hundred yards and higher than Synoplex offices

1. The SKIY. Offices of various companies and restaurants. 63 yards (57.6 meters) distance from highest point of Synoplex Building. 48 yards (43.9 meters) higher.

2. Asper Building. Offices of Asper International. 75 yards (68.6 meters) distance from highest point of Synoplex Building. 12 yards (11 meters) higher.

3. Troy Building. Offices of various companies. 92 yards (84.14 meters) distance from highest point of Synoplex Building. 41 yards (37.5 meters) higher.

"The SKIY," Simone smiles. "Home of the revolving Szechuan restaurant."

"Y_RAM, where can I get a get a zipwire?" Jane asks

"Like Batman? You will find a black case in Locker 3 in the garage basement. It has a firing range of eighty-two yards (seventy-five meters). I will bring up the instructions for its use."

"What's that?" Simone asks when Jane shows her the hard,

black briefcase.

"It's our route into Bing's offices tonight," Jane answers, opening it up.

"A giant gun?"

"A gun with a high tensile steel wire coiled inside. We attach it to this grappling mouth and zip our way across to the helipad on top of Bing's building."

"I'm not sure I can do that, Jane. I'm a PA, not Sarah Connor."

"I'll set it up and show you how it works. Don't worry, you'll be fine," Jane reassures her. "It's sixty-three yards across from The SKIY building. But before we run through the details, let's dig out some glad rags, because we are going to dinner later. I'm sure you've got something among all that stuff you bought went you went shopping the other day!" Jane teases.

Simone sashays back wearing a long, black sparkly dress, her smile wide.

"You look great. But I'm not sure that's the best thing to wear for zipping across London on a wire!" Jane laughs.

Simone disappears to find something more appropriate for action. Her dark trouser suit gets the thumbs up from Jane.

Then it's her turn.

Jane returns in a floral dress, looking uncomfortable.

"Lorraine — my grandmother — made me wear things like this. I hate it but I bought it in case I needed something that made me look girly."

"You look great! But won't it ride up when you're in the air?" Simone asks, trying to get her own dig in.

"I've got my running shorts on underneath. I'll be fine. Let's get to the tech room and run through the plan. Y_RAM can help us. I've done it before. It's not too difficult," Jane says fearlessly.

"Easy for you to say then. I'm as nervous as a kitten." Simone smiles, desperately trying to make it look genuine.

"Y_RAM, get me a reservation for two in the Szechuan

Plateau for tonight at eight," Jane instructs the super computer.

"You do know this one of the hottest restaurants in London at the moment? It's fully booked four weeks in advance, so I will have to hack their system. Under what name?"

"Er, go for Roberta Stevenson."

"OK. Table booked for two for Roberta Stevenson at seven. I just hope you don't see Mr. and Mrs. Hermione when you are there."

"One more thing," Jane says to Simone, reaching into the drawer in the tech room.

"This is a stun lipstick. You might need it. Push this end hard into someone's body and it will disable their muscles instantly. They'll still be awake but won't be able to move."

It is seventeen floors to the Szechuan Plateau, but the lift shoots Simone and Jane up rapidly before they have had time to say "spicy prawns".

"What do you mean we don't have a booking? We booked this weeks ago for our anniversary," an angry woman says to the maître d'.

"I'm sorry, madam, but you are just not on our system."

"This is outrageous. We even received a call from one of your people yesterday asking us to confirm our booking."

"Roberta Stevenson for two," Simone says.

"This way, Ms. Stevenson. We have a lovely private table for you as requested. Straight from work, I see," the maître d' says, eyeing Simone's office-style suit and black briefcase.

"What the hell is going on? You people are incompetent. What sort of booking system do you have?" Jane hears the lady scream as they are shown to their table.

After a few minutes, a Deluxe Szechuan Platter is delivered to their table and Simone requests they are left alone to enjoy their food.

"The fire exit is near the toilets," Jane tells her. "We can access the rooftop from there. Maybe Mr. and Mrs. Hermione will get their table back once they realize we have gone," she

212

adds while placing two fifty-pound notes on the table.

They slip out of the booth and up the fire stairs to the rooftop. A few stars are still managing to glint though London's permanent electric light show below.

"That's it. Bing's building. I can see the flagpole for his helicopter pad."

"It's not lit up very well. That's good," Jane says as she unpacks the zipwire gun, attaches the cable securely to a fixing on The SKIY rooftop and sets up the pulleys.

"I've got to hit that flagpole. This works like a bulldog's mouth. It opens on impact and then claps shut again like a trap. It's impossible to open once it's attached, just like a rabid dog's mouth when he's got his grip on you."

Jane taps her watch.

"Y_RAM. Fix the device on the target."

The sensor from the gun locks onto the flagpole as Jane gets ready to fire.

"Gadget girl," Simone mutters.

The dog's tooth clasp whistles through the air, with Kapoor Steel's cable unraveling in its wake. It hits its target, locking onto the flagpole with a clunking noise that alerts the guard who is slumped against the wall on the other side of the rooftop. They wait, watching his movements but after a couple of half-hearted flashes of his torch he slumps back down into position. This is the easiest guard's job ever. The only thing that ever comes up here is the boss's helicopter. And the odd secretary the guards persuade to join them for a cigarette and a bunk up.

"You go first. I'll follow when you give me the signal that it's safe. That lazy guard might actually get up and do something this time."

"What if it snaps or something?" Simone asks nervously.

"It won't!" Jane laughs.

Jane cracks her knuckles then checks the fixings, then firmly pushes the shaking Simone into the night air before she has time

213

to think.

"Ahhhhhhh!"

Simone hurtles across the road below toward Bing's helipad and Jane watches her smack into the flagpole a bit harder than she'd expected before wrapping her legs around it and sliding to the ground. Graceful it is not. This time, the noise is too loud for the guard to ignore. Simone is dazed but signals to Jane to stay put as they watch the guard racing across the rooftop in search of whatever it was that made the noise, the beam of his torchlight flicking back and forth as he runs. He spots Simone and just as she manages to release her hands from the leather ties, he is upon her. Simone has still not fully recovered from her beatings from Sven, and despite her dexterity, she is soon overpowered by the muscular guard. As he drags her from the flagpole to toward the edge of the building, Jane knows it is time for her to act.

"Now, Jane. Now. It's up to you."

Jane feels the warm summer air on her face as she shoots through the air and watches the guard land a heavy round-arm punch to Simone's face, his legs straddled across her torso and pinning her down.

It's the last punch he gets in. He just has enough time to hear the whistle and whirr in the air behind him and turn around to see Jane's raised feet heading toward him. Her soles smack him under the chin and twist him around fully so he's now splayed on his back with his backside squashed into Simone's face. Simone wriggles out and slaps him in the face.

"You're making a habit of that with Bing's guards," Jane says, raising her eyebrows. "Pass me the cable ties, Simone. They are in the bag," she adds, before removing the colorful wrap from Simone's head and gagging him.

Even though he is out cold, Jane can feel the man's body jerk unconsciously as she pulls the ties tight around his wrists. She feels strong and angry. She's ready for a fight now. She hates Bing and all these people who back him. She tightens the ties a little more, and is surprised at the pleasure her strength gives her.

"Let's go. There will be more of them. We can be sure of that," Jane says, relishing the thought of it.

One floor down, she hears a guard patrolling the fire exit. Simone raises a finger to indicate that she should hold her ground, but Jane is in no mood to wait and taps on the door immediately. The footsteps stop. Jane taps again. The door swings open and the doorway is filled with a man so huge that even Jane is shocked. He growls something unintelligible and steps forward. Jane attacks in haste and is brushed away by the man's slap before skidding across the ground.

"Timing is everything in attack, Jane. You know that. You just let your anger and overconfidence take over."

Jane stumbles to her feet, staggering backwards and trying to find time to compose herself but soon finds herself with her back to a cold wall. She has nowhere to go. The giant approaches her, seemingly unaware Simone is to his right. When he is upon Jane, she pushes two fingers into the depression under his Adam's apple and pushes hard. The man gurgles for breath but Jane keeps pushing as hard she can, walking forward for extra leverage. Simone senses her opportunity and leaps on the guard, scratching his face with her false nails. Jane is now firing in a series of open palm blows and despite his attempts to fight back, Jane's clever maneuver with her fingers to his throat has left his lungs empty. His resistance ends and he stands frozen as the blows continue to rain into his neck and face. Then his bulk starts to topple, almost in slow motion at first, before he hits the concrete floor with a shudder.

"Nice trick. Where did you learn that?" Simone asks as she gets to work with the cable ties.

215

"Krav Maga. If it's good enough for the Israeli Defense Force, it's good enough for me."

"Good Jane. Overcoming an opponent is not just about strength. Never forget that."

They know from Y_RAM's plans that they are on the service area, full of ducts and wiring. It's one more floor down to Bing's office. They exit on the twelfth floor. The offices are still heavily lit but are empty apart from the humming of vacuum cleaners and the distant sound of a cleaner singing badly.

"Wait. There is probably a guard outside his office," Jane says. "You go. I'm pretty sure you can distract him with your looks," Jane teases. "And get that stun lipstick out of your bag. You're going to have to use it."

She's right about the guard. Simone sashays up to him sailing, the stun lipstick gripped tightly in her right hand. He straightens as she approaches, admiring Simone's well-dressed slim body.

"Can I help you, ma'am?"

"I have a delivery for Mr. Bing," she says, eyeing the black case she is carrying.

"Nobody tell me nothing," he replies, and Simone immediately latches onto his Jamaican accent.

"Hey! A bredda from mi home!" Simone exclaims, feigning a broad, toothy smile as she switches into Jamaican Patois with ease.

"Hey! A sista from Jamaica," the man replies, his shoulders noticeably dropping in a release of aggression. "Yu have dun well fi yuhsself!"

"I'm a May Pen gyal just trying fi get mi funds."

The man roars with laughter at the mention of the town outside Kingston where his grandmother is from. As he tips back his head, mouth wide open in his guttural laugh, Simone senses

216

her chance and rams the stun lipstick hard into his chest. He convulses and she just has the chance to see the shock in his eyes as his falls and slides down the oak door that is the entrance Bing's office.

It's locked as expected and there is complex-looking keypad on the wall. Simone has never seen one like it before. Jane runs down the corridor, smiling at the sight of the man on the floor.

"I heard the noise. Glad it worked!" Jane exclaims as Simone looks at what she has done to the man while holding up the lipstick in triumph.

"The door's locked. Y_RAM, can you get this door open?" Jane asks, pointing her watch toward the keypad.

A red light on her watch flashes as it darts across the numbers and letters on the sensor pad. After a few seconds, they are moving so quickly that to Jane's eyes, the keypad is just a haze of red. The door whirrs smoothly and clicks open.

"What? No slap in the face this time?" Jane jokes as they step into the office.

The office is lit, but unlike the Blackpool Illuminations of the corridors, there is no LED lighting. Bing's office is more like a gentleman's club from a bygone age than an office, with soft lighting from lamps and recessed down lights coming down from mahogany panels. Simone quickly identifies the burgundy Chesterfield couch and the artwork of Ouroboros.

Ouroboros

Also spelt uroborus. A circular symbol of a snake (sometimes called a dragon or serpent) eating its own tail. Its perfect circle identifies the eternal cycle of life, death, and rebirth, while the shedding of the snake's skin represents the transmigration of souls, particularly its reincarnation. Ouroboros symbolizes eternity, especially in Ancient Egyptian, Greek, and Hermetic philosophy. The symbol was later adopted by Christian and Jewish sects which emphasized personal spiritual knowledge above their traditional beliefs, and in alchemist circles.

Jane slides back the artwork and strokes the front of the safe respectfully, as if it is an honor to meet such a challenger. Her magic bag has the tool she needs: a cordless magnetic drill press.

"What are you doing?" the ever-inquisitive Simone asks.

"Every lock has a weak point. I'm using it to get into the safe."

"How do you know where the weak point is?"

"The manufacturers release that information for locksmiths."

"That's handy."

"It is if you can remember the weak points of all the safes out there. I know a fair few and I know this one."

Simone looks around nervously as Jane works away with the drill, but she soon has it open. Jane grabs some files and a small box of memory sticks then flicks through the papers.

"It's Bing's schedule and more. These memory sticks might have information too. And those watches, Simone. Take them and put them in a bag. We have to make them think this is a robbery. Photograph the schedule and put it back," Jane instructs.

As Simone is stuffing the bag with watches and Krugerrands, they hear a noise at the door. Jane slides back the artwork and pulls Simone down behind the Chesterfield, raising her finger to her lips. The door swings open and the room is suddenly lit up fully.

"Hello, who's there?" a heavily accented Swedish voice calls out.

Simone rolls her eyes and looks at Jane. It's Sven. She knows the voice only too well after hours of being beaten by him in the A.M. HQ.

She stands up from behind the couch and Sven smiles.

"Lovely to see you again, my beautiful," he drools.

Then Jane stands up.

"Haha. I'm Spartacus!" Sven exclaims in a booming laugh.

He removes the gun from his holster and places it on the coffee table.

"I won't be needing this."

Jane launches herself from the couch, but Sven has been stung by what happened at Bing's mansion in Wales and is ready. He grabs her under the arms as she nearly upon him and twists, then slams her onto her back with all his weight. Jane lets out a loud whistle of pain as the air is expelled from her body. Simone jumps on his back, clinging on and using her long nails again. He tosses her like a ragdoll, but she has given Jane just enough time to get away from his grip.

"You have to change your tactic, Jane. Remember what I said about anger. Use your opponent's own anger to bring him down."

Jane is up and circling around the room, almost like she is avoiding Sven.

"That's right, little girl. Run! You will not be so lucky this time."

She feels powerful inside, but knows there is another way to get him. As he approaches Bing's desk, she resorts to a childish sing-song voice, remembering how Simone's taunts had gotten to him in Bing's mansion.

You're fat,
You're ugly,
You got beat by a little girl.
You dumb,
You're thick...

Sven face reddens in anger and shame as Jane sings and he charges at her like a crazed bull surrounded by taunting clowns

219

in a ring. Jane bends down and grabs the base of Bing's ornate, ivory standard lamp beside his desk and swings it in a low, wide arc. What's left of the once impressive African elephant tusk delivers a blow as mighty as when it was still part of the great beast, whacking with a fierce crack into Sven's shin. Jane has no doubt the blow has splintered his bone from the cracking noise she hears as he lets out a blood-curdling scream.

But driven by pure anger and adrenaline, Sven is up again, ignoring his immense pain as he grabs Jane and charges across the room with her in his arms with all the power he can muster. He slams her into window and the glass shudders. Jane feels as if every bone in her body has been rattled as she hits the window, but she hangs on to Sven grimly, her arms under his biceps and hands clasped around the back of his neck. Jane's hold is restricting his ability to punch effectively but he counters by continually bashing Jane into the glass. But she can feel the energy slowly sapping from him. His adrenaline can only keep him going so long.

"Shoot him, Simone! Shoot him!"

Simone points the gun but the tussle between Sven and Jane is frenzied and she can't get a clear shot.

"Shoot!" Jane begs, desperately trying to keep her clasp tight as Sven fights desperately to shake her free.

Jane hears a loud crack behind her as the bullet hits the glass.

"Again. Now!

At that moment, she manages to twist Sven round so his back is pressed to the cracked glass and as the second bullet hits the glass just by his ear, she releases her grip and falls to the ground. The window shatters and with his weight on it, Sven is sucked out into the darkness. But the guard is still being driven by his animal instinct and one of his ogre-sized hands clasps the aluminum window casement as he falls. He's hanging on by his fingers.

"Give me your other hand," Jane screams.

Sven reaches up and clasps Jane's hand by fingers and she tries to pull him up. But Sven's thirst for revenge is overpowering his instinct for survival. As he pulls himself up, his hand holding the window casement grinds into a glass shard and pierces his palm. He lets out a cry as his grip is lost and he falls, with only the streets of London waiting for him.

"*Nooooo!*" Jane exclaims, as Simone approaches to catch the last sight of her tormenter falling to his death.

"We have to get out. Quick!" Jane yells.

But noises from the corridor make it clear it's not going to be easy. The exit will be teeming with guards.

"There are some cables hanging outside the building. They look close enough to reach. It's our only chance," Jane tells Simone as she climbs onto the casement and leaps without waiting for an answer.

Simone looks out to see Jane already hanging on the cables, her arms and legs wrapped firmly around it like an octopus. She's safe. Simone takes a deep breath and jumps. She grasps for a grip, her panic making her claw wildly. For a moment she thinks all is lost. Suddenly, a strong arm reaches out and the firm clasp of Jane's hand grabs her arm and soon she feels the cold comfort of the steel cable in her palms. They slide down the triple cable network, desperately hoping it continues to the ground floor. A few floors down they reach a small metal cradle.

"Window cleaners! Thank heavens for them! How's this thing work?" Jane asks without really wanting an answer, as she works out the controls.

The cradle clunks and swings slightly before grinding downwards.

Zing.

A sharp sound pieces the night air just as they are approaching the street level as a bullet ricochets off the side of the cable. The security guards have spotted them. But the light is still not good enough to offer them a clear sighting. Jane heads for cover by swinging her lithe body over the side of the cradle and grabbing hold of one of the cables below, so she's hidden from the guards' aim. Simone pauses and looks up as another bullet zings off the cradle. Closer this time. She needs no further prompting to scrabble around the cradle and join Jane under it.

"Those umbrellas below. Aim for them. They'll break our fall. They won't shoot there because there are too many people. It's only one floor. Me first."

Jane swings her hips to build momentum then flies through the air toward the restaurant below. She hits one of the large umbrellas full on and braces herself for the crash to follow, but it holds firm and instead she bounces back up like she's hit a trampoline then slides down the canvas, landing with a bump on the floor between two tables of bemused diners.

"Hello," she says, standing up gingerly and brushing down her dress.

Moments later Simone comes crashing down. There is no bounce this time, her extra weight crushing the canvas of the umbrella inwards, and she lands on the table below, which collapses as food, drink, cutlery, and plates shoot in all directions amid panicky screams.

Jane grabs the case, pulls Simone up, and they run off as fast as their battered bodies will allow. Simone is hobbling but soon they are safely lost in the throng of central London, desperately looking for a dark area to catch breath. Jane pulls out her pen and activates it to disable the CCTV cameras.

"There are too many of them around here. They've already seen us, but we can't let those cameras guys track us back to the house."

They are soon back at the Mews house. Isabel is already asleep, as per her regime. After swapping stories of their injuries, they burst into relieved laughter that they are OK.

Simone unpacks the case. Watches. Expensive watches. A Patek Philippe Henry Graves Supercomplication, a F.P. Journe x

Francis Ford Coppola FFC Blue, a Rolex Daytona Unicorn, and a Breguet & Fils, Paris. A handful of proof Krugerrands. A single British Britannia gold coin. And a block of five-hundred euro notes.

"I'll take these to the safe deposit box at Harrods tomorrow," Simone says.

Jane checks the information on the memory sticks. They are all encrypted, but Y_RAM quickly breaks their codes — basic financial reports. But there is one Y_RAM cannot solve. The memory stick is black with silver edges and has the symbol of a snake on it. Jane fingers it. It's different to all the others. Somehow impressive. Important. On it is an algorithm.

"Why can't you break the code on this one?" she asks.

"It's not complete," Y_RAM replies.

"There are bits of the algorithm missing, you mean?"

"Yes. This must be part of an algorithm. You need the rest of it before it will make any sense."

This has to be the key to something important. But what? Jane knows she has to find out more about what it is. She *will* avenge the death of her mummy and daddy. Bing *will* pay with his life.

"Y_RAM. Reply to that message from the Keyholder Order. I will meet them as requested."

Chapter 12

"Safe deposit box thirty-one," Simone says to the executive at the entrance to the Harrods Safe Deposit department after passing the watchful eye of two security guards.

The executive shuts the intricately etched glass door and theatrically looks around the otherwise empty room to emphasize that nobody is within earshot.

"Your password please, ma'am."

"Navckid Keyd."

"This way please, ma'am," the executive smiles as he leads Simone to the Victorian three-ton steel door protecting the strong room. "This will be locked behind you. Please ring the bell when you have finished."

Simone marvels at the rows of ornate wooden safe deposit boxes in the beautifully appointed room with the mahogany leather-inlaid desks topped with gold lamps for viewing items.

"Thirty-one. Wow!" Simone exclaims.

It's not like any safe deposit she has imagined; this is a huge vault big enough for her to stand upright in with comfort if was empty.

She inserts the key before twisting the brass handle and is surprised at how smoothly it opens despite its obvious weight. It's certainly not empty. She slides out a couple of drawers, dazzled by the whole experience and not knowing where to start her search. Simone quickly realizes the drawers inside the vault have been meticulously organized. In one there is jewelry, in another blocks of cash in different currencies, then gold ingots, coins, stacks of blank passports and identity cards. It's a treasure trove of wealth and intrigue. But there is one drawer that catches

Simone's attention in particular. There is just one item inside: a small red notebook, embossed with three interlinked rings and filled with names.

Use codes through Y_RAM + master code. Payment will be automatic.

Hamish McCleus (Private jets) 23g89?H8
Julie Ashworth (Private boat hire) 9!48HU6y
Abdul Sattar (Surveillance) 076£Ykha23
Andre van der Merwe (Handguns) kE99&7hYR
Jonathan Westwood (Armored vehicles) Ki6R*v062
Thomas Anderson (Forger) 29yTpH9%E
Haneul Bahk (Land arrangements west Asia) 9Y+56Fgj6T

"There are pages and pages of contacts, each with their own specialization and a password, Jane. It's everything we need," Simone says back at the Mews house. "But we need a master password as well. There was no sign of it."

"It's my head," Jane replies, smiling.

It's less than an hour on foot to the Tower of London. Despite the warmth of the day, Jane marches with her hood pulled up over her cap and keeps her head down as she walks along the river from the Mews house. Simone is following from a distance and every so often Jane stops, pretending to look at the view to check she is still in sight.

She arrives at the Tower at just past four, and hordes of zombie tourists are still milling around, seemingly being controlled by their smartphones which they all hold up high in front of them to get a clear shot of the old building over the heads of the other zombie tourists.

Entering across the middle drawbridge, Jane strolls along the path to the Tower of London's former parish church next to the Waterloo Block and the much-gawped at Crown Jewels.

Despite its immense history, there are only a handful of tourists looking for solace here; not surprising when there are tales in abundance of wealth, blood and gore so close to attract them. The Chapel Royal of St. Peter ad Vincula is small compared to its illustrious neighbor, but Jane is impressed nonetheless. She is immediately struck by a sense of calm as she looks around the well-proportioned Tudor design. There are a few people sitting praying in the simple wooden pews and one tourist taking photos, but in front of a board listing names in gold letters, there is a tall, bent figure, covered from head to toe in a black cloak. The figure pauses for a while, then walks to a pew beside a stone archway, far from the other visitors. Jane cautiously settles herself in the same row a few seats away and thinks how gracefully the figure moves as it walks, almost as if it is gliding. The figure immediately extends a bony hand, bloated slightly by dark varicose veins, and beckons her forward.

"Did you know that a church stood on this site as far back as the twelfth century?" a deep, husky, but clearly a woman's voice asks, but not pausing long enough to allow an answer. "Do you think that is a long time? Do you think people should live that long, Jane?"

"I'm not sure. It seems too long to me," Jane replies.

"Yes, you may be right. But it would be nice to live just *a little* bit longer, don't you think?"

The tall, hooded figure is bent over as if praying, partially hidden in the shadows of the archway, and does not look toward Jane while talking.

"How old are you?" Jane asks.

"One hundred and thirteen."

"What? I thought you were with Bing?"

The hooded figure cackles with laughter.

"Not exactly *with* Bing. But I think I know what you mean. So yes, I am in a program and I won't be old much longer. It is nearly time for me to be young again."

226

"So you've had previous lives?"

"A few times, Jane. A few times."

"What? When were first born then?"

"That was a *long* time ago, Jane. The world was a very different place then," the old woman laughs huskily.

"Bing and his people get cloned much younger. Why do you live to be so old if you can be young again?" Jane queries

"A.M. know the basic process, but they have not perfected it. We have been around for hundreds of years. We do things differently. We believe we should enjoy every life we get to the full — not rush to stay young all the time. Age has many advantages that youth does not."

Jane nods, trying to come to grips the enormity of what she is hearing.

"We've been following you with interest, Jane, so I know you will soon understand what I am telling you."

"Who is we?"

"We are the Keyholder Order, Jane. Anil Kapoor, whom you met, was working with us. It was him who told us you were special. Do you think it was a co-incidence that he was working with your father?"

"You knew my daddy?"

"Daddy? So sweet, my child. Oh no, we did not know him personally. We left that to Anil. He told us that your father was strong and clever. His mind was sharp, just like yours. And he told us that if you could have the transfusion, you would be *very* special. That is why we want to help you."

"Help me do what?"

"Get to Bing."

"Why would I want to do that?"

"To kill him."

Jane is stunned by the bluntness of the words and sits silently for a while, absorbing them. The hooded lady is motionless, waiting with patience for a reply.

"Why would you want to help me do that?" Jane asks after a long pause.

"We have tolerated Anno Methusala until now, but Bing's recent actions are risking everything we stand for. The experiments, the live organ trade. He's gone too far and it is a danger to us. We simply cannot risk being discovered."

The lady slowly turns her head toward Jane, but her facial features remain hidden in the darkness of its cover.

"Have you heard of Ouroboros?" she asks.

"Sort of. There was a picture of it in Bing's office."

"Yes, we assumed that break-in was you," the hooded figure cackles. "And you saw the same symbol on something else?"

"Yes, on a memory stick."

"That is the first part of an algorithm that will help you get to Bing," the hooded figure says, handing Jane an identical looking memory stick. "The second part of the algorithm is on here. You will find the third and final part in Bing's apartment in the Burj Khalifa in Dubai. Only when you have all three parts will you get the plans to Signature Island where he is hiding. He is well protected there. You need the plans."

"How do I know you aren't working with him and you aren't just leading me into a trap?"

"We could kill you or kidnap you now if wanted to," the hooded figure says as Jane notices two of worshippers stand up and show their physiques to be a lot bigger than they looked when they were bent over praying.

As the hooded figure stands up, she hands Jane a small piece of paper.

"Here are some names of people who can help you get the third part of the algorithm and kill Bing. You'll find their contact codes in Anil Kapoor's red book."

The hooded figure glides out as her security guards reach her pew, leaving Jane alone with her thoughts. She stares at the snake symbol on memory stick and strokes its silver edges to distract

228

her thoughts. She is the only one left in the chapel and her heart is beating so fast she is sure she can hear it.

"To kill him."

The words race through her mind.

"They are just words, Jane. You need to mentally adjust your mind now. Get it ready for action."

As Jane is exiting the Tower, she sees soldiers from the Honorable Artillery standing in line on the Wharf beside four large guns pointing out across the Thames. It is just a rehearsal.

"The real thing will come soon enough," she says.

Encoded message to Keyholder Order

Contact successfully made with JB…

Part two of algorithm passed to JB to assist in assassination of the danger to the Order…

Location Signature Island…

A dark blue Bentley Mulsanne pulls up on Tower Hill and a chauffeur leaps out. The woman in the dark hood slides into the car, stoically refusing assistance from her driver. Only once she is alone in the third-story town house overlooking Regents Park does she remove the cloak.

She stares at herself in the mirror. Her skin is paper thin and blotchy, and her almost translucent ears point up to patches of wispy gray hair. She strokes her face, grimacing at the hideousness of it, but buoyed by the knowledge that it will only be a few more years before she is young again.

The woman sits down and strokes her blue silk dress.

"How nice it will be to have skin that feels like this again," she says, smiling.

Simone is pacing about under Tower Bridge by The Tower Hotel. She has heard nothing from Jane for an hour and is nervous. She twists the heart hanging from her neck and listens for Jane's response. Nothing. She stares at the piles of empty cardboard boxes and wheelie bins at the back of Tesco Express and the stark entrance to a car park. It's a far cry from the grandeur of the nineteenth century bridge nearby.

"All right?" Jane asks casually as Simone paces past the same bin for the umpteenth time.

"What happened? What did they say? Are you OK? I was worried. I thought you'd been kidnapped," Simone blurts out breathlessly.

"I'm fine. I just needed a bit of time alone to think things through," Jane says as they walk past the hotel's brassiere and onto the wooden decking toward St. Katherine's Dock Marina. "I'll tell you everything as we walk. I'm still not sure if we should trust them or not," Jane says.

"Me neither. I don't like it," Simone says as they lean on the white railings overlooking some moorings for the river boats.

"But she knew about the algorithm. How would she know about that? She also knew about Anil Kapoor's red book that is found in the security box. She gave me these names. Look!" Jane exclaims, holding up the piece of paper.

Names of Contacts

Kavita Dev (Communications and surveillance)
Euan Leybrind (Sniper)
Annette Strang (Pilot)
Amanika Machava (Explosives)

"It just seems too simple, Jane. I'm not comfortable with it."

"OK. We'll see what shows up with this part of the algorithm. Then we can decide. Come on, let's walk east. It'll give us time to think. I've had enough of antiseptic central London for a while.

230

"It's time to make your move Jane. Now is the time."

"Y_RAM, please contact these people. I need to speak to them. The master code is H0+ey*J8u&7d9e. Simone will give you their individual codes. You have them from the book in the safe deposit box, right, Simone?" Jane checks.

"Yes, I have them. But are you sure? We haven't decided if we can trust that group yet. We don't even have a plan yet."

"I do," Jane says. "I need to work on it. I'll be on the rooftop if you need me."

"Please give the codes for the people in the algorithm," Y_RAM asks Simone.

"Not yet, I need to check something first," Simone says.

She is not happy. Jane is charging into this confidently but Simone is still not sure.

Y_RAM s**earch results…** Count St. Germain
    …Surface web post and mentions: 814,343…

Theosophist, adventurer, alchemist, spiritual master in ancient wisdoms (1710-1784). *The Great Secret Count St. Germain* by Raymond Bernard claims the Count was Francis Bacon (1561-1626) by birth and authored plays attributed to Shakespeare. It claims that clues were left in the plays using Bacon's cipher. Theosophists to this day continue to claim that the Count is still alive and that they have met him.

Y_RAM **search results…** Vampires
    …Surface web post and mentions: 2,753,886…

In folklore, a vampire is an undead being that feeds on the living (usually their blood). Vampires have existed in folklore for thousands of years, with depictions of creatures drinking blood from humans found on pieces of excavated Persian pottery. There are written records of the term in 1718 when the invading Austrians noted that local people were "exhuming and killing vampires" in Serbia and Romania. Unlike the pale depictions in modern films, vampires in legend were ruddy faced and bloated — physical traits caused by the drinking of blood. In legend, vampires can only be identified by a virgin boy riding a virgin stallion through a graveyard. The stallion will rise up at the grave if it passes a vampire.

Y_RAM s**earch results...** Human sacrifice
...Surface web post and mentions: 1,856,904...

Ritualistic kills, often as offerings to gods, demons, ancestors, or a living ruler. The sacrifices were believed to offer protection against bad fortune or to pacify the gods/demons. They were also carried out for prosperity, to bring fortune in warfare, or to boost fertility. They were practiced across the world in the prehistoric era and, although sacrifices are now viewed as barbaric and are outlawed, they are still believed to continue in secret among certain groups such as cults, Satanists, extremist groups, and remote communities cut off from civilization.

Y_RAM s**earch results...** Cannibalism
...Surface web post and mentions: 987,774...

Eating flesh or organs of other humans. In many cases, the person eating the flesh believed they would take on the strength and power of the person they are eating, so it was especially prevalent before or during battles. Eating another person's heart, liver, or other organs was also carried out as an act of vengeance on the conquered after war. Right up to the nineteenth century, cannibalism was also used in Europe for medical purposes, with people believing that it would ward off diseases and keep them healthy. In some parts of the world, people ate their own dead relatives as part of the grieving process.

"Simone! What's going on? Y_RAM says we have not contacted

these people yet," Jane yells.

"We are not ready, Jane. There's something too easy about this whole thing. I'm not comfortable with this at all. We don't even have a plan," Simone protests.

"*I* have a plan. Meet me on the rooftop in a couple of hours. Just give Y_RAM those codes. We don't have time to waste."

Jane opens out a map, spreads it on the large table and smooths down the folds. She runs her finger down the Bay of Biscay, through the Strait of Gibraltar, the Mediterranean to Port Said and the narrow Suez Canal. Once through, the journey will take them to the Red Sea, opening up into the Gulf of Aden and round to the Persian Gulf. She punches her finger on the tiny dot that is Signature Island off the coast of the small state of Abu Yash.

"This is where I will get you, Bing. This is where you will die."

Jane retraces the route when Simone appears, looking sheepish and reporting that Y_RAM has the codes needed.

"We pick up someone here," she says rapping her finger on the word 'Gibraltar'. "And someone else here," pointing to what looks to Simone a deserted part of the North African coast. "A diver and someone who can deal with some friends we might need."

"Do you want me to contact them?" Simone asks, despite her continuing reservations.

"I've done it already. I've spoken to both of them," Jane replies, leaving Simone in no doubt that this plan is going ahead. "I need you to organize a yacht through the boat people from Kapoor's book. Something rich tourists would use but not the flashiest thing they have. We won't be inconspicuous but we don't want to stand out too much."

Jane hands Simone a scrap of paper.

"We need passports in these names. Can you find out how quickly the forger can have them ready?"

"Which one am I?" Simone asks, eyeing the names written on the paper.

"You won't need one. I want you here coordinating everything with Y_RAM. You'll be in constant contact with us the whole way."

Simone nods and heads off to the tech room.

"Mr. Bing. So nice to see you again."

Sheik Ahmad greets Bing warmly as the tech giant enters the sumptuous marble-lined entrance hall to his palace. Bing eyes a large, solid gold carving of a phoenix rising from the ashes.

The sheik has dark skin and his chubby face makes his deep brown eyes appear more sunken than they actually are, making it impossible for people meeting him to get any clues as to what he is thinking. His robe clings tightly to his huge belly which he has the habit of stroking, particularly after he makes what he thinks is a clever comment. He has ruled Abu Yash with an iron fist, accepting no criticism and putting down dissent without mercy in the eighteen years since he took over as leader from his father.

"You like the phoenix? Poignant, don't you think? A being that lives for five hundred years then is reborn to live its life again. Just as we are planning. But first we need the flames. We now need to burn down what has already been built. Is everything going to plan?"

"There is always resistance to change at A.M. naturally. But I have that in control. David may think he is charge now, but there is much he does not know. They will always need me. And yourself, of course, your Excellency."

The two men settle down on high-backed chairs in a cavernous reception room, cooling air drifting in from the beautifully carved multifoil archways as a string of immaculately dressed servants bring in silver trays laden with tea, juices, fresh and dried fruits.

Bing eyes the servants as they enter, all men dressed head-to-toe in white, apart from their black agals perched on top of their heads, the circular cord keeping their keffiyehs — the traditional Arabian headdress — in place. They bow as they place the food and drink on the table and again as they depart the room.

"You must try the dates, Mr. Bing. I promise you they will be nothing like you have ever tasted before. We grow them in our gardens here," Ahmad says. "Now, tell me about the Bedouin. Do they make good subject for our experiments? We have many of them if you need more. I will no longer tolerate the insurgents from the desert. They are people we need cleansed from the earth of Abu Yash. But let us use them first."

"They are excellent. Strong and hardy characters. They are very interesting because their bodies have had to adapt to survive in that harsh desert environment they call home. In some ways it's a surprise they can live at all, let alone enjoy long lives," Bing says. "They are bit headstrong, but we have ways to make them compliant for our experiments." Bing laughs, as if he is enjoying the thought of it. "But I understand the families of those taken to the island were not happy and there has been some trouble?" he adds.

"A little trouble. Unfortunately, the families do not understand that their sons and daughters are doing a great service for mankind. A small loss for them to pay. An honor that they have been selected in fact. But we have quashed the trouble and those families who refused to accept the honor are now guests of the state."

"Guests?" Bing queries.

"Oh yes, Mr. Bing. Did you notice a blue five-star hotel as you traveled to my humble palace today?"

"I did," Bing nods.

"The families are being hosted at that hotel. We ask them to remain in their rooms, for their own safety of course. Our doctors are able to check the bloodlines of all the families for the everlasting greatness of Abu Yash. We will continue to eliminate those who are not ancestors of the mighty Parthians. Abu Yash must remain pure and free of *ajnabis*."

"*Ajnabis*?" Bing queries.

"How do you say? Strangers, aliens. Those people do not belong in Abu Yash and I will rid our country of them until my dying breath."

Chapter 13

The triple-level-deck motor cruiser pulls out of Southampton as Kavita Dev eases forward on the lever.

"I'm still worried this will stand out. I told Simone to get something that wouldn't stand out," Jane says, not taking her eyes off the water.

"A 140-footer won't look anything special once we are in St. Tropez and Dubai. There are plenty of more impressive yachts out there," Kavita replies.

Kavita and Amanika Machava are dressed as captain and first officer respectively. Euan Leybrind and Annette Strang are playing the roles of Jane's parents. The three of them are a wealthy family off for a holiday at sea. That's the story, at least. In reality, all of them are former special operatives with extensive knowledge of the water and will crew the boat themselves. It's too risky to use the crew supplied by the charter company.

"It's fast and big enough for what we want. Not bad for two-hundred thousand dollars a week!" Kavita smiles.

Jane has had a few days to finetune her plans with Simone as she waited for the team to arrive; Kavita from India, Amanika from Mozambique, and Euan from South Africa. Annette only had the short journey from West Sussex. They have had two intense planning meetings before setting off but have a few weeks to iron out any problems. Kavita is meticulous with her planning and has insisted they not only have a plan B, but also a plan C and D for every step of the operation.

"Operation Hancock underway. Travel well everyone," Simone says from the tech room in the Mews house.

"Received with thanks, HQ. Please confirm all systems are

fully operational," Kavita says.

"Location confirmed. Satellite images confirmed. On-board cameras confirmed. All aural connections confirmed."

The first three days are easy and calm as they cruise through the English Channel and Bay of Biscay toward the marina in Cascais, near Lisbon. The motor yacht has a range of three-thousand nautical miles, but they will stop off every so often to back up their rich-family-on-holiday story.

The early days are spent in a haze of planning, re-planning and training, and the team has little interest in enjoying the luxury of the yacht with its stylish curved bar and sundeck Jacuzzi. Jane spends most of her time with sniper Euan. The first day is one of frustration.

"This is something for the open sea. We can't practice with guns off the coast of North Africa or in the Red Sea," Euan says as he grabs a yellow buoy and lets it out onto the water on a thin line of polypropylene rope. He secures the rope with the buoy at fifty yards.

The sniper is a tall man, well-tanned, with long, sinewy limbs. He hardly speaks, but when he does the breathy-voiced, slow pronunciation of his words immediately displays his South African roots. He is slow to smile but has an inner calmness that easily radiates out to others. He spent twenty years in the South African Special Forces, which he refers to simply as the Recces.

"OK. Let's see what we are starting with," he says.

Crack!

Jane watches, somewhat embarrassed as she sees the water explode upwards as the bullet hits it a few yards wide and well behind the intended target.

"Again," Euan says calmly.

Crack!

The water explodes nowhere near the buoy again.

"Again. Again," Euan says, not showing an ounce of emotion.

After five shots he kneels down and moves Jane's position,

one limb as a time.

"Close your eyes and feel it. This position will work for you. When you are ready hold your breath for three seconds and try again."

It misses, but it's closer.

"That's enough for today," Euan says, clasping his rifle in his right hand.

"I can get it. I can get it!" Jane cries.

"I know you can. Tomorrow. I will playback the video and make a few adjustments tomorrow."

Jane is furious. Furious at her failure and furious that she has to wait to get it right. She is not used to failure.

"Failure can use you or you can use failure, Jane. Learn to use it."

The next day, Jane settles into position. Euan makes only one small adjustment to her right knee.

"Excellent, Jane. You have excellent muscle memory."

Crack!

The bullet grazes the yellow buoy.

"Not bad. If that was a head, you'd have grazed the ear. Again."

Crack! Jane smiles as she hits the buoy full on. Jane's ability to learn quickly impresses Euan and he can't avoid a smile of satisfaction.

"Good. But remember, you only get one shot at a target. People don't hang around in the same position like a buoy when you graze them with the first shot."

Euan takes the gun from Jane and starts letting out the rope until Jane can barely see it without binoculars. He settles into position and Jane notes the small adjustments he makes to his position. He holds his breath and is still. Stone still, as if dead. One second, two, three, four, five, six, seven, eight, nine… At ten seconds, Jane hears the crack of the sniper's shot.

"You missed it!" Jane exclaims.

"You think?" he replies, standing up and reeling in the rope.

The buoy is no longer attached as the end of the rope is yanked aboard. Aiming at the fixing, he has pierced the rope clean through.

"Don't worry Jane. It takes years of practice and thousands of shots to get that accurate. From what I've seen, you will get there quicker than most. There's something about you; I've never seen anyone absorb information and learn so fast."

Transcript of encrypted satellite radio call between Jane Banks and Simone Grant
16th August

Simone: Are you ready, Jane? We can't afford any mistakes with our cover story when you meet people.

Jane: Yes, I'm ready. Simone, we've been through this a dozen times already.

Simone: Should be easy then.

Jane: My name is Jane Kuter. My father is Euan, originally from Johannesburg in South Africa. My mother is Annette from Sussex. Together they run a stud farm, which we own. My horse is called Jingles, a brown, three-year-old Haflinger. I go to school at Hurstpierpoint College. We are on an extended holiday on the yacht. I don't avoid answering questions but always move the subject on by asking them a question about themselves.

Simone: Excellent. Remember, most people are more interested in themselves. Let them talk.

Encoded message to Keyholder Order
16th August

JB has arrived in Portugal en route to destination... Assassination target has returned to Signature Island following visit to Sheik Ahmad...

Kavita Dev has an elegant, elongated face that makes her look like royalty and a sparkling smile that is infectious. Originally from a wealthy Sikh family in Delhi, she is a self-taught surveillance expert and was encouraged by a mother determined she would not be overshadowed by her three older brothers. Aged eleven she installed the family's home protection system much to the surprise of her father and at eighteen she was recruited into the Research and Analysis Wing — India's external intelligence agency. For large parts of the trip Kavita has been holed away downstairs talking to Simone as they try to gather information on Bing's island and its surrounds.

Kavita folds down the creases in map on the table, more out of habit than need and points to Gibraltar.

"Next stop. We should be there the day after tomorrow. Greg will meet us at the Queensway Quay at noon."

Greg Thompson is a much-traveled diver, having worked on oil rigs in the North Sea, Persian Gulf, Kara Sea off Siberia, and Gulf of Mexico, frequently punctuated by what he calls working holidays in places like the Bahamas and Bermuda when he hits the booze. He spent five years in the SBS, followed by the same time in a military prison after his court martial. Originally from Cornwall, he tells everyone he has spent more of his life in the water than he has on land. His mood swings, often quickly, from being a jovial, friendly uncle to a grumpy know-it-all grandad.

He's waiting as the motor yacht pulls into the quay at quarter to midday and after the round of greetings, some of the team head off to the nearby Morrisons for supplies. Jane stays on the yacht to get Greg up to speed with their plans. He will lead the attack on Signature Island.

The nine-day journey through the Mediterranean would be an idyllic holiday in a motor yacht if it were not the endless planning meetings and training sessions. Jane is pleased to see that Kavita was right — there are much more impressive yachts out there. She uses her time poring over maps, liaising with Simone, tapping into Y_RAM's seemingly unlimited library of information, and learning the skills of her team.

"There is no one better to learn from than someone who has dedicated their life to becoming an expert in their field."

Jane is the always first one up in the morning, raising a smile from whoever is on watch. She sets out her mat on the sundeck and stretches her sleepy muscles into action. Once she feels ready, she is twisting and turning, leaping and thrusting the *iklwa* she took from St. Edith's. She has found perfect balance with the African stabbing spear; it feels an extension of her body now. With every thrust she thinks of Bing, feeling it enter his body as it pieces his skin. She is determined to be mentally prepared when the moment comes again. This time she *has* to succeed.

A stop-off in Sicily provides the ideal time for Jane to get a crash-course in diving from Greg. Greg has already shut down Jane's original plan for her to dive to Signature Island with him. He prefers to work alone and does not have the time to get her diving skills up to the level required for her to get to the island undetected, he says. Jane accepts his word reluctantly. She will follow in a small boat once he has set up the explosives to distract the security guards for the boat's landing.

But not surprisingly, given that she has inherited her father's love of explosives, Jane spends most of the journey with Amanika. Although now in her mid-thirties, her slim figure and perfect, almost glossy skin, coupled with her endless laughter make her appear much younger. Growing up in Tete region of Mozambique, which borders Zimbabwe, Zambia, and Malawi, her every move as a child was dictated by explosives. By the time the Mozambique Civil War had ended in 1992, the country had become one of the most heavily mined in the world. Tete was littered with land mines, most scattered indiscriminately, and there were no records of where they were. She quickly had to learn which areas were safe to play in and which were no-go areas. Fields with signs displaying skulls and crossbones were a common sight; many of her neighbors had been killed and the large number of them without limbs provided a constant reminder of the danger all around her.

Her mother fussed endlessly, living in permanent fear for her child. But her father was fearless. He worked for HALO, a Scottish NGO dedicated to clearing the land mines and it was a path she followed. She needed no training — her father had taught her everything. Jane feels close to Amanika instantly and they swap stories about their fathers and explosives.

"The best way to understand an explosive is to defuse one knowing it can blow you sky high at any moment," Amanika says.

Jane thinks about the early childish exploding bags her dad had made and feels guilty at how she had squealed with delight in her well-tended London garden as if these were toys. To Amanika, explosives were anything but.

They prepare the devices they will use on the island: mini barrel bombs Annette will drop from her microlight, smoke bombs for cover and distraction, timed devices that will release rockets, and general-purpose bombs for blasting open doors.

"You should make this one yourself," Amanika says, handing Jane a metal vial. "Pour it three quarters full of the clear liquid then top it up with this green liquid."

Jane watches as the mixture fizzes and lets off a bad-smelling smoke before screwing on the lid, which has a one-way

243

valve inserted into it.

"This is my back-up plan for Bing. It is safe for now. I will only prime it through the valve when I get to the island. Then it will let off one hell of a bang! If you don't get him earlier, of course," the Mozambican says matter-of-factly.

At the southern coast of Greece, just before the Gulf of Kalamata, the team turn the yacht south toward the Libya. Europe is behind them now. Africa and the Middle East awaits. Dark falls as they make their way toward a deserted part of the coast some miles to the east and turn off the lights apart from the mast light. After twenty minutes, they spot the signal from the land. Kavita signals back and waits for the confirmation signal. Jane joins her, Annette and Amanika in lowering the inflatable tender and climbing in, leaving Euan and Greg on the yacht.

"Guns ready, girls," Amanika says.

Another signal comes as the boat approaches the scrub-covered beach. Annette turns off the engine and they drift in, guns at the ready.

"Lovely night! Any chance of a lift?" the figure, wrapped up from head-to-toe, jokes in a thick Geordie accent.

Sam Beade is the last part of Jane's jigsaw — an unconventional warfare expert who hires out her skills to the highest bidder — governments and companies who want to assist insurgents in foreign lands for their own ends. She peels off her headscarf and Jane sees a face weather-beaten, dirty, sand blasted, and deeply tanned. But beneath all the grime, she sees a pretty face, punctuated by a small pug nose and framed by a blonde, albeit messy, bob.

"The Army told me a blonde woman could never make it in UW in Africa and the Middle East. I wear this bloody headdress the whole time anyway. Anyway, sod them; I make way more than they would pay me," Sam says.

The other women laugh knowingly, bound together by the prejudice and hurdles they have had to face. Jane smiles at the

244

scene of them enjoying themselves, happy and contented despite the dangers they face daily. She feels safe and secure with them, like she belongs.

Encoded message to Keyholder Order
25th August

Invitation to World Economic Forum in January next year...
Main location: Davos...
Regional conferences: Latin America, Africa, East Asia, India...
Davos attendees: CB1643 and GS1674...
Latin America attendees: TG1725 and PK1833...
Africa attendee: MH1824...
East Asia attendee: KD1782...
India attendees: JR1698...
Details of secure call for this year's aims to follow...

Small children run around the Bedouin camp, screaming as they play, happy to enjoy the cool of the night after yet another day of relentless blazing sun. The leaders of all the Bedouin tribes are meeting, so the night air is filled with sounds of raucous laughter as old friends greet other, exchange stories, and embellish adventures of the past as all people are inclined to do. A row of skinned goats is sizzling away as they are turned on crackling open fires, while a group of women is at work cooking huge pots of rice and vegetables. People drift by a large red mat away from the fire, where there is a giant pile of dates and jugs of camel and goat milk. A group of men sit at the edge of the light given out by the fires, the younger men puffing on cigarettes while the older men pass around shishas contentedly. It is rare for the children to see so much food and they are excited by the feast being prepared.

The Bedouins have been pushed to the outer extremity of Abu Yash, not wanted in their homeland and not welcome by neighboring countries. They are used to being pushed from place to place and surviving in the harshest of conditions. They are used to not being wanted.

A tall, young woman signals to the children with a wave of the hand. She is dressed in a light blue cotton thawb, the robe reaching down to her ankles and brushing her camel-hide sandals, and wears a blue keffiyeh on her head, which remains unrolled to signal she is unmarried. Not that she has not had offers. Her light skin, pretty looks and determined nature make her worth fifty camels, her father jokes, but he knows his single-minded daughter will never accept an approach. Every one of her fingers is ringed, and they glint briefly when the moonlight catches them.

Camels grunt loudly as the children settle down on the sand, and they start mimicking the sound of the beasts, poking each other as they take it in turns to let out a grunt. Fatima Allasad Mehedi abu-nabia smiles broadly, her thin nose and dark eyebrows obscured by the smoke of the cigarette in her mouth. Although only twenty-four, she has led the Bedouin insurgents for nearly two years since her brother was killed by Sheik Ahmad's security forces. She is one of the few Bedouins still living in the desert to have been to university; she spent three years living in Al Tinamah, the capital of Abu Yash, a glittering city that is a far cry from the conditions around her. But she is happier here. These are her people.

"Children, settle down. Tonight, I tell you the story of our ancestors. The people who brought us to this land two hundred and fifty years ago. They lived across the Great Sea, herding their goats and camels, and sometimes growing crops when they could find land to sustain them. Life was peaceful and happy, but then outsiders arrived and they were pushed away. They built a new life but again they were pushed away by outsiders. This happened again and again until the leader Abdul Karim Zaki abu-nabia decided they had to cross the Great Sea to a new land.

"Some of his men had skills in fishing, but none had crossed the Great Sea. But Abdul Karim knew he had no choice. They packed all their belongings: tents, pots, goats, and camels on the boats for the journey. The weather was good when they left but once at sea, a storm appeared. Abdul Karim was determined and would not turn back. The storm whipped up into a wild frenzy around the boats like it was testing him. One of the ships was lost to the water and we pray for those people lost to this day. The people were screaming; they thought all was lost. But just when it seemed as if the end was coming for our ancestors, Abdul Karim spotted some tall trees poking up through the waves. It was land.

"He guided the boats to safety and our ancestors took shelter in a cove. When the storm had passed, they found water, regained their strength and fixed the boats. We know that island today as Intasala. The next day, the sea was calmed by God and the boats sailed to the New Land where we live today.

"For many years, when a young boy came of age, he had to travel by boat to this sacred island to give thanks to Abdul Karim. Only then would he become a man. For eighteen years now, no journeys have been possible because the island was given to an outsider. *An outsider!* Our boys still wait to become men. But one day, we will get back the island and give thanks to the great Abdul Karim and our brave ancestors."

The children all clap and cheer at Fatima's story. They have heard it many times but they never tire of it. Parents and elders look on, smiling with pride.

"Children, now get your food and goat milk and then to bed," Fatima says as the children jump up and run toward the feast excitedly.

When they have all been fed and put to bed, the leaders of all the Bedouin tribes gather around Fatima.

"As we know, the outsiders and Sheik Ahmad have been taking our people to the island. But our spies have now reported news of missing children, fires burning, and screams — even

247

cannibalism."

There are angry shouts from the crowd.

"Our spies have seen these things with their own eyes and I have seen images of this terrible things. Our people are being used for experiments too horrible to imagine. Worse than anything Sheik Ahmad has even done. Not even the great Abdul Karim and our ancestors faced such persecution. Now is the time for us to act."

"What can we do? We have been fighting Sheik Ahmad for years and all we find is death. There is not a family who has not lost a son, daughter, brother or sister. The white sand is filled with our blood," a man shouts.

"If we do not act now, there be not one of us left. Sheik Ahmad has already said he will to purge Abu Yash of our people. We fight or we die. And we start with our sacred island," Fatima says to cheers.

"In a few days a friend — someone I have been working with — will arrive with weapons. Boats are arranged and we will attack the outsiders and free our people. This is just the start. Sheik Ahmad must fall. Go back to your camps and gather your fighters. We meet back here in eleven days."

Port Said is a bustling port, with boats of all sizes. Minarets stand tall across the skyline, jostling for attention with the giant cranes that service the boats. None are more symbolic or impressive than the two minarets of the Port Fouad mosque, which stand like guards at the entrance to the Suez Canal.

The team has been stuck in Port Said for two days as they complete paperwork with the Small Craft Department at the Canal Authority for the canal crossing. Jane works out her frustration by exercising endlessly. The others leave her alone as she leaps and jumps across the sundeck until she is exhausted. Jane feels her strength rising during this time. She feels powerful through her strength and can sense a new anger bubbling inside her. Revenge is no longer what she wants. She *needs* it.

Early on the morning of the fourth day the department calls and they are told to collect the pilot at Port Fouad Yacht Club, complete the immigration formalities and begin their journey.

The waterway, which passes from the Mediterranean Sea to the Rea Sea, is one hundred and twenty miles long and the journey will take nearly two days. It feels as if they are barely moving at the reduced speed enforced in the canal, with little more than empty land and odd scrubby bush to look at. The pilot guides them to Ismailia, where they stay overnight; no small ships are allowed to travel through the canal at night.

The next morning, a new pilot boards the yacht and guides them to the exit at the Port of Suez, passing for hour upon hour through yet more stark and desolate land that has been scorched to a deep golden brown. Once at Suez, Jane feels as if they have been transported through a magic gateway: one day they were in waters shared by southern Europe and North Africa and a couple of days later they are in the Middle East's Red Sea.

At their cruising speed of fourteen knots, it is still nine days to Dubai. They drop off Sam on a deserted part of Arabian Peninsula coastline. She will make her way across land to the narrow strip that is the state of Abu Yash where she will meet the Bedouin insurgents, picking up a shipment of weapons along the way.

"Take these," Kavita tells Sam, handing her two small, gold earrings as she gets ready to leave them. "They've got tracking devices in them. It will help me co-ordinate things when we can't talk."

Jane feels sad as they wave goodbye to Sam, who is again wrapped from head to toe, with just her eyes peeping out to the world. Jane has felt strong and happy surrounded by the women mercenaries. The bonding between them in the inflatable tender had continued unabated in the days that followed on the yacht. Jane runs her left hand up her right arm and feels the strength of her muscles, now browned and salt-stained by days at sea. Her muscles feel strong. Her mind feels strong. But deep inside her, there is a strength she has not felt before. It is a strength that will get her what she wants.

Although incidents of hijackings from Somali pirates have dwindled since international patrols have increased in recent years, the team proceed with extra vigilance through the Gulf of Aden and around the Arabian Peninsula to the Gulf of Oman. Now for Dubai to get the third part of the algorithm — the key to the plans for the island. Without it, they'll be attacking Bing blind.

"All ready for your explosions, Amanika?" Kavita asks as the Mozambican bursts into her characteristic laugh.

"The firework display is booked, if that's what you mean. I'll be there to co-ordinate with the restaurant so they let them off on your signal while I'm having dinner with my darling husband for our anniversary," Amanika replies sarcastically. "Greg. I hope you've got a clean shirt if you are my husband for the night," she adds.

"Tonight and tonight only," Greg snaps back angrily.

"Grow up, Greg. It's an important distraction as Jane and Annette are coming down that ridiculously high building to get into Bing's apartment. And at least you'll be enjoying dinner while the rest of us are working," Kavita chastises Greg.

"All good for your position, Euan?" Kavita says while ticking off the next item on her list.

"Scouted, checked, and secure," he replies.

"Absolutely no shot unless it's an emergency. The last thing we need is the Dubai authorities get worked up."

"I know the drill," Euan says, still showing no emotion.

Annette Strang's posh horsey accent, entitled eyes and po-faced upper-class facial features belie her tough character. In the years of piloting in war zones in an effort to kick back against her family's conservative constraints, she has learnt to use it to her advantage. Being underestimated gives her an edge.

She smiles at Jane as they stroll casually through Burj Park that surrounds Burj Khalifa, making sure to drift to the back of the desert rose-shaped building where the Building Maintenance Teams enter the building in their ever-rotating shifts.

There are dozens of workers dressed in overalls and cleaning uniforms. Some hold umbrellas above their heads to shield themselves from the sun and Jane imagines them floating away into the perfectly blue sky above. Many of them smoke as they wait for the buses to pick them up at the rear of the building; dirty work should be done not seen. The maintenance staff view Jane and Annette with interest while they walk closer to the gates as the buses pull up.

"Oh sorry!" Jane exclaims as she bumps into a couple of the men at the same time while pretending to look up.

The men's faces redden and they bow slightly, apologizing continuously even though they have done nothing wrong. Some of their friends stare on while others continue to climb onto the buses.

"I'm terribly sorry," Annette says, stretching her posh accent to its limits and patting another man, who looks like a supervisor, by way of apology. "My daughter can be so clumsy."

"You get one?" Jane asks Annette when the buses have left.

Annette moves her eyes down secretively to her open palm which displays the security card she pick-pocketed from the supervisor.

"And you?"

Jane mimics Annette's actions exaggeratedly and fans out two cards before beaming with satisfaction.

"Cocky," Annette jokes.

The busy entrance to Burj Khalifa is filled with office workers, business people and tourists. The structure has become a magnet in Dubai, with apartments, offices, viewing decks, restaurants,

251

bars and a hotel. The apartments were snapped up quickly after going on sale and Max Bing was characteristically at the front of the queue. And Bing being Bing, he secured one on the hundred and fourth floor — one of the highest of all the residences available. They sign in using their false passports and are handed passes to the Lounge.

"We'll get out at the Lounge and find the maintenance lifts."

Secure radio system (Channel 1)

Kavita: Confirm your current locations, team.

Annette: We are in the Lounge on Floor one-five-two.

Euan: I am in place and have a clear view of Bing's apartment and the entrance.

Amanika: We are in the restaurant. Fireworks are set up. I just need to give them the nod.

Jane: We need to find the maintenance lifts to access the platform on Floor one-one-zero.

Simone: You can access the maintenance lifts through the security door down the corridor to the left of the main lift doors for the Lounge.

Amanika: Each one is restricted to a particular level. Did you get maintenance access cards?

Annette: We got three.

Kavita: Good work. Make your way to the lifts as soon as it is safe.

Jane and Annette slip past the people waiting for the bank of lifts to leave the Lounge. It's busy and everyone is too excited to take any notice of them. A short way down the corridor a security door blocks their way. Jane holds up a pass to the sensor and watches the light turn red. She tries her second one. Red again. Annette holds her breathe as she tries the third pass. The light turns green and the door pings open. Immediately, the glitz is behind them; this part of the building is purely functional — just a corridor with unpainted concrete walls and the type of lift doors you'd find in any other building.

Inside the lift, they scan the maintenance levels. Floor 110 lights up but the lift stays unmoved.

"Scan the card again. It wants to know we have access," Jane says.

The lift moves smoothly, almost imperceptibly.

Secure radio system (Channel 1)

Jane: We are on Floor one-one-zero. In some sort of tube on the outside of the building.

Simone: That's one of the maintenance tubes. Turn left and walk fifty yards to access the platform the window cleaners use. Go out to the far right of the platform to get to Bing's apartment.

Kavita: Timings please, Jane and Annette.

Annette: One minute to platform and four minutes to get the harnesses on. Make it five minutes thirty from now.

Kavita: Did you copy five minutes thirty for the fireworks to start, Amanika?

Amanika: Yes, we confirm the timings.

Once on the platform, Jane and Annette quickly gear up with the harnesses and check each other's kit for safety.

"Thirty more seconds, Jane, wait for the fireworks. No bouncing on these. Just walk down steadily. They are made for cleaners, not commandos."

The first rocket fires into the sky with a trail of white light. Jane peers over fearlessly then turns and climbs over the rail, leans back and walks in unison with Annette. They count down the floors then Annette pulls out the glass cutter and gets to work creating a large circle. The fireworks are in full flow: yellows, reds, blues exploding in a blitz to their left. Greg groans as Amanika strokes his hand sarcastically.

253

"So romantic, darling," she tells him.

"As long as it helps them get through without being seen."

Annette has already scored the glass twice.

"Once more time should do it. Twelve mill glass won't give that easily."

Annette bounces and crashes through the glass before bouncing back off the next pane behind it. She immediately gets to work cutting the second layer of glass that has spent its life keeping the intense Middle Eastern heat out of the apartment. She crashes through, peels off her harness then helps Jane who has already swung through behind her.

"Let's find that pen drive. It was in the safe in his London office. Can you see a safe?" Jane asks.

They search around behind paintings, in cupboards, and along the walls.

"The bowl on his desk. It's full of pen drives!" Jane exclaims.

"He wouldn't leave it in there!" Annette says incredulously as Jane rummages through the bowl.

"He would, you know," Jane replies, holding up a black pen drive with silver edging and a symbol of a snake on both sides. "This is it. It's just like the others we already have. This is the third part of the algorithm. He hid in a bowl of different colored drives. This is the only one with a snake on it."

"Let's go. We go out through the front door this time."

"I still don't know why we didn't do that to get in," Jane says.

"Come on, we've been through that in the meetings. It was too risky, even with a residence pass. The place is crawling with security and the checks to get in are fierce. Leaving is a different matter. Who gets checked *leaving* a building?"

She's right. Annette's posh accent and dismissive stare and the occasional flash of the residence card are enough and apart from an uncomfortably long look from the concierge as they scuttle past, all they encounter are a few "goodnight ma'ams".

Back on the boat, Jane contacts Simone and links the black pen drive into Y_RAM.

"That's it, Jane. That's it! You've found the missing part of the algorithm. Can you see the plans?" Simone screams excitedly over the video link.

"Yes. Yes, I can. This is perfect," Jane replies.

On screens in the tech room in London and on the motor yacht in Dubai, detailed plans of Signature Island are displayed: aerial and 3D views, surrounding water depths, potential landing areas for boats and helicopters, buildings with details of entrances, interior layouts, positions of CCTV cameras, even the hidden electrical pipework services and underground entrances.

Now dressed as captain and first officer again, Kavita and Amanika guide the motor yacht out of Dubai as the rest of the team pore over the new-found plans and start to adjust their strategy of attack accordingly.

Everything seems quiet in the Bedouin camps as the trucks roll in. After another blazing hot day in the desert, only a few old men sit around with cigarettes and shishas outside. Fatima emerges from her tent at the sound of the vehicles and sees Sam jump from the first truck. They embrace as the men look on.

"It is good to see you, my friend," Sam says. "Your delivery, as promised," she laughs.

"Everyone is ready. The other tribes are here. The fighters have been resting today, ready for the journey," Fatima responds.

"Good, we need to go now. We cross the border into Oman and travel through the desert then back into Abu Yash. We attack just after dawn, so we only have a few hours to get there. Boats will be waiting for us at the meeting place on the coast."

In the time they have been talking, the camp has come to life as fighters, young and old alike, emerge from the tents, dressed and ready. On Fatima's signal, they start to board the trucks and within minutes they are gone, leaving behind them only those who are too young or old to fight and a giant dust cloud.

Chapter 14

Kavita eases the motor yacht into a secluded position in a quiet cove on the coast of Abu Yash. They are only minutes from Signature Island. The atmosphere is a cross between a farewell party and a wake — a mixture of excitement at what is to come and sadness that this is their last night together. After the attack, the team will disperse and head off in separate directions. They have only a few hours left together.

Greg stands alone, staring out in the direction of the island as he checks his diving equipment one last time. He will be the first to go, in the early hours. Jane and Amanika ready the inflatable tender. With Euan, they will go second, just before dawn. Annette will be the last to go. She is assembling the wings of the microlight to attach to the body of the lightweight aircraft that has been stored below deck.

Kavita hands round snacks and drinks. She will be constant contact with Simone in London and Sam with the insurgents to co-ordinate the attack. She runs through the plan in her head once more, making sure she has calculated the arrivals of her team to perfection. Then she runs through Plan B, C, and D. She knows she has to make decisions fast during the attack; the lives of her team depend upon it.

When everything is ready, the team settles down on the sand. Talk is sparse, with only a few exchanges about minor equipment details. It is the calm. The storm awaits. Jane feels ready. She feels calm. She has been mentally preparing herself for the moment for years. For revenge. To *kill* Bing.

"When you feel ready inside you have nothing to fear, Jane. Success will follow."

"That's it. Holiday over, everyone. We've got the best team and we've got everything planned. Let's get this thing done. It's time," Jane says, standing up and flicking the sand from her toes.

The rest of team murmur their agreement and jump up. They wish Greg good luck as he waddles into the sea with a long, black waterproof bag. Then he is gone, submerged by the water and the last darkness of the night. It will take him an hour to swim to the island. By then, dawn will be breaking and the inflatable with Jane, Euan, and Amanika will be on its way.

Max Bing has not been to sleep. Getting out of Synoplex and coming here full-time is the best thing that could have happened, he thinks. To spend more time doing what he loves the most: working closely on the human experiments. For the sadistic Bing, to be surrounded by so many subjects, with no medical controls and virtually no security concerns, it feels like heaven.

Bing peels back more of the skin on the top on a young man's head and the man writhes in excruciating agony in his restraints, letting out a deep moan of pain that is barely stifled by the huge plastic gag inserted into his mouth. Bing stares at the back of the raw skin with a magnifying glass.

"Fascinating that the head is covered by something so thin. It's almost see-though," he says looking the man in his eyes, which roll into his head as the pain shoots through every inch of his body.

Bing turns around and picks up large drill.

"But the bone won't be as thin. Did you know that in prehistoric times people had holes cut into their skulls to release the pain or the demons that troubled them. Some of them went on to live afterwards," he educates the man, who is struggling with every ounce of strength he has left.

Bing smiles maliciously. The last thing the man hears is the sound of the drill grinding into his skull before he passes out.

Greg crawls out of the water, dragging his bag with him. He looks up at the cliff face that runs straight down to the small beach where he briefly catches his breath before stripping off his diving suit and flippers.

Secure radio system (Channel 1)

Greg: Have reached the island. Starting climb now.
Kavita: Estimated time for climb, Greg?
Greg: Five minutes for climb. Ten minutes to set up the rockets. Three minutes to get to meeting place with boat team.
Kavita: Boat team. Are you ready?
Jane: Ready.
Kavita: Go now. Greg will be waiting.

Greg slides his hand carefully onto the top of the cliff ledge and eases himself up before peering over. Security should be thin on this side of the island, with the cliffside providing natural security and no obvious landing places for boats. Dawn has still not broken so he has vision of only a few yards, but his hearing is keen, and once he has confirmed to himself it is clear, he pulls himself up and makes his way northwards along the cliff edge. After a couple minutes, he kneels down and unzips the bag. Amanika has set up a number of rockets with timed devices for him to set up and he starts to unpack them, placing them in order as he was instructed. One, two, three, four, the bag seems to have an endless capacity as the devices keep on coming. Ten, eleven, twelve, and they keep on coming from the bag. Then the coil of rope he'll be using later. Greg peers in and shakes the bag, confused as to how the bag could hold so much.

He checks and rechecks the instructions for the angles and direction of each device.

Secure radio system (Channel 1)

>Greg: Rockets all set up. Ready to activate.
>
>Kavita: Boat team. Time to landing destination?
>
>Jane: Four minutes.
>
>Kavita: You're a minute behind schedule, team. Greg. Wait one minute before activating the timers then make your way to the meeting place.

Greg depresses the timer switch and sees the lights on the rockets flicker green. He looks around nervously for guards. Dawn is about to break, but it still dark. He gives the bag one more querying look, scratches his head at its seemingly infinite capacity then heads back to where he climbed up the cliff. Not far past it the team has identified a gully where he can set up a rope relay. Greg throws the rope down the gully just as he hears the inflatable purr onto the shore. His throw is short and the rope is caught on a rock. He yanks it hard to get it loose, pulls it back quickly and coils it again as Jane, Amanika, and Euan climb out of the tender. In the rising light, he can just make out the sight of their arms waving furiously below. The rope flies through the air this time, landing in the shale a few yards ahead of them. Jane instinctively scrambles on her stomach, reaching desperately for its end. As she reaches, she slides back. Frustrated, she readies herself to try again.

"Teamwork, Jane. Sometimes you have to accept you cannot do everything yourself."

"Euan. Lie flat and stretch forward. You are the tallest. Amanika. Hold his ankles firm so he doesn't slide down. I'll climb over him to form a human chain."

She scrabbles over Euan's back and digs her feet into his shoulders. His face is buried in the shale and she can feel his body shaking slightly as she pushes. Just inches short of the rope.

"Push me up, Euan. Use your hands."

With the extra push, Jane is able to grab the end of the rope just as the loose ground collapses and comes down in waves. They tumble to the bottom, all three of them falling in a heap at the bottom of the shale. Jane holds up the rope triumphantly.

Euan drives a piton into a crack in a solid rock, then tugs the rope to make sure it is tight — he knows Greg will have secured it at the top already — and ties a figure-of-eight knot into it. He pushes the rope sideways to check its tightness, then signals to Jane to head up first. The climb is short but arduous, the loose ground giving way under her feet with every movement, and despite her leg strength she can feel the muscles in her legs burning from the exertion. The loose rocks pile down in a rush as she climbs, making it even harder for Amanika and Euan, who are following her up on the rope.

Secure Radio System (Channel 1)

Greg: Boat team are now at the top.

Kavita: You're behind schedule. Move it. Sam and the insurgents are on their way.

Annette: I'm four minutes out. Do I stick to the plan or circle back?

Kavita: Continue. The insurgents will need your cover. Simone, go to Channel 2 and guide Annette. I will co-ordinate with Sam.

Simone: Message received.

Signature Island security radio

Head security guard: Mr. Bing. We have a breach on the island. There are multiple explosions to the north and south of the island. They appear to be coming from rockets. We are still trying to identify where they are coming from. Our scanners have not picked up a boat.

Bing: Bloody hell! Send guards to the scene of the explosions. And use lookouts with bins to look for small boats. They won't show up on the scanners.

Security guard 1: Another rocket incoming to the south.

Bing: What the hell is going on? Check the cameras. And secure the experiment rooms. Get this mess sorted.

Secure radio system (Channel 2)

Simone: Annette. Confirm position.

Annette: Circling round to the south-west of island. Explosions from rockets to the south below me.

Simone: Time to drop zone one in south-west?

Annette: Thirty seconds… Approaching now.

Simone: Release, then proceed to drop zone two in east.

Annette: Confirm all three explosive devices have been released in drop zone one…

Signature Island security radio

Head security guard: More explosions in south-west. They are coming from a small aircraft.

Max Bing: Shoot it down. Shoot it down!

Security guard 1: Aircraft swooping to east. Multiple explosions. It's under fire but too high for our shooters.

Surveillance officer: Large dhows spotted off the east coast. They don't look like fisherman.

Max Bing: How many?

Surveillance officer: Ten. Maybe two hundred men. Repeat. They are not fishing boats.

Max Bing: How far out?

Surveillance officer: A few minutes. They are traveling very fast.

Max Bing: In dhows?

Surveillance officer: They are not like any dhows I have seen before.

Max Bing: Engage them with everything you have.

Head security guard: We pulled most of the guards to north and south to deal with the rocket explosions. There are only a few men on this side of the island now.

Max Bing: Reposition a team to the east immediately. Those explosions were just bloody distractions. Whoever they are, you idiot, they've played you!

Secure Radio System (Channel 2)

Annette: Under fire. Heading higher. Shall I continue to release explosives?

Simone: Hold off for now. Head out and guide in the dhows. They are just off the east coast now. They will need cover from you as they come in.

Secure Radio System (Channel 1)

Kavita: Boat team. Confirm locations.

Jane: I'm heading to the main compound. Three minutes to location.

Amanika: In place with Euan at helicopter pad.

Euan: Two targets identified. One by helicopter and one in the tower.

Kavita: Can you take out both targets?

Euan: I have a shot to target in tower. Other target has lots of cover he can use once the first shot is fired.

Kavita: Amanika. Can you get the one by the helicopter?

Amanika: Yes. Moving into position.

Kavita: Only fire once Euan has taken out the target in the tower.

Euan: Confirm that I have a clear shot to target in tower.

Amanika: In position for target.

Kavita: Take shots.

Euan: Target eliminated.

Amanika: Target eliminated.

Kavita: Euan. Take up position in tower and await instructions. Kavita, put Plan B into operation for back-up.

Euan: Message received. Moving into position.

Amanika: Message received. Making way to helicopter.

The island is ablaze. Fires from the explosions continue to burn and more of the timed rockets zip down to their targets in the south and the north. The dhows come under increasingly heavy fire as more of Bing's men arrive in the east and the main landing area. Annette releases a bank of smoke cover then moves in to cover the dhows' landing by dropping more explosive devices. Bing's men are panicking; being pulled from here to there and not knowing what to do next. Their minds are scrambled and the instructions from their leaders mixed and often incoherent. They shoot randomly at anything, often shooting wildly at smoke or pointlessly at the explosions.

Signature Island security radio

Head security guard: The dhows have landed on the main landing area. It's Bedouin insurgents. There are too many of them. They have overwhelmed the men. We are being overrun. They are heading to the main compound.

Max Bing: Hold them back. Hold them back with everything you have!

…Radio connection goes dead…

Jane is confronted by two security guards as she heads down the small slope toward the main compound. They have been left confused and dazed by the sudden attack to the island. Their minds are racing. This was supposed to be a nice easy job in the sun. Nobody told them they'd be facing explosions and gunfire. Jane is feeling pumped. She is stronger than ever and adrenaline is pumping through her veins. The men are no match for her as she fires in rapid blows. She lands a blow to the groin of one guard with her foot while landing an upper cut to the other with a rigid flat palm. As the first man bends over in agony she swings her leg again, a fierce blow into his fibula. She hears his bone crack like a twig and he falls, screaming in pain. The next man looks up, with fear frozen in his eyes and blood streaming from his nose. She lands another fierce low roundhouse kick, this time to the tibia. *Crack!* Jane stares, shocked at what she has done. Something inside her, an inner rage, has taken over. She looks down at herself, amazed at the strength inside. Astonished at the rage inside her.

All around the island Jane can see smoke rising, and away to the east she hears the guttural roars of the insurgents approaching. She must get to Bing before them. This is her revenge. Bing sees her at the entrance to the compound as he is attempting to make his escape. Most of the guards are running, fearing for their lives and making their own escapes. But one guard steps forward. Bing smiles. The guard races ahead, hoping to catch Jane unprepared. But she is too quick. She reaches down to a strap on her thigh and with one smooth movement pulls out the *iklwa* and holds it firmly forward. Against his ongoing force, the razor-sharp blade plunges deep into the man's stomach and blood spurts from the wound as he collapses on Jane. She wriggles free and pulls out the *iklwa* with a pop as more blood shoots onto her face. Her training tool of so long has tasted its first blood. The dark red liquid of his death drips from the blade as she looks toward Bing. He laughs nervously, letting out a stream of abuse toward her and Jane can feel the anger rising in her once more. His words are barely intelligible.

265

"The weak talk and the strong take action, Jane."

Bing laughs loudly as they stand facing other, trying to show his bravado, but Jane can hear the fear deep inside him and remains silent. She twirls the *iklwa* expertly in her fingers, nimbly flicking it around like a majorette, as drops of blood spit into the air. She stares at Bing, still saying nothing. He steps back, now silent himself. At that moment, a young girl, a cleaner, runs behind Bing, screaming. Bing grabs her and continues backing off, his arm around her neck threateningly.

"Keep back. Keep back," he says, any semblance of bravery abandoned as the girl sobs and whimpers.

He eyes a building a few yards away and backs off, eyeing Jane nervously, then opens a door and slips inside with the girl. Jane runs furiously toward the door and slams into it. It's locked. She runs around but the building is connected to others. He could have gone in any direction.

Secure Radio System (Channel 1)

Jane: I've lost Bing. He's in the main building complex somewhere. He could be anywhere. It looks like a maze.

Kavita: Head to the helipad. It's his only way to escape. He'll use one of the tunnels to get out of the building.

Euan: In location at helipad tower. Have clear shot of helicopter.

Amanika: Thirty yards from helicopter behind maintenance shed.

Simone: The insurgents have taken over the main landing area and Sam reports that most of the guards still alive are deserting Bing. They are facing almost no resistance and will be at the main building complex in minutes.

Bing is with two men when he arrives at the helipad. Two other men are urging him on as he looks around continuously. He has lost his tech company and he has lost his island but he still has A.M. If he can just get to the helipad, he can escape and take refuge in Sheik Ahmad's palace, where he will be safe. He will regroup from there.

Secure Radio System (Channel 1)

Amanika: Bing is here. He is heading to the helicopter. Two other men. Look like pilots.

Euan: I have a clear shot of the target. Permission to fire.

Jane: No! He's mine. Do not fire.

Kavita: How far are they away?

Jane: I'm close! Wait!

Amanika: They are boarding the helicopter. Rotors have started.

Euan: Permission to fire.

Jane: No! No! He's mine!

Kavita: He's going to escape. We are going to lose him. Jane, you have to let Euan take the shot before it is too late.

Amanika: Wait! Jane is here. We can use plan B.

Kavita: Confirm that it all set up. Otherwise, we must take the shot while we can.

Amanika: Confirmed. Bing is Jane's now.

Secure Radio System (Channel 2)

Simone: The insurgents are all over the island, you need to be quick, Jane. There is no telling what they will do if they get to Bing first. Sam, do you copy?

Sam: I have instructed the tribal leaders to hold back from the helipad, but the fighters have smelt blood and some of them are starting to run wild. You need to move now!

"Are you all right?" Amanika asks Jane, staring at the blood splatters on her face and clothes.

"Yes. It's not my blood."

"Okay, then take this," Amanika says, handing her a black box with a red button. "The metal tube with the two liquids you mixed on the boat. It's in a bag that was on the helicopter. It's activated and ready to blow. Just press this button."

Jane looks down at the black box and goes to raise her hand. Amanika grabs her wrist.

"Not now. Wait until the helicopter is off the ground. Only blow it then."

Jane walks out from behind the maintenance shed and looks toward the helicopter just as it wiggles awkwardly to leave the ground. Jane sees one of the men raise a pistol and aim but Bing grabs it and stops him. Even though he wants her dead, he knows she is too valuable. The chop-chop of the rotors is getting louder and the downdraft from the helicopter's takeoff pumps into Jane face like a gale. She stands resolutely, fixing her eyes on Bing and just making out his words mocking her.

"You'll never get me. You'll never stop me."

Jane simply smiles and raises her hands, mimes holding up a bag, then points to the imaginary bag, urging Bing to look. Bing looks down at his feet. There is a small beige bag. He unzips it, and to his horror, he sees a metal vial with a wire hanging from it. He picks it up, feels its heat and hears a faint sound of fizzing. Horrified, he looks back toward Jane. She is smiling.

Jane stares back, her eyes shining fiercely. Then she presses the button.

The Daily Telegraph
11th September
Tech Giant Max Bing Killed in Helicopter Explosion

Max Bing, the man responsible for some of the world's greatest advances in technology, has been killed after his helicopter exploded in the Middle East.

Bing, who resigned as the head of Synoplex to concentrate on building an undersea city linked to Signature Island off the coast of Abu Yash, was trying to escape to safety from Bedouin insurgents who attacked the island (which they call Intasala) when the explosion occurred. Two other men, a pilot and security guard working for Bing, are also reported dead in the explosion.

Officials from the tiny Middle Eastern state have been unable to confirm the cause of the explosion, as the insurgents continue to hold the island. Overnight, it has been reported that further attacks have taken place on key government installations and offices on the mainland and riots are spreading to all major cities. Sheik Ahmad, the long-time leader of Abu Yash, is said to be in hiding in his palace just outside the capital Al Tinamah.

David Rogerson, Bing's successor as the head of Synoplex, said that he will leave a legacy that will be felt for many years to come.

"Max Bing was a giant in the tech industry. He was also a friend and will be missed. But in the innovative work he leaves behind, he will continue to live on. Right up until the day of his death, he was working on new ideas that will benefit mankind. I promise you that I will continue to build on *everything* that he was working on."

Bing was responsible for creating technology that people love, from phones — one in three people with a mobile phone own a Synoplex phone — virtual reality headsets, computers, and self-driving cars.

Under his leadership, Synoplex became one of the biggest and most influential companies in the world. But he was also a man who liked to create grand projects that attracted excitement and controversy in equal measure. Four years ago, he launched MethusalaCo, a life science company that was dedicated to finding solutions into extending people's lifespans. Bing said at the time, "If we succeed, we will have turned the most awful paradigm that we know on its head. The inevitability of death."

Only last month, he announced plans to launch Synoverse

— Synoplex's ambitious own metaverse. The new world will be themed around technology and science and will hire a hundred thousand young people from disadvantaged backgrounds around the world.

In recent months, Bing has been mired in controversy following MethusalaCo being linked to leaks in the media that involved cloning people for medical research, something Bing strongly denied.

Max Bing obituary on page 48.

Epilogue

The light glints through the balcony doors to the fifth-floor apartment and onto the face of Cordelia Charrier as she looks out on the Place du Trocadero. Parisians swarm around the many chic cafés, enjoying the afternoon sun.

"Such beautiful, well-dressed people," she says to the tanned young manservant who is naked, bar his tight white shorts.

"Your tea, Miss Charrier. It is three o'clock."

"Oh, thank you, Fabio," she replies, arranging herself on her cream chaise longue as if she is preparing for *Vogue* photoshoot, her piercing blue eyes locking on the young man expectantly.

"Of course, Ms. Charrier," the man replies knowingly. "Can I give you anything else when you have finished your tea?" he asks suggestively.

"Oh Fabio, you will make the other boys jealous. But how can I resist that beautiful body of yours?" she replies, squeezing his tight buttocks and giggling. "Wait for me in the bedroom. I shan't be long."

She picks up her copy of *La Figaro*. Max Bing's death has been dominating the news for days.

La Figaro
18th September
Was the Tyrant Sheik Ahmad bankrolling Max Bing?

New evidence has emerged that Max Bing was being secretly funded by Sheik Ahmad, the recently deposed leader of Abu Yash.

Papers released by the Eyes, the international human rights organization, shows that millions of dollars were paid to Bing over the last few years. Bing traveled regularly to Abu Yash and leased Signature Island (which is known locally as Intasala), just off the coast of Abu Yash, from the state's enterprise company.

The Bedouins discovered secret bunkers on the island that were being used for experiments on people. Many of these people were Bedouins who had been abducted from the desert camps by the Abu Yash state police, say Eyes. They believe that the funding was linked to the sadistic work being carried out in the bunker laboratories.

Sheik Ahmad ruled Abu Yash with an iron fist and put down dissent ruthlessly. Thousands of people have been reported as missing from the small Middle Eastern state under his reign, many of them Bedouins, a people he has publicly stated he wanted to destroy. During the coup, hundreds of Bedouins were found incarcerated in five-star hotels near his former palace.

Bing was, until recently, the CEO of Synoplex, the world's largest technology firm, but following allegations that one of companies — a life science company called MethusalaCo was connected to human cloning, he announced that he would be moving to the island to set up an ambitious underwater city called the Persian Sea Kingdom. The Bedouins, who now form part of the transitional government in Abu Yash, have vowed that the development will never go ahead.

Following the links of MethusalaCo — another of Bing's companies — to human cloning, these latest allegations will further shatter the legacy of the man once known as technology's great innovator.

"Oh, Max. You had it all, but you pushed things too far. We could not trust you any more," she says, while sliding off her chaise longue.

She strokes the tall, cylindrical glass case in the corner of the room.

"Jane did us a huge favor killing Bing, George. But we now need to find her. She is the key to the future of Anno Methusala."

Inside the glass case, the muscular body of George Travers stands erect and unmoved, frozen in a state of cryostasis. Charrier stares into the whiteness and feels the cold of the case against her hand as she presses her palm against it.

"Not long now, George. We will need you soon. Your little girl will soon come out of hiding for her daddy. Especially as she thought you were dead all this time."

Charrier places a long lingering kiss on the glass.

"Maybe we can repeat our afternoon on the bonnet of the car in the woods? It had been years since I had been fucked like that. Oh, how I enjoyed you that afternoon, George. But this afternoon Fabio will have to do."

She smiles.

"Fabio, I'm coming, darling," Charrier shouts in the direction of the bedroom. "Or at least I will be soon."

ENDS